The Zealot's Bones

Also by David Mark

The DS McAvoy Series

D.M. MARK

The Zealot's Bones

MULHOLLAND
BOOKS

HODDER

First published in Great Britain in 2017 by Mulholland Books
An imprint of Hodder & Stoughton
An Hachette UK company

1

A CIP catalogue record for this title is available from the British Library

Hardback ISBN 978 1 444 79819 7
eBook ISBN 978 1 444 79818 0

Typeset in Plantin Light by Hewer Text UK Ltd, Edinburgh
Printed and bound by Clays Ltd, St Ives plc

Hodder & Stoughton policy is to use papers that are natural, renewable
and recyclable products and made from wood grown in sustainable
forests. The logging and manufacturing processes are expected to
conform to the environmental regulations of the country of origin.

Hodder & Stoughton Ltd
Carmelite House
50 Victoria Embankment
London EC4Y 0DZ

www.hodder.co.uk

For my dad

And I saw the woman drunken with the blood of the saints, and with the blood of the martyrs of Jesus: and when I saw her, I wondered with great admiration.

Revelation 17:6

From Hell, Hull and Halifax, may the Good Lord deliver us.

Medieval Prayer

Prologue

Don't smile, Lily. Don't let it out. Don't look at yourself in the glass. One glimpse of your reflection and you'll piss your drawers . . .

'I can feel them. They draw near.'

The ladies shuffle in their chairs. They cast excited glances at one another and tuck their elbows tight against their corsets. Shiver, in the cold and the dark. Grow thinner, older, more cadaverous in the flickering candlelight.

Lily lets her eyes roll back in her head and coughs, like a cat bringing up fur. Her hands hang limp by her side, and the light of the solitary flame illuminates only half of her young, pale face. She gags. Swallows. Feels her gorge rise and hopes that the light is catching in her tears.

Time for the show, ladies . . .

She barks. Her mouth snaps open. The spider she had secreted beneath her tongue suddenly scuttles, multi-legged and primal, across the pale flesh of her neck, escaping the dark, wet cave beneath her tongue where it has squatted since before the ladies entered the room. The tendons in her neck stretch and she hears a popping in her jaw. She seems to go into spasm, face pointed at the high ceiling and hands forming into fists.

Lily opens an eye, carefully, and takes in the view before her. She can see well in the dark: she has spent the past couple of years growing accustomed to rooms like these, a brief visitor to stately homes and lavish castles, indulging bored and well-fed women in their fantasies as she pioneers a new religion that thrills the rich and allows girls like her to make a living somewhere other than on her back. She is used to cold like this. Better used to the chill of this snowy January night than any of her audience. She likes her ladies to suffer a little, to watch as their breath gathers, like summoned ghosts. Likes to watch them shudder and then grow red across their chests as she thrills them to their marrow, and robs them blind.

More money than sense.

Bored beyond reason.

Gullible old fools.

It's a cold house, this. The breeze feels like a whistle from dead lips. Lily has long since stopped believing in the superstitious nonsense that feeds and clothes her but she had experienced a sensation of eerie disquiet as she passed through the double doors and into the darkened hallway. She had expected servants, gaslight and bustle. But the door had been opened by an ogre, in near total silence. He'd said his name was Wynn. He'd looked like he was chiselled from rock, as if pagans should have danced naked around him as he stood, obelisk-like, beneath a solstice sun.

Lily recalls her mentor's words. Recalls the man who told her she could make better money in the parlours of the high-born than on the stage.

Don't feel sorry for them. They've got more than you, Lily. Even in their grief, they're winning . . .

She opens the other eye, sees the blackness rush in like a tide.

At the head of the long, rectangular table, the lady of the house is a blob of spilled ink. She is dressed from head to toe in black and only lifts her veil to sip from the glass of clear liquid that the big man had brought her as she slithered, boneless and broken, into her seat. The big man had held her arm as if she were about to float away, but Lily had seen small chance of that. She's as plump as a pregnant horse. Lily had to force herself not to burst out laughing when the thought occurred to her

She's watching, Lily. Eager. Ripe for the plucking . . .

Lily retches. Makes a strangled, angry noise, as though she has a boot on her throat. And then the spirit comes.

Around the table, the half-dozen ladies recoil. The high-ceilinged room is already cold, and the snow from their dainty shoes is melting all over the hard wooden floor. But their skin still rises as goose-flesh when the thing emerges from Lily's mouth.

'Grace . . .'

The lady of the house sobs the word. She lifts her veil and flicks her head to the big man, who leans, uncomfortable and sullen, by the grand fireplace.

You poor credulous fool . . .

It took Lily a long time to learn this act. To swallow the muslin in a way that allowed her to breathe, and talk, and make the right sounds as she entered her trance. It took her an age to learn which muscles to employ to bring it back up. To make it dance in the half-light. How to writhe and buck and connect it to the gossamer twine she had hung from the rough ceiling beam during her preparations an hour before.

'Grace, is that you?'

Her ladyship is sitting forward now. Her face is like dough, shapeless and malleable in the gathering dark.

Lily wishes she could give the poor cow some real answers, that she could tell her that her dead daughter really is happy and well in the spirit world. She wishes she were more than an actress who has learned to puke up cloth. Instead, she twitches the twine bound to her wrist, and revels in the whispers and gasps that meet the movement of the muslin.

Lily marvels at herself. She fancies, for a moment, that she is looking at herself through their eyes. They see a spirit, a translucent pale shape, spinning and twirling in the air above the slumped girl. They hear a low moaning and feel the chill that sweeps down the chimney and scatters the ashes in the cold hearth.

'My baby. Please, tell me you are happy. Tell me you forgive me . . .'

Lily feels the familiar unease. A moment's guilt. She presses her toe against the coin in her shoe, feeling its weight: the certainty of food, of shelter, of handsome things and comfort. She gags, again, as she prepares to start the speech she has given a hundred times . . .

'Do not cry for me, dear mother,' she whispers, in a guttural, rasping voice. 'I am in a better place. A perfect place. There is no pain. There is no suffering. I do not hold you to account for what . . .'

3

Lily barely notices the twine snapping overhead. There is a fraction of a second in which she wonders if she attached it to too rough a beam, and then the cloth has fallen upon her face. She starts. Jumps in her chair. Curses in a voice that is less reedy and ethereal than the one she has used during the performance. She's broken the spell. Betrayed herself.

Lily seethes. *Fucking cheap twine.* Going to cost her. They won't pay up now. She'll be lucky if the big man in the beard doesn't wring her neck. It'll cost her a slap or two more when she gets back to her lodgings and tells her employer that she dropped the bleeding ectoplasm in the middle of the damn séance . . .

She kicks out and connects with the table, knocking the candle onto its side. The lady of the house gives a shriek and lunges forward, glass in hand.

Cloth, flame and liquor meet in Lily's lap. For an instant, she fancies that she can save the evening. She can blow out the candle, stuff the cloth up her skirts and fall to the floor in the swoon that signals the end of her performance. But the fire catches. The noise that accompanies it sounds to the assembled ladies like somebody blowing across the top of a glass bottle. It is almost a whistle, the sound of air being transformed and reshaped. And then it is lost in Lily's screams.

At the head of the table, the lady digs grooves into the wood with her fingernails. She sees her daughter's spirit wrap itself in flame and twist, angry and purposeful, around the shrieking girl who has brought her forth from the afterlife.

She cries out as she watches the spiritualist burn.

Smoke rises from the girl, coiling upwards as the spirit had done just moments before. The lady of the house follows the smoke with her eyes. She does not see the other ladies scream and push back from the table. Does not see the drinks spill or the fresh fuel upon the fire. Does not see the big man run forward and throw a coat around the spitting, hissing shape of the woman in white as she cooks and smoulders in her chair.

Her ladyship stares through wet eyes and black lace, seeing the smoke take shape. She sees a face she recognises and a glimpse of Hell . . .

A man. Naked. Sweat-streaked and wide-eyed. Harlots. Teeth like gutter-rats. Long hair matted with sweat and spilled drink. She sees fornication. Perversion. Sees the man. Some skinny, mewling girl. Sees Grace, beating against the windows, trapped and fearful. Sees the smoke swarm and dance and curl above the wails below.

She falls forward, face landing in candle-wax, sticky and warm against her cheek, losing consciousness as she stares at the ceiling and watches, before the vision dies, the spirit of her dead daughter dwindle and perish, sucked into the midst of the ethereal forms that laugh and moan in the dark.

PART ONE

From Diligence Matheson, c/o The Vicarage, Limber Road,
Croxington, North Lincolnshire, England
27 August 1849

Dearest sister,
I had hoped to spout poetry upon my first viewing of the great river
whose name so closely ties the communities where you reside and
where I now halt my recent itinerant travails. Yet the Humber River
of our blessed Ontarian childhood and the River Humber, which I
glimpsed for the first time today, are as alike as fork and spoon.

I am temporarily residing in the village of Croxington, some
seven miles south of the estuary, which cuts like an axe wound into
the English coast. It does not bear comparison with the river which
plays such a significant part in my recollections. It is a slash of
mud. A soup of silt and shifting sands. A vapour rises off its surface
like the stink from a corpse, and were one to wade into its shallows
in an attempt to wash, the sloppy mud would have one within its
grasp in three paces. I found this last to my cost.

Upon revising this last paragraph I realise I sound down-at-
heart. Allow me to allay your fears. I am in fine spirits. My enthu-
siasm for this adventure knows no limits and I regret nothing about
the circumstances of my departure. Father may wish me ill, but
inheritance be damned. I am learning, sister. I am discovering. I am
making my way in the world and absorbing its majesty and wonder.
You would not recognise me. My many miles of dusty progress
upon the holy pilgrim trails have left my skin brown as tree bark,
while the soft cushion of my belly has deflated, like a punctured
bladder. I would almost call myself handsome, were it not for the

poor impression I make beside my admirable escort! I cannot thank your fine husband enough for his recommendation. I can say, with my right hand upon my heart, that without Mr Stone my expedition would have ended prematurely and in disaster. As I outlined in my last missive from Europe, he has proven an invaluable companion, though the portrait painted by your husband would not match the somewhat formidable aspect of the man I now call a friend.

Major Stone is somewhat piratical in appearance. His long years spent in the employ of the Bombay Artillery and in Her Majesty's Government have taken a considerable toll upon him: he has the scarred, beaten appearance of a man who has witnessed too many horrors. And yet there is handsomeness still. Women fairly swoon when he turns his dark eyes upon them. He has the brooding air that ladies who read a certain type of poetry seem unable to resist. Ha! Do I sound like some besotted maiden? But this is the Hero of Herat! He was celebrated in the periodicals for his single-handed defence of that damned Afghan city long before he survived an expedition that killed sixteen thousand of his fellows. He has advised chieftains and kings, and claimed more lives than ice! And yet, were it not for having read of his heroism, I would not believe it from the way he comports himself. Though thoughtful and intro-spective, he is also capable of extraordinary temper and sometimes does not seem entirely in control of his actions. Still, his loyalty is unquestionable. He reminds me of a dog, beaten beyond compassion, who will still bite anybody who touches his abuser. I only hope he thinks of me as a gentler, steadier hand than those that have held his collar in years past. He would not thank me for relaying this, sister, but beneath the silk rag that he wraps around his head, he has a completely hairless scalp that looks, upon examination, like an egg boiled in onion skins. He is unwilling to talk about the nature of this wound but, while in drink, revealed to me that on his travels in India, he underwent an ordeal known by base sorts as 'pitchcapping', in which molten pitch was poured on to his naked skull. The injuries sustained may perhaps explain his decision to abandon his previous career and to make a living as an escort for unworldly gentlemen such as I, though if truth be told, he had already walked away from soldiering and diplomacy following the atrocities he witnessed on the road from Kabul. I thank the good Lord for his decision, for I believe I would have been dead several times over without his poise and military prowess.

I do not wish to spew praise like some flighty debutante, but you would be right in believing me to be quite taken with my new fellow. He has proven himself friend, counsellor and protector, and continues to serve me without the need for admonishment or remonstration. I only wish he were able to find more pleasure in our mission and calling. I ask you to forgive my brief descent into the gutter, but in your last letter you requested information about Major Stone's impulses and asked not to be spared. His demons take the form of whisky, laudanum and women, and the latter of this deadly triumvirate respond to him as a glutton to the scent of roasting pork. I do not wish to sound like an expert in the human mind, but I know that my disapproving response to his nocturnal sins brings him as much pleasure as the physical couplings he undertakes so joylessly with every halt of horse. And still I cannot judge him. He has lost those dearest to him and has washed his hands far more in the blood of Her Majesty's enemies than he has in the Blood of the Lamb. His eyes are inkwells, sister, and I cannot begin to fathom the story they could write.

Hark at me! I must remember my place. I must remember the nature of my undertaking. We are here as envoys of God. We search for the last remains of an immortal. We are decorated in the scallop shells of St James and seek the last resting place of a miracle. Why then, sister, does he continue to rely so heavily on the intoxicants that have aged and withered him? Why does he still swim in his bottomless pool of black grief? I hope to energise him. I hope to help him find his way, as the good Lord has helped me find mine.

I will curtail my ramblings now, dear Constance, and vouchsafe to alert you to any developments in my search for the Zealot's bones. Tell Father I regret nothing, and please, in your next missive, include a leaf from home. Crush it in your palm to release the aroma of my beloved Ontario. Picture me holding it to my tanned,

11

grimy face and smiling at the memory of a Humber River that is never far from my thoughts.

I include, for your pleasure, the leaves of a laurel tree from the garden of my temporary home, alongside a fine purple mulberry, hand-picked in the garden of the great liberator, William Wilberforce. How I recoil at imagining what he would think of the city that reveres him as a favoured son. I hope the fruit's divine scent survives the many miles between us.

Your loving brother,
Diligence Fraser Matheson

I

This landscape is a quilted blanket, draped upon an unmade bed. It is a coverlet of greens, browns and golds, neat patches stitched together from squares of turned soil, of trampled grass and gently bending corn. The setting sun is clawing long pink scratches in a soft blue sky.

A man in a tall hat and soft leather coat draws upon a clay pipe. He is slumped, like a marionette with its strings cut, at the boundary fence behind the large, white-painted vicarage. The building, in turn, stands at the rear of a squat sandstone church, which forms the centre of the small village at the eastern edge of nowhere, sitting at the junction of five roads, like a stone in the palm of a soft hand.

The man is short and trim. He has the broken hands of a private soldier and his face has been suffused with a look of brooding malevolence by the disfiguration above and below his left eye. The swatch of silk around his skull gives him the appearance of a buccaneer, and a black constellation of gunpowder scars has dug deep into the fine lines of his tanned face.

His name is Meshach Stone.

Stone looks at a skyline of elderberry trees and angular privets, of creaking laurels and weeping willows. He imagines the cool shade beneath the branches, the cushion of dead grass and dried earth, then looks up and considers the two hawks that hover overhead, forming splinters in the blue sky. He wonders where his tears have gone. When that part of him died.

He finds his mind filling, once more, with pictures of his dying wife, his imagination overspilling with vile projections of her final moments.

They didn't believe her.

That's the part he cannot put aside. She had told the truth, that she didn't know where he was, could give them no address. He'd seen to that. And they had treated her words as lies. So they had beaten her until her heart gave out, then left her body on the cold flags of the kitchen.

Stone sucks the smoke into his lungs. Holds it until it burns. Breathes out through his sleeve and raises the glass of brandy and laudanum to his lips. Toasts his dead wife's memory as his vision blurs and sleep smudges the edge of his consciousness. The fence is all that is keeping him upright. 'Claudia,' he mutters, and the name burns him like hot coal. 'I will say sorry for ever.'

It is more than a year since the news reached him. The letter had been forwarded countless times before it found him at that tavern on a dusty road in southern Spain. His wife was dead. The money he had sent her to settle his gambling debts had not covered the interest accrued during his absence. His house was now forfeit. His life would be, too, should he ever return to the small town in rural Germany where they had met and spent too short a marriage. He had failed her, had let her die in pain and terror because he had been too ashamed to face her and apologise for his hopelessness. He has managed to locate only one of the men who killed her. He forced him to recount her final moments, then snapped his neck as he prayed.

Meshach Stone. The man the newspapers called the Hero of Herat and one of only a handful of men who survived the Afghan road of death from Kabul.

Stone rubs a hand across his forehead. He closes his eyes and lifts a boot to the lowest rung of the wooden fence. He misses, scrapes his shin and curses, leaning, half drunk and floppy, upon the barn door to his rear.

Croxington. North Lincolnshire.

The back of beyond.

Home for the past few weeks, but not far enough away from the demons he is fleeing.

Slowly, he opens his eyes and drinks it all in. The warm evening air. The soft blue of the summer sky. He gazes out across fields of swaying barley, past the site of the large new property taking shape on the edge of the church land. He breathes in and smells the churned earth and freshly scythed grass, the ale and animal fat. He sniffs noisily, and catches her scent. Rosewater and fresh sweat. Feels her watching him.

'A fine evening, Mr Stone. Close. I shall require a servant from warmer climates this evening. Perhaps a large man to fan me with a leaf as I doze.'

Stone pinches the bridge of his nose. He'd known she would follow him outside. That she would spoil this intimate moment. It is the best part of his day. The part that sustains him. Here, in the open air. Drinking. Remembering. Brandy in his glass and a chunk of fine Turkish resin smouldering in the well of his clay pipe. He's enjoyed its effects for more than ten years, having first discovered its qualities while trying to find some kind of comfort amid the heat and dirt and disease of the Afghani campaign of 1840 that had made his name and then destroyed it. He was an instant convert to the drug's caress. Had liked the liquidity it brought to his thoughts. He mixes it with slugs of laudanum so he does not become too dependent on a substance he doubts his ability to purchase on these shores. He needs these times. The times he feels closest to his dead Claudia.

He turns and looks at his landlady. She must be able to smell the pungent, thick aroma of the medicine that helps him sleep. He wonders if she can catch the faint whiff of burning hair that adds a whisper of tragic elation to his evening's leisure pursuits, whether she would judge him for adding the solitary strand of his dead wife's blond curls to the base of the pipe. Whether she would think him damnably pagan for sucking his wife's burning hair deep into his lungs and imagining that she is climbing inside him and rubbing her pale cheek against his heart.

'Fewer flies than in Bombay,' says Stone, his words sluggish things upon a furred tongue. 'That's all you hear on a quiet night. The buzzing, and the slap of hands on skin.'

Mrs Verinder regards him from the open doorway. She is a plump, dark-haired woman, with skin the colour of milky tea. She is at least ten years older than her husband, the good reverend, who has allowed Stone and his companion to share their home these past weeks. The Reverend Mr John Verinder is a thin, nervous man, who seems constantly on the verge of tears. Stone finds it hard to imagine their courtship. She treats him as a naughty child treats a doll. She has been wed before. She has a worldliness in her eyes that Stone recognises. He had been in her home only two nights when she asked him about his past, the lives he had taken. She told him, with a ghoulish breathlessness, of the execution she had witnessed a year ago in London, then handed him a sculpture of a small red barn, and told him it commemorated a murder for which she had felt a peculiar fascination: the foul deed of a yeoman farmer who had shot his sweetheart through the eye when she dared ask him to marry her.

'They cut off his skin and bound his confession in it,' she had said, through wet lips. 'The back of his head is being studied by anatomists. Can you imagine the feel of it? Would the flesh smell, Mr Stone? If one were to eat it, would one absorb that viciousness? Would one become a killer too?'

Stone had found himself drawn to her. He had liked the vitality and honesty of her demeanour. He had wondered whether she thought of herself as a sinner to be consumed, or as one eager to partake of another's sinful flesh. Quite how she persuaded the young theologian to marry her has not been vouchsafed to Stone or his companion, but Stone fancies she almost certainly captured him with her body. She has the look of a woman who knows how to please a man, though from the noises that emanate from the master bedroom each night, it would seem that Mrs Verinder is more concerned with her own delight than with any notion of wifely duty. She emits the reckless, shameless noises of the whorehouses above the squeaking of wood and the frightened, ghostly mewing of her husband.

'Your Mr Matheson,' she says, without leaving the doorway, 'do his eyes still trouble him?'

Stone turns slowly, hoping she does not see the dilation in his own pupils. She is holding a glass of wine, a curve of smudged red liquid like the hoofprint of a pony upon her lips. 'He bathes them in salt-water,' says Stone, letting out the last of the smoke. 'I don't know if it helps. Perhaps the act of activity itself is beneficial.'

'The act of activity?' repeats Mrs Verinder, softly.

'Sometimes it is better to do something that has no value than do nothing at all.'

He sees her smile, and wonders what she may be reading into his words.

'That may be a reflection of his entire endeavour.'

'Yes,' says Stone, turning back to the view. 'It might.'

Stone has been in the employ of Diligence Matheson for more than six months. He is at once guide and bodyguard to the short, portly Canadian, who is spending his father's money freely in pursuit of adventure. Matheson's father seems to own most of Toronto. Diligence is his youngest son and named, in the Quaker tradition, after an ideal. He measures up to his name. He is hard-working, committed and enthusiastic. The problem is the direction of his enthusiasms. He cares nothing for his father's businesses. Instead he yearns for understanding of otherworldly, transcendental matters. He longs for excitement and experience. He fled university with enough money to fund a year of discovery, took ship to southern Spain and sent word to a man who had been of help to his brother-in-law during a similar journey some years before. He offered Stone enough money to buy his services for a full twelve months. He needed protection, assistance and comradeship. In his mind, he was Don Quixote and Stone his faithful Sancho Panza. He longed to seek out mysteries and excitement. Longed to find exhilaration on a continent far from home. So far he has found only saddle-sores, sweat rashes and a variety of allergies, but his eyes still shine with the zeal of a man having the time of his life.

'He seems happy,' says Mrs Verinder, crossing to his side. 'I heard him singing in there.'

A quick smile flashes across Stone's face before he can bite it back. He has grown fond of the young Canadian and finds him both agreeable company and a generous employer. Over the many miles of their bandit-littered pilgrimage to Santiago de Compostela, he came to think of Matheson as a man for whom life is a source of endless fascination. He found his joyfulness and zest contagious. In contrast to his own laconic demeanour, Matheson is a man who wakes excited at the prospect of what each day will bring. Stone saw enough horror in Afghanistan to keep his ambitions and hopes simple. He hopes for less pain and more brandy, that one day he will forget the things he has done and the horrors he has seen. In this last, he has been disappointed. His memories are now overlaid upon his new experiences, like a veil.

'How will he react when he finds nothing?' asks Mrs Verinder.

She leans towards him as she speaks. He gets another whiff of her and wonders, for a moment, whether there is sweat behind her knees. Whether the hair between her legs is streaked with the same line of grey that she tucks, so artfully, between ear and bonnet. He shakes the thought away. Wishes his glass were still full. Wishes she would leave him to his private communion. He watches as she leans forward and picks a long blade of grass. Enjoys watching her mouth opening, suckling, as she softly chews on the bone-coloured stalk.

Stone draws again on his pipe. He misses the cheroots he smoked in Afghanistan but has not been able to tolerate them since he saw a half-smoked stub poking from the dead lips of one of his officers on the second day of the march from Kabul. The man had frozen, along with so many others, on that hellish road, and his dying breath had formed icicles around his beard and the stub of the cigar. Stone, who had survived the night by blanketing himself with the body of a dead sepoy, had thrown away his own cigar at once.

'Mr Stone?'

He considers her question. In truth, he does not expect Matheson to be downhearted. Few things have dispirited him on their journeys. When riding in rain he is thankful for the refreshment. When robbed by vagabonds during their two-night stay in Dover, he gave thanks for the possessions he had kept upon his person and not left in their lodgings. Stone does not expect any significant lull in his spirits when his spade hits rock and the body within the casket turns out to be that of a mere mortal, not the mouldering remains of an apostle crucified two thousand years before.

'He may find him,' says Stone, with a twitch of his mouth. 'He may shock you all.'

Mrs Verinder gives a dry laugh and drains her wine. She licks her lips and, for a second, Stone's mind is a palette of mixed images and shapes. He sees his dead wife, pale and perfect, crying at his failure to be the man he promised. He sees Mrs Verinder, bare-footed and with dirty soles, pushing him back onto his straw-filled mattress and taking him in her hand. And he sees her, Laura, the girl who made him whole again, if only for a night.

'Simon the Zealot?' scoffs Mrs Verinder, and as she laughs she shows where teeth are missing at the rear of her mouth. 'In Croxington? The only zeal I see is Mr Matheson's. Though I do not judge him for his hopes. He has certainly brightened our lives these past weeks, as have you, Mr Stone. I know it does my husband good to have a man here. He is kind and generous, but it is reassuring to find oneself in the company of one who knows how to wield a sword as well as a crucifix. And, believe me, Croxington was a dull place before your arrival.'

Stone says nothing. He has no feelings either way about the tiny Lincolnshire village between the market towns of Caistor and Brigg, some few miles south of the Humber. He has never thought of England as his home. He was conceived on a Spanish battle-field amid the blood and pillage that followed the sacking of Badajoz in 1812. His mother was a servant in the house of a wealthy merchant. When the British breached the walls of the fortress, the soldiers of Wellington's army gave in to base desire. Some half-dozen men had already taken their turn with her before Major Arthur Stone put a bullet in the head of the man between her legs, and chased away those who had already enjoyed her favours. Major Stone was only twenty-four. His sword was bloody and his ears were ringing with the sound of shot, shell and screams. When the pretty, dark-haired girl scrambled to her feet and clung to him, he did not know how to shake her off. He felt her sob against him and his heart dissolved. She said her name was Adriana. She spoke no English. Within days he had resigned his commission and brought her home to his father's house in County Durham. The action threatened his inheritance. The major's father had no sympathy for her plight. He told his son to set the whore adrift and to deny ownership of the bastard in her belly. Arthur said no. His father cut him off from the family purse and left him to make his own way in the world, protector and patriarch of a family he had not sought.

Arthur chose love over wealth, did his duty and kept his promise. He lived for a time with his lover and her newborn infant in a tumbledown cottage on the outskirts of his father's estate. The perfect picture was ripped to shreds inside a year. Adriana died of influenza and Arthur was left with a child he had not fathered and no income. Arthur had named his baby Meshach, in honour of the Old Testament zealot who had refused to worship an image of King Nebuchadnezzar and been thrown into a fiery furnace for his pains. It was a curious name to give a child. Meshach has long felt it would have been more apt to be named in honour of the wealthy king instead. After all, Arthur Stone valued gold above all else. He proved it when Meshach was still a child; capitulating to the family's demands and marrying a simpering young girl his father had chosen for him and whose family had status and wealth. Then he had turned to drink.

Meshach was always introduced as the eldest child of the new union but, in truth, he looked so little like his so-called father that it became an embarrassment. He grew up wild and angry, aggressive and sly. He was attractive and exotic, unloved and hateful. The brothers and sisters who came after him were quick to ask about his physical difference, and Arthur's new wife was only too happy to tell them about the bastard cuckoo in the family nest. At fourteen he was disinherited. Lawyers drew up papers that ensured he would not receive a penny when his father succeeded to the estate. Instead, he was sent to a military seminary, given money for uniform and horse and learned how to be an officer, never a gentleman. At twenty, he was a lieutenant in the Bombay Artillery. His family had done him a favour. Had he stayed in England his temper would have ensured he was hanged for murder. In India, he discovered he was a good soldier, and could handle sword and rifle. He knew how to earn the respect of the men beneath him and how to stay out of sight of those above. He knew when to use violence and when a kind word. Stone had expected to live and die in the military. He never sought more than the respect of his fellows and the occasional good woman beneath him. He had never expected to be noticed by friends of his father and rewarded with a position as a diplomat. He trained as an adviser and spy, learned to cut throats and pour honey into the right ears. He could do more with a bag of coin than a general with a regiment. He advanced. He mattered. And in 1837 he found himself in a place called Herat, marshalling a handful of natives against forty thousand Persians in a war he did not truly understand.

Stone lets his thoughts drift. He remembers that cursed place, the stone wall of heat during the day and the cold each night that sank through skin and bone to chill the soul. For months he woke and fell asleep amid the stench of death, holding out in the face of devastating odds. He was given medals for gallantry and feted as a hero in the press. As brevet major, he was newly arrived in Kohistan when the uprising against British rule become a full revolt. But even that was nothing to what came later in the retreat from Kabul. Stone was one of the advisers who bartered a deal that allowed the British and their loyal followers to leave the city unmolested. The train of sixteen thousand men, women and children that left Kabul was annihilated. Stone saw his fellows freeze to death on mountain passes and be cut down by wave after wave of vengeful Afghans. He survived by good fortune alone, climbed from the grisly pile of death, began to walk and kept going until the landscape changed. It was only months later that the army heard of his survival. In his absence, he was court-martialled for desertion. He turned to drink, to women, to games of chance and tinctures of opium. He made his living keeping the rich safe on their grand tours of exotic locations. He fought and kicked, scrapped and whored. He lost what little capacity he had for love.

For a time, Claudia had healed him. Her father ran a tavern in a small Bavarian town. Stone was passing through, making his way south following a brief return to London that had almost ended with him in chains. The drink was sour in his belly and he wore the expression of a man seeking violence. But Claudia had smiled at him with an innocence and sweetness that had stripped the venom from his gaze. He had stared at her so hard that her hand shook as she handed him his ale. She blushed beneath the intensity of his glare. She was young. He had felt that to press his lips to hers would be to sully something pure.

He left the tavern without a word, the ale undrunk. He went two whole months without touching a drop and came back to her clean and pristine. He courted her with poetry and pictures, grew addicted to her laughter, became a friend to her father and kept trouble at bay in the tavern. When he kissed her for the first time he felt as though he were drinking pure water. He married her in a small black-timbered church in a forested valley, tears streaming down his cheeks. He had taken to her bed with good intentions, promising her sweetness and delight. He had been unable to provide either. For all that he had tried to fool himself, he knew what darkness ran in his blood. Within a month he had started to drink again and had beaten a customer half to death. Claudia began to fear him.

He left her without a goodbye. Before long he was in the debt of a tall, one-eyed former cavalryman, who ran the games of chance in the slums of Hamburg. His name was Axl, and he was not to be crossed. Stone was several days from Hamburg when he learned that Axl was pursuing him. He feared for Claudia's safety, sent a bag of coin and turned south. He was in Spain when news reached him that the money had arrived too late. Claudia had died because of him.

'Mr Stone?'

He drags himself from his reverie and turns to his landlady. Would she mind if he took her hair in his hand and crushed his mouth on hers?

And then he hears it. Raised voices. Metal on stone. Temper and drink . . .

'Grant,' he says, and closes his eyes. 'Why now?'

Trouble has been simmering between Matheson and Grant ever since the Canadian arrived at the vicarage and word spread regarding his intentions. Grant is the leading farmhand at the manor house in Brocklesby, a thick-set, coarse and brutal man, who has fathered half the bastards in northern Lincolnshire and whose wife lies buried at the town crossroads with a stake through her chest. She was interred as a suicide, pinned to the dirt of the village so her spirit could not roam. She had known what would happen to her mortal remains even as she put the rope around her neck, but eternal damnation and a burial beneath the boots of her fellows was better than living with the savagery of her husband.

Grant had been displeased to lose of two of his labourers to Matheson's deep pockets. He claimed that digging up the floor of the Mosby family vault next to the parish church was the work of the devil. He made life difficult for the men Matheson had hired and threatened dire retribution if he did not cease work and leave the village.

Stone wishes the horse trough were nearer. He would like to douse his head in its water, to expunge the opiates and drink from his system. Instead he slaps his face and half smiles to Mrs Verinder. He lifts his hat and scratches at the scarf that covers his patchy skull. He winces as his fingernails pull at the old wounds. Then he feels a frisson of pleasure at the thought of violence to come.

There are at least twenty people at the edge of the graveyard. They form a loose semi-circle behind the broad-backed man who stands, shirtless and drunk, before the stone mausoleum built four centuries ago by the vicar of this quiet parish.

Diligence Matheson has mud upon his hands and blood upon his upper lip. He is dressed in a labourer's smock, though his riding boots and spectacles betray his wealth. He is leaning back against the stone, his face pale and his hair stuck to his forehead from his exertions and the fear of the moment.

23

For hours, Matheson and his two labourers have been digging through the floor of the crypt. Matheson believes that the man who built this tomb did so to conceal the final resting place of a soul resurrected by Christ. Each swing of the spade has been done enthusiastically. Each mound of earth tipped on to the grass has been done with the glee of a man on a mission from God. He believes he is close to finding the bones of Lazarus. He seeks Christ's most mysterious disciple, Simon the Zealot, whom a handful of theologians believe to have been the man Jesus resurrected. He is certain that Simon is Lazarus. The research of many learned men suggests that Simon came to Britain two millennia ago, preaching with the impassioned zeal he had heard in Christ's company, and was ultimately crucified at the garrison town of Caistor for his beliefs. Matheson has already searched there – has sifted and dug and scratched at the mud and stones of the poor farming town, enduring disappointments and resentment. His faith had been restored by a chance conversation with a local scholar, who had told him of the vicar who moved to Croxington from Caistor and built himself a great mausoleum. He had told him, too, of the peculiar inscription it carried: 'Son of Bethany, brother to Mary and Martha'. The vicar had no such siblings. Lazarus, in the Gospel of John, was from the village of Bethany. His sisters were mentioned by name. Matheson had immediately made the connection and given thanks for the blessing of new direction and fresh hope.

Stone absorbs the entire scene as he vaults the fence that separates the grounds of the vicarage from the edge of the graveyard. He wonders if there could be a peaceful resolution. Whether he could offer a purse to Grant in exchange for a cessation of hostilities. But such thoughts make him feel like a diplomat and thus an assassin. Stone wants to feel neither.

He skips between the gravestones and pushes through the throng of spectators. He does not produce a weapon. His cavalry sword sits above the hearth in his bedroom. About his person he keeps a small curved dagger and an Indian axe with an ornamented handle. A flintlock pistol digs into the small of his back. Were he to produce any of his toys, he would cause a major disturbance. Instead he jostles his way to Grant's rear and stops. When he speaks, he realises that the crowd has fallen silent.

'You don't want to do that,' he says, and means it.

Slowly, Grant turns. He has red upon his dirty hands. He has already struck Matheson. The Canadian's spectacles are not in their usual position on his round, cheerful face.

'I don't?' asks Grant, grinning at the crowd. 'I do. You think I'm scared of you? I've seen you, smoking that filthy foreign muck and drinking like you're a drowning man. You're here to protect him? I could pull his breeches down and spank his fat arse and you couldn't do a damn thing to stop me.'

Stone looks at Matheson. He sees the fear and relief in the younger man's eyes. Matheson has witnessed all of this before on a dozen different occasions.

'I don't mean to be rude,' says Stone, 'but if you don't go away I shall have to break your arm.'

Grant tugs his beard. His chest glistens with sweat and the matted hair upon his gut seems to form into some indecipherable language as Stone stares at it. Grant has lived his whole life in this part of the world. He has formed his opinion of himself based upon his reputation as a merciless man of strength. He enjoys the humiliation and pain of smaller, weaker men. He has never suffered. Never smelt his own skin cooking . . .

'It will be expensive,' says Stone. 'You can't work with a broken arm. I can spare you that. Walk away now.'

Grant sneers. Clearly he's been looking forward to this fight. He took against Matheson the first he heard of him. He wants to show who matters most around here, to smash his fist into a chin he hasn't hit before.

Stone sighs. He shrugs, then raises his hands and beckons the big man towards him.

Grant takes no persuading. He turns from Matheson and lunges forward, throwing a boot and a fist at Stone.

Stone watches the fist whistle past him. He grabs the big man's greasy wrist, brings his other hand up, palm first, and hits Grant just below the elbow.

25

The crack sounds like somebody snapping a log.

Grant turns pale.

Falls.

Pukes all over the grass and the headstone of a child taken by cholera twenty years before.

Stone turns to the crowd. He says nothing, simply nods in the direction of the gate.

Hands grab at Grant and drag him over the grass. The two workmen whose absence from his crew had caused such upset follow the crowd. Stone takes coins from his own purse and throws them after the disappearing men. They stoop to retrieve them, and give half-hearted, awkward nods as they scatter.

'I told you,' says Stone to Matheson. 'I said not to take his men.'

Matheson looks down, finds his spectacles on his brow and puts them on his nose.

'Are you hurt?' asks Stone, and examines the wound on his friend's lip. 'Any teeth loose?'

'Put a roast turkey in front of me and you'll see whether I'm impaired,' says Matheson, then grins bloodily. 'I was just about to break through, Meshach. That oaf had no sense of occasion.'

Stone smiles and wipes sweat from his face. He wishes the fight had lasted longer, that he'd been able to kick the man in the ribs until more bones snapped and his insides turned to jelly. 'Were you really?' he asks. 'You've been saying that . . .'

'Another day and night,' says Matheson, excited. 'We're nearly there.'

'And he's down there, yes? Simon the Apostle? Lazarus? Diligence, we don't even know they're the same man, let alone that they're buried in some English churchyard in the middle of nowhere . . .'

Matheson smiles warmly and rolls his eyes as he listens to Stone repeat himself. 'I thought you might use the flames on him,' says Matheson, with a note of regret. He nods at the bottle in Stone's hands and looks at him, like a child eager to see a trick.

Stone feels a sudden affection for him. He sighs, then treats him to an act that always makes him squeal with glee. He takes a sip of the liquid in his bottle and holds it in his mouth, lights his tinder box and sprays the liquid through the flame. Diligence's face splits into a grin at the sudden explosion of light. Stone winks.

Matheson seems about to demand a repeat performance when a voice brings him up short. The landlord of the village inn is striding towards them, a piece of paper in his hand, the familiar stink of beer and tobacco about his stout frame. 'Came to me,' he's saying, his hands raised. 'One of those new devices. All dots and drums. But it's for you, Mr Matheson, sir . . .'

Matheson takes the piece of paper, peers at it and turns to Stone, childlike in his excitement. 'A direction! A development. This is good news.'

Stone closes his eyes and wishes he were still smoking his wife's hair – that he had been any kind of husband . . . that they had never met.

'We must pack! We have business in Kingston-Upon-Hull.'

Something jolts inside Stone. The picture of his dead wife vanishes, as his mind fills with Laura, she who offered him something he did not think he was capable of feeling, and whom he abandoned before he was wooed by ill-deserved notions of redemption. He has so much to be sorry for. He has done so many terrible things. But walking away from the pretty whore who held him as he cried is the regret that eats through his heart.

2

It is a little before midnight and this room, in a festering hovel at the far end of Pig Alley, has been transformed into a tapestry of charcoal hues and loose silver threads by the light from the expensive tinder box, which flickers on the rotten wooden boards.

She's still where he left her. She hasn't been claimed, hasn't been moved from the position in which she dropped and to which he returns in his every thought and fantasy.

He extinguishes the flame. Lets the smell of burning dissipate so he can appreciate her properly. Vile, and yet so beautiful he is unsure if he can stand it.

He takes a breath . . .

In another man's nostrils, such a stench would be unbearable. It is an invasive, thrusting reek that clambers down the throat, licks at the eyes and feels like the fingers of an abuser. It violates the senses and fills the room.

The man on his knees by the straw-filled mattress does not find the smell intolerable. He fills himself with it, feels it settle in his lungs and closes his eyes to concentrate. Stiffens in his breeches.

Thinks: *I shaped this.* This is my creation.

The girl drew up her knees as she died, curled inwards, like a foetus, in her final moments, though whether it was for comfort or to stop her guts spilling out, he couldn't say. He'd been too busy watching, too enthralled by the expressions that passed over her face, as if she were staring up at a sky of fast-moving clouds.

He should not have come back here. He simply couldn't help himself.

She has been dead for days. She stinks like the wagons that

wind their way to the cemetery each hour of the day and night to dump another load of bloated corpses into the mass grave that grows with each sunrise.

He had expected her to be gone, had feared she would have been discovered and shovelled away. But her neighbours are too consumed with their own ruination to have entered a room that reeks of an even worse death than the one that climbs further inside them with each breath.

The city is decaying, turning to putrid flesh and brittle bones. Death has thrown a cloak over Hull, and beneath its folds, the people are gasping final breaths that taste of corruption and rotten skin.

'I missed you,' he says, looming over the bed. 'I needed to see you again. You've been my favourite, though your friend with the curls was sweet too. She did not fight as hard as you, seemed willing to accept what must be done, though I think she would rather I'd stuck my blade through her heart than taken my time. I saw the fear there. Real, genuine fear. With you it was rage. A sense of loss and injustice. It was beautiful, my girl. You were beautiful, though never more so than now.'

A shaft of yellow moonlight finds her. It spears down from the high, broken window, with the rag she had stuffed into the frame to keep out the cold, illuminating the half of her face not pressed into the straw. Her lips are pulled back in agony. Her eyes are still open, though the orbs within are little more than rotten acorns. He gasps at the beauty of her.

A noise behind him causes him to turn. Is somebody watching? Would anybody dare? He had slipped into the room like nightfall, having managed the stairs, the creaking floorboards and the screeching hinges of the door without a sound. He is good at this. He once cooked a whore on a roasting spit and dumped her body in the river unseen by anything but birds and the baleful glare of the moon.

He moves back from the bed silently, slips into a patch of absolute darkness and holds his breath. Hears rotten wood creak beneath a bare, dirty sole.

He grabs the girl by the hair as she hovers by the door, stares into wide eyes, sees freckles and pale, dirty skin.

29

She does not have time to scream before his hand is across her mouth. He looks deep into her shining brown eyes and notes a flash of recognition. Had she seen? Did she know? He remembers the sensation of being watched as he went about his work. The prickling, crawling sense that he was being observed as he took his knife to the creature on the bed and began to split her skin in the sign of the cross. Had she watched him? And, if so, why had she not told? He looks deeper into her eyes. Is she a simpleton? Perhaps she had not been believed, or her family had decided it was none of their business and that the dead whore should be left to rot.

He slackens his grip. She babbles a few words in a language he recognises but does not comprehend.

The man smiles. He's safe. The girl is not much more than a child and a damned Irish one at that. Probably unable to read or write. A pauper. The lowest of beings.

'Better to be safe than sorry,' he says quietly, and pinches her cheeks between finger and thumb until her tongue slides out, like a slug. He grasps it in strong, thin fingers, enjoys the look of absolute terror as he takes the blade to her mouth.

He sets about his work, knowing, with certainty, that he is making something beautiful.

3

The carriage bumps and skids across cobbles, dirt and horse-shit. The rear wheel slithers on the leathery remains of a fish dropped by one of the gulls that wheel and scream in the dying light above.

It is a little after nine p.m. and the road to Hull is quieter than it has been in weeks. The tollbooth had been empty as they passed by and only half a dozen carriages were waiting at the quayside when the small ferry split the mud of the northern shore.

The scent of the sea has yet to register in the nostrils of the carriage's two occupants. The smell inside is of tobacco and soap. Matheson and Stone have made an effort with their appearance. They are scrubbed and ready for an evening in a city that the newspapers liken to Gomorrah's lowest slum.

Stone feels as though he is preparing for battle. He cannot control his hands. There is cold sweat upon his neck and sickness in his belly. He wonders at the similarities between fear and love, and at why his body is responding to the prospect of seeing Laura again as it did when he was running through the deathly hail of enemy cannon fire.

'She's got under your skin, this one, hasn't she?' Matheson lowers his newspaper. He nudges his companion in the ribs and dispenses manly wisdom. 'She made you smile, Meshach. Few manage that. I don't approve, but I understand.'

Stone leans his head against the wooden interior of the small carriage. He is wearing a scratchy shirt and his breeches came back from the laundry too stiff and small. His weapons dig into his skin, and he is making a colossal effort not to reach for the whisky in the deep pocket of his soft leather coat. 'I shouldn't have told you,' he says. 'Some diplomat I was, eh? Can't keep my mouth shut.'

He is still surprised that he confided in his companion. He had not even been intoxicated, simply giddy with the feelings Laura had produced in him. He had gabbled about her smile, about the way she held him – even caught himself grinning as he spoke of the way she rubbed her nose against his and breathed tobacco between his lips. He had only stopped talking when Matheson had asked him why he had left her without a goodbye. Stone had no answer. He could not explain, in a way that the other man would understand, that he did not deserve happiness, and that she had not sinned enough to be punished by the nearness of *him*. But now, as he moves closer to the city where she spreads her legs for money, he cannot stop the giddiness that is fluttering inside him. Would she consider it? Would she come with him? He screws up his eyes and finds himself grinding his back teeth, the familiar self-loathing settling back in his chest. He imagines her looking at him blankly, perhaps laughing dismissively, as he offers to save her from such a life. He pictures her staring straight through him, failing to recall the night when she offered tenderness to a man who deserved only pain.

Matheson grins and returns to his newspaper. He's holding it only inches from his eyes.

'You'll give yourself another of your headaches,' chides Stone, trying to be companionable. 'Maybe that's the plan, eh? An excuse to ask one of the young ladies to give your shoulders a rub.'

Matheson does not rise to the ribbing. Instead he lowers the paper again. 'This plague is doing strange things to you English,' he says, shaking his head. 'I read here of the butchery done to one innocent who made the mistake of talking about illness.'

Stone grunts, only half interested.

Matheson takes it as permission to proceed. 'Found on Dagger Lane. Dagger Lane, Stone! By the good Lord, that's a name, eh? Neighbours say she was eighteen. Ripped apart by her younger brother when she spoke of illness in her belly. They found him chattering nonsense, still pulling the guts from her corpse. He took intimate parts as souvenirs, so they say. Seamstress, she was, fine-looking.'

Stone does not turn his head from the window. He has seen worse. 'If she was down Dagger Lane she was a whore, Diligence,' he says. 'That's not to say she deserved it. "Seamstress" is what the papers say to protect a city's reputation. Poor girl. But he probably saved her a worse death. Shitting yourself is no way to end a life.'

Matheson grimaces at the vulgarity. 'Chief Constable Andrew McManus says the boy was already known to them. His sister had been his protector and sole support. An act of madness and barbarity but one that pales beside the enormity of the affliction confounding Hull . . .'

Stone stops listening. There is no room inside him for misery or compassion.

'We will not tarry here,' says Matheson, peering out of the small viewing slit in the carriage wall. He curses as the vehicle lurches, causing him to bump his face on the wooden wall and his spectacles to fall into his lap. 'It's a grim city.'

Kingston-Upon-Hull is no better or worse than the many cities Stone has passed through on his journeys. It has its rich merchants and politicians, its philanthropists and entrepreneurs. And it has its slums, a sprawl of overcrowded, stinking hovels where the poor beg, borrow and whore their way through short, brutal lives.

Tonight, Matheson will dine in a fine hotel by the new railway station. He will drink from crystal glasses and smoke cigars in the company of a wealthy man. Stone will seek out debasement. He will stumble through the gloom to the one-room brothel on Pig Alley and lose himself in the young, pretty girl who held him close and didn't judge him as he sobbed. He had followed Matheson to Hull several weeks before, when the cholera was only affecting a handful of people in the lowest slums. Matheson had a meeting with a local cleric who had expressed interest in his research. Stone was there as his protector. He had not expected to see anybody he recognised and had been astounded when he heard somebody say his name. He had turned to find a middle-aged man wearing the uniform of the Hussars staring at him, as common soldiers might at the lice in their undergarments. Stone remembered him from the military seminary. He recalled him as a bigoted bully whose family owned land in Ireland and who seemed convinced that Stone's dark skin was the sign of his being the bastard of a bog-Irish tinker. Stone made a fist upon recognising him but had no time to throw it before the Hussar unmanned him. He told his companion that the man before him was a coward and a traitor: a deserter and abuser. Stone had been powerless to defend himself, unable even to speak. He was still standing mute when the Hussar turned upon his heel and stalked away.

Laura had saved him from murdering either himself or another. By Christ, he had needed her. He had sought death that night but nobody would fight him. Had tried to drink until he drowned in a city gutter, only to find himself steered by a man in a bright coat who told him where he would find a whore who could better bring a man to his knees. The pimp had been right. Laura was all he could have wanted and more than he deserved. Beneath her ragged smock she was so slim that, in his arms, she felt like a baby bird. He had wanted to crush those bones. Had wanted to close his fist around something delicate and feel it break in in his grasp. She was beautiful, too, and as broken as Stone. In a pretty dress, with the dirt wiped from her face and hands, she could have passed for a society beauty. But removing that dirt would be to rub her out. Her long black hair shone in the flickering light of the solitary candle and her mouth tasted of stale bread and the desire of other men. He had planned to push her down and force himself in. Instead, he had collapsed upon her, breeches half undone. He had woken an hour later in such pain that he feared he was in Hell, with a great curved beak pecking at his liver. Then he remembered the girl and searched his memory for reassurance. Had he hurt her? Please, God, let him not have hurt her . . .

Laura was still there. It was her home as well as her workplace. She had resisted the pimp's entreaties that they strip the man and dump him. Had taken a blow to the face for her trouble. She had seen something in him that she understood, had felt something stir when their eyes locked. He intrigued her. And when she had searched his pockets, she had found a broken beauty within him.

She was sitting there when he woke, looking at the drawing she had found in his coat. It showed his dead wife, staring off into the distance. It captured the errant curl that would never stay behind her ear, the shadow upon her neck and the hollow of her throat where Stone had planted his kisses. It was a picture drawn in love and it had brought tears to the girl's eyes.

Somehow Stone had found his voice. He answered her questions about the woman he clearly loved so much. They spoke for hours, lying together on a straw-filled mattress, and found comfort in telling painful stories. Laura was only seventeen. She had a sister and two brothers somewhere in Scotland. She had come to Hull to look for work and found only misery and disease. But she had learned how to please a man. Stone had felt no pity, only connection. He had seen a soul that was suffering and pressed it against his own. They had made love, softly and tenderly, as the sun rose and the filth of the gutters began to steam in the morning's unforgiving gaze.

Afterwards he had wept, then made some half-drunk apology about returning to save her. Then he had staggered away.

It was fear that forced him from her bed. Fear of causing more pain. Fear of hurting her. Of loving her. Of being loved by her. Fear of having to be a good man, and terror at the certainty of failure. He did not deserve redemption and she did not deserve to be degraded by him. He had wanted to take her from that place and run to where the past could not find them. But he had known that, wherever they went, *he* would be there. And *he* had no business attempting any kind of life that was not tethered to the rigid spine of his own self-destruction.

Laura has not left his thoughts. She has been as ever-present in his mind as the spectre of his dead wife. He does not know what he wants from her or even quite what she did to bring him that moment of peace. He simply knows that, somehow, she saved him. She had seen something in him that seemed kinder, gentler, than the rest of her life. And she had stayed with him when it would have been better to slit his throat and throw him in the river.

'You can take care of your own lodgings, Meshach?'

Stone nods. He bites down on his lip and makes his hands into fists. He doesn't know what he will do if she doesn't remember him. What if she turns those soft eyes on all those who enjoy her favours? What if their moment of connection was merely his reward for the silver in his purse?

The coach comes to a halt on the main thoroughfare outside the gleaming new railway station. Stone and Matheson disembark into the muck and dust of the street. Matheson smells it immediately and raises a hand to his face.

'By Christ, Stone, but that's the smell of a city rotten to its core,' he observes.

It is mid-evening and the gaslights have been lit. They cast a peculiar glow on the fog, which collects at the base of the straight brick buildings lining the far side of the road. The streets are quieter than they were on their last visit. The sound of horses' hoofs had been deafening then, but tonight the pair could speak at a whisper without fear of misunderstanding. Stone takes a breath. 'Cholera,' he says softly. 'Shit. Sweat. Something sweet – and shallow graves. Poor bastards.'

Matheson is normally averse to cursing but cannot seem to find the will to remonstrate with his companion. Hull smells of death. 'Are we wise to stay?' he asks, as he looks in the direction of the large hotel where he is due to dine. 'I cannot claim to be consumed with appetite ...'

Stone's eyes are closed. He is remembering the vile conditions in which he ate, slept and fought during the siege of Herat in Afghanistan. He had thought he was glimpsing Hell during those long months. He has seen worse than this and endured far more. Even so, he could make a case for leaving. His job is to keep Matheson safe. It would be prudent to climb back into the carriage and return to the dock, take the next available crossing and be back at their lodgings in Croxington before midnight. Yet that would rob him of his opportunity. To leave would be to fall asleep without Laura's scent on his skin.

'Perhaps if we were to conduct our dealings with haste,' says Matheson, tactfully. 'My own business could surely be dealt with promptly, if you could undertake a similar swiftness in your own.'

Stone swallows. He places his hat on his head and straightens his shirt. Matheson helps him adjust the silk scarf that ties around his throat. 'Be safe, Meshach. We each deserve our happiness, in whatever form it may take.'

Stone ponders his employer's words. They reek of naïveté. He has witnessed the kind of brutal happiness that men have taken in the belief they deserve it. He is the product of one such encounter, the son of bloodshed and lust. He knows himself to be the son of a rapist. He feels that blood inside him every time he looks at a woman and feels himself harden.

He spits sour whisky as he walks through the yellow light towards a whorehouse where he hopes to feel something other than despair.

'Pretty boots, my lord. They don't pick up the shit, I'll wager.'

Stone turns. Two men are leaning against the wall of a draper's, passing a bottle between them. One has a wet face and a shiny patch on the sleeve of his thick coat. He has been snivelling into his gin.

'Better class of gentleman heads west,' says the other man, between mouthfuls. 'I wouldn't head further east, sir. You'll get yourself hurt.'

Stone considers the two men. Harmless, really. Working men, of a kind. They are dressed in a better class of rag than the poor slum-dwellers further east, but they would not be above cudgelling a skull in exchange for a purse of coin. 'The bottle,' he says quietly. 'How much?'

The two men exchange a glance, surprised at the turn in conversation.

'I need it,' says the crying man. 'All bloody gone. The whole lot. And me, alone . . .'

He dissolves into tears and the other man looks at Stone directly. 'Cholera,' he says, and spits. 'Three days ago he had four children and a wife. Today he's got nobody. Nobody but the bottle.'

Stone takes a coin from his pocket and crosses the street. He smells drink and mildew on the two men. He proffers the money. After a moment's pause, he feels it disappear from his palm. He takes the bottle, swigs hard and deep without wiping the lip.

'You know how to drink, sir,' says the crying man. He wipes his cuff across his face, seeming less inclined to do violence. 'You won't be wanting to go any further. They're dying faster down that way than we can bury them. Take the bottle and your fancy boots and head the other way. This part of the city is going to Hell.'

Stone sips from the bottle again, then hands it back to his new companions, who pass it between them wordlessly. *This is diplomacy*, he thinks. The same tricks that worked in palaces can solve a dispute in the gutter before it even begins.

'I have a friend,' says Stone, and the two men take his meaning. 'Down Pig Alley.'

He feels a sudden catch in his chest. He is about to ask whether the plague has taken her, the way violence took his last love. If it were so, he might not be able to stand it. He snatches the bottle back and gulps greedily.

'Pig Alley,' says the first man, quietly. 'They should be painting crosses on the door, sir. Heart of it. Worst place in the bleeding city. Carrying them out two at a time . . .'

Stone's head reels and he stumbles back. The bottle falls from his hand and he feels a sudden heat upon his skull. For a splinter of time, he can smell his own skin burning again, the hot tar eating through his flesh to glaze the white of his skull. He staggers away and half runs, half falls in the direction of the river, the stench growing stronger in his nostrils as he goes.

The sound of snivelling hangs like a cloud in the still night air. Stone hears his own footsteps disappear into the fog of wailing and tears. The properties to his left and right grow poorer, dirtier, darker as he thrusts through the narrow streets. They seem to close behind him. He feels his dead wife's presence, hears, suddenly, a reproachful voice. He never ran for her. Never burst through the door at the last moment. Never saved her. He was drinking and whoring in some distant brothel while she died. And now he runs to save a stranger from a plague. Runs to save a girl he barely knows from a torment that is not his fault . . .

He turns a sharp left into the stench and gloom of Pig Alley, pushes aside a ragged strip of sailcloth, hung there by the undertakers as their men removed the latest bodies in this city peopled by the walking dead.

'We can't unfold her, boss. All kinds of foulness leaking from her. I don't want to touch her.'

Stone puts a hand out to steady himself. He just *knows*.

'The girl,' he says, his voice echoing with the weeping of the streets he has run through. 'Laura . . .'

On the street in front of the dismal garret, a cart is piled high with the dead. Swollen bellies, green skin and clawed hands. A man stands beside it, a rag pulled tight across his face. Next to him are two young men. They do not have masks, and Stone is able to see the deathly white pallor of their cheeks.

'Sorry, sir, didn't see you there,' says the nearest man, dipping his head respectfully. 'Would you be lost now? This is a bad place. Hell on earth, sir.'

'The girl,' says Stone, swallowing hard. 'One of the smaller rooms at the back. Dark hair. Green eyes.'

The men exchange a glance.

'A lot of misery in that building, sir. If you have fond memories of the young lady I'd preserve them. Say a prayer. You won't be wanting to say goodbye any other way.'

Stone feels the rough brick scrape against his skull as he slumps onto the wall. 'Cholera?'

'Plague, sir. Taking us in handfuls, it is. Vicar, Mr Sibree, can't get the gravediggers to keep up with us. Only opened the cemetery two years ago and it's half full already. You're not a local man. What the devil brought you to this place?'

Stone isn't listening. There is a high-pitched whine in his head. He can hear his own blood. He tries to concentrate. Focus, for a second, on what he heard as he arrived.

'The body,' he says, trying to put some authority into his voice. 'She was there a long time?'

'Days,' says the nearest man. 'Weeks, maybe. Might have been one of the first. She's gone stiff as a board, sir. Curled up like a baby with a bad belly. She died bad. We can't even untangle her. She won't go on the cart . . .'

39

Stone crosses the distance between them in four strides and takes the man who had spoken by the throat. He pushes him back to the wall and feels himself reaching for the curved blade at his waist. Only grief stays his hand. 'I'm sorry,' he says, shaking. The men are looking at him in fear and confusion. He wonders how he appears to then. How they reconcile themselves to this well-spoken stranger turning up at a whorehouse as they spooned bodies from the floor.

'Take this,' he says, and thrusts a handful of coin at the leading man. 'Soak her body in water and vinegar. Massage the limbs. Build her a coffin and line it soft. I'll pay for a proper burial.'

The man takes the coin and turns his gaze on Stone. 'Mr Sibree won't bury her. Not 'cause she were a whore, begging your pardon, sir. He just don't have time. We'll build her the coffin, say what you will. Word has it that the carpenter up Hessle is building coffins the shape of them heathen pyramids, sir, to put in the bodies that won't bend. We'll see her right, but don't expect there to be any soft words spoken over her grave. Funeral factory it is, sir. Carts and corpses all up Spring Bank, the lights at the cemetery burning morning, noon and night. I appreciate the coin, but it won't be buying any special place, not here or in Heaven.'

Stone is pulling a small, corked bottle from his pocket. He's spilling the papers that had cushioned the clinking sound every time it bounced off his blade. He fumbles, and a solitary piece of paper falls like a leaf. It is a sketch of a dark-haired girl with bewitching eyes, arms wrapped around the smock that covers her thin frame. It is a drawing done by a tender hand and loving eye. He cannot bring himself to see what she looks like now. Cannot stomach the devastation visited upon her. He cannot be here. Cannot breathe in this stench any longer. The shadows and gloom are clawing up his legs, like dark spirits.

He picks up the picture and crushes it to his heart.

Wonders whether, in her dying moments, she had a single happy memory in which to hide.

4

The tavern smells of mildew and spilled ale: a sour, heavy, unwashed fug.

Diligence Matheson feels as though he is breathing through a damp sleeve. He had expected this evening to be all polished silver and twinkling crystal, had hoped to be spearing tasty morsels of pink meat and roasted vegetables with a waiter at his elbow and the sound of violins in his ears. Instead he finds himself in a public house on Spring Bank. This is the road to Hull's new cemetery, and beyond the dark glass of the tavern, great vats of tar burn with a fury that turns night to day. The flames illuminate a pitiful straggle of mourners, trudging behind coffins and carts towards the great mound of turned earth where their loved ones will be interred by the light of a solitary lantern, and where the sounds of grief are muffled by the resonance of spade on earth and the wet coughs of those soon to die.

Cholera has had the city in its grip for a month now. Matheson has said several prayers of thanks that, after their first visit, he and Stone had left it at such an opportune time. The dead number in their thousands. Scarcely a family within the city's boundaries has been untouched by sorrow, and the stink of death hangs low and thick between the cobbles and the clouds.

Matheson has his back to the windows. He saw enough on the brief walk here and is not sure he can let himself see much more. He feels uncomfortable, with his fine clothes and full purse. He would never have ventured into such a place without Stone at his side, were it not for his fear of appearing rude to his new acquaintance. The man had not even allowed Matheson to remove his coat or select a fine brandy upon their meeting in the lobby of the expensive hotel they had chosen for their rendezvous. Instead he had taken Matheson's elbow and promised they would go 'somewhere they could be themselves'. Matheson had let good manners get the better of him and followed the other to this half-empty alehouse, lit by stumps of burning tallow, where a man is snivelling into his beer and occasionally screaming, 'God's wrath!' at the passing funeral trains.

'A colourful fellow,' Matheson had said to the tavern-keeper, with a nod in the direction of the weeping man. 'Touched by the angels, perhaps?'

'Lost his wife and seven children, sir. All within a day and night. Touched by the angels? Cursed by devils, if you be asking me.'

Matheson sips his beer and tries to ignore the grumbling in his belly. He listens to the sounds of a city consumed by plague, and the muttered conversations of the muddy, half-stooped men at the near table who rest shovels against their dirty trousers and drink as if trying to cleanse their souls.

'Stank like the devil,' says one man. 'She was pouring out the gaps in the coffin. Been left in the heat, so they said. Turned to stew.'

'I can't breathe through the rags,' mutters another. 'Can't get my breath. But vicar says it stops the poisons. He ain't wearin' one, though, is he? Takin' deep breaths like the air's scented with roses. Shakin' hands with everybody. Pattin' arms and strokin' heads. Like kissin' a fuckin' leper.'

'He's a man of God. He's protected.'

'God's left us, John, like a horse leaves shit. God's gone somewhere pretty.'

Matheson closes his eyes, tight. He has been in the city for an hour but he has heard several such blasphemies. He cannot judge those who speak. Truly, this city seems to have sinned. Matheson has always believed in a good and benevolent God; a kindly, grandfatherly deity whose punishments are few and whose rewards are immeasurable. That is the God he grew up with and whom he honours with his search for religious relics and greater understanding. He does not recognise the Old Testament God, a

42

reckless patrician who smashes His fists against those who sin, then demands loyalty and love.

'Another ale, Mr Matheson?'

Matheson gives his companion his full attention and wonders at the scale of his mistake.

Phillip Ansell is the son of a lord. He is a flamboyant dandy, a willowy, long-limbed peculiarity of a man. To Matheson, he seems a person out of time. He would be better suited to an age of powdered wigs and beauty spots, sequins and stockings. He is a splash of purple amid the muddy autumnal hues of their surroundings. He wears rich velvet and spotless silk, and his waistcoat is a gaudy concoction of gold and pearl. Half-moon reading glasses sit on the bridge of a fine, pointed nose, though the blue eyes survey Matheson over their rims rather than through the glass. A thin cigar smoulders, continually, in the corner of the wide, thin-lipped mouth, and Ansell's hair has been artfully arranged to stand in ruffled, jagged peaks over his head. There are no whiskers on his weak chin, though his sideburns have been razored to neat points. It is his hands that fascinate. Rich, dark ink has been carved into the backs and up the length of his long, elegant fingers. These are not the tattoos of a common sailor. They are exquisite patterns that remind Matheson of the fine stencilling around the door of a crypt he visited in Spain. Matheson has never seen a man with tattooed hands before. He longs to ask the meaning of the pattern and to press his companion for details of the process and the pain he must have endured. He has not yet found a convenient opportunity to question him – Ansell has not stopped talking since they arrived.

Matheson shakes his head in response to Ansell's query but finds himself ignored and a full tankard placed in front of him. Ansell takes a pull at his own drink and draws upon his cigar. It is merely a deep breath ahead of another burst of speech, peppered with extravagant hand gestures and peals of high, girlish laughter. Matheson finds his stomach knotting with embarrassment at the incongruity of the man's behaviour within earshot of so many mourners, yet he is drawn to the devil-may-care demeanour of the scandalous rascal.

43

'Your letter came as a true treat, Mr Matheson,' Ansell says, for what must be the fifth time. 'My mail is so dreary. Missives from old friends pressing me for coin. Sickening pleas for my involvement with good causes and charitable works. Do they think me my father? I would fight a beggar for a ha'penny, sir, though as you may judge upon inspection, I would not anticipate victory. Some are fighters, some are lovers, and others are nothing at all. That is I, Mr Matheson. I am the degenerate son of a great man. In my father's pure white flock I am a sheep of ebony. No, I would go further. In his eyes I believe that I am barely of the same species. Perhaps I am a pig, rutting in filth and gobbling up the putrid leavings of his perfect white lambs. But son I am, sir. Son and heir. And though he keeps his purse-strings drawn tight as a nun's quim, there will come a time when I am sufficiently in coin to respond to correspondence with gleeful affirmation. Until then, it makes good kindling.'

He says this last with a loud guffaw, which turns into another peal of giggling. Matheson winces and glances over Ansell's shoulder at the other drinkers. One man is considering them closely. He is a large, broad-backed figure in a black coat. His red hair runs to grey at the tail of his long, coarse beard and he stares out between the brim of his hat and the lip of his cup with an angry, brooding malevolence. It sets Matheson's teeth on edge. He wishes to goodness that Stone would push open the door and greet him. He hopes his protector has received the note Matheson had paid a young boy to courier to him. He hopes, too, that this evening will soon provide good news.

'I would surmise, then, Mr Ansell, that your father has a similarly strict policy regarding access to the family's other notable treasures.'

Ansell takes a sip of ale, then grins widely. 'You wrote to him first, I'm led to believe.'

Matheson had written several letters to Lord Ansell and received only the most peremptory of replies.

'Father has little interest in the collection, save the pleasure he takes in knowing nobody else is able to enjoy it. He will be displeased that you even know about it. It was Mother's hobby and, as with so many things, he was merely the name on the promissory note. That being said, he has grown oddly proud to possess such a trove and I know he has purchased fresh curiosities since her departure.'

'I was informed of your mother's death, sir. You have my sympathies.'

'A tad belated, Mr Matheson,' scoffs Ansell. 'It is a dozen years since she shuffled off, though your wishes are still appreciated. She was a fine woman. I see more of her in me than I do of my father. But, then, my father was bedding his second wife before Mother's body was cold, so perhaps I am to be grateful for that.'

Ansell seems to be waiting for his companion to laugh but Matheson seems too uncomfortable to oblige him. He merely raises his eyes, as if seeking clarification.

'The present Lady Ansell is an altogether different soul,' Ansell says. 'She tried to be a mother to me but I was not an easy son. I was already a man when she married my father, though it must be said I still played with childish things. She did her best to marry me off but my courtships always ended in scandal or shame. When I did take a wife it was akin to cutting my own throat. I lost her dowry and half my own fortune and scuttled back to Father. It was not the good lady's fault, and I believe she is happier now, married to an ageing colonel who believed her when she said we had not consummated the union in any way that the Bible considers holy. A fine annulment is worth its weight in gold, is it not? I am their shame, though I dwell in a home that has seen greater misery than the little I heaped upon it.'

'Explain, sir.'

'My sister,' says Ansell, looking away. For the first time he seems to be experiencing some real feeling. His eyes glitter in the guttering light. 'Dead a year this Christmas. Always was a frail thing but we imagined she would shake off the fever that ailed her. She did not. Her death has crippled the current Lady Ansell. Driven her half mad, sir. She takes solace now only in the knowledge that some day they will be reunited, but until that sad day, she is a rain-cloud floating through Randall Hall. Believe me, you will find more joy in the reliquary.'

Matheson feels a tingle of excitement. He has all but given up hope of the evening yielding fruit but he senses in Ansell's demeanour that he has good news to impart. 'As I explained in my letter, sir, I am not some grave-robber or idle collector of the unusual. I would consider myself a student of the interesting chapters of humanity's past. They may be from the Good Book, or the kind of adventurous tale that so displeases my father.' Matheson pauses. He finds himself about to share a confidence and realises he has nothing to lose in unburdening himself. 'I share your discomfort at being considered unsatisfactory,' he says quietly. 'My father is a kind and good man but the child he hoped for and the one he received are some distance apart. He does not share my enthusiasms and I do not share his. This journey is my compromise, sir. He will fund my great adventure and at its curtailment I will endeavour to be what he asks of me. These past weeks I have been scraping through stone and soil, flesh and bone in search of the bones of Lazarus. Why, sir? Because I am intrigued. I am enthused. Because a scrap of parchment written centuries ago suggests that Simon the Zealot and Lazarus, the man risen by Christ, are one and the same. I have followed a trail and I believe I will find what I seek. I have discovered much already. Have you heard of the great British warrior Boudicca? The man who had her daughters raped and unleashed her fury against Rome was the same who had Simon crucified! He commanded the garrison at Caistor. Do not be fooled by those who would point to the dates of Boudicca's uprising. Simon lived to a grand age because the power of the good Lord's miracle still lived within him. Believe me, I have studied the manuscripts until my eyes felt like glass.'

Matheson is warming to his subject now, growing more animated and earning bemused glances from the other patrons. He shuffles forward on his hard chair, and his voice falls to a whisper. 'There is a legend that tells of an agony I have yet to comprehend,' he confides. 'The nails that drove Simon into the wood of the cross would not hold, sir. They splintered. It took three nails to secure him to the wood. Those nails may still survive. They may hold the clue to his identity. Imagine such a thing. Do you see in my eyes somebody with only a passing interest in study, or a man for whom this journey is a true quest? And yet I have broken off from my divine work to make your acquaintance. I believe our paths were destined to cross. And so, I ask you, are you in a position to assist me?'

Ansell sits back in his chair and makes a sudden, sharp movement with his head. It is not the first time he has done so and the gesture seems to be some kind of affliction. Matheson hopes the other man will not procrastinate. His father's reliquary contains some of the most fascinating artefacts imaginable. Matheson longs to look upon them. To touch the dried blood of martyrs and inhale the scent of saints. For thirty years, Ansell has been collecting relics from around the world. The original project was his first wife's. It was she who lapped up tales of the healing powers of holy relics and began to purchase items touched by Christ and His followers. She spent a king's ransom on a rag said to have been used to mop the breast milk of the Virgin. She travelled to southern Italy and traded guineas for the shinbone of St Thomas. When she began to collect in earnest, her husband ordered the construction of a secure reliquary beneath the foundations of the family chapel. It now houses some of the treasures of the Christian world. Lord Ansell's first wife is rumoured to rest within the reliquary clutching a piece of the True Cross to her chest. Matheson heard about the collection from a fellow pilgrim while tramping the long, dusty path to Santiago de Compostela. Lord Ansell had just paid a fortune for a piece of cloth used to wipe the blood of the martyred Thomas Becket from the floor of Canterbury Cathedral. Matheson would have spent his entire fortune to be able to touch such a relic. To hold it to his face and inhale its wonder. Instead he had despatched a letter to Lord Ansell, begging an audience. After continued failures to persuade him, he turned his attention to his son. And now Phillip Ansell sits before him, promising much.

47

Ansell drains his ale and calls for brandy. He licks his palm and stubs out his cigar. Then he gives a giggle that causes those in earshot to shiver. 'I believe that for adequate remuneration I could risk my father's wrath one more time.'

Matheson is about to breathe a sigh of relief when one of the grave-diggers at the nearby table loses patience. 'You laugh like a girl,' says the man who spoke of God's abandonment of Hull. 'We hear tears and wailin' all day but it's your laugh that's givin' me a headache. I'd sup up and spend your money somewhere else, mister. You're goin' to get yourself into mischief.'

The bar falls silent as Ansell turns to the other men. Matheson holds his breath, his guts chilled. He wonders if it is possible to summon up Stone using prayer and hope alone.

'I do laugh like a girl, sir,' says Ansell, lighting another cigar. 'I run like a girl. I dance like a girl. But when I stick my prick in your wife, believe me, I make a noise very much like a man.'

There is a moment's pause as the assembled drinkers consider Ansell's words. It takes the space of several breaths for the grave-digger to realise he has been insulted. And now he stands, face filling with rage as he crosses the space between himself and Ansell: boots heavy on the floorboards, shovel clanging against a raised nail as he hauls it to his shoulder . . .

The broad, ginger-bearded man is out of his chair before Matheson has time to find his voice. He stands, rising to a height that Matheson has never seen outside the circus tent, and throws his tankard at the back of the grave-digger's head with a sickening thud.

Matheson watches, horrified, as the huge figure passes the table where the other grave-diggers sit, pushing it, and them, back against the far wall. It pins them fast and the shouts of protest are muted as his piggy eyes glare upon them with an expression of pure malevolence. Then he turns his attention to the man who had dared insult Ansell. He has both hands to his head and blood is leaking from a nasty gash. The giant strikes him, and he goes down in a heap. The giant brings back his foot and kicks the man several times in the ribs. There is the sound of bones breaking.

And now the giant is reaching beneath his trousers to his right knee. He wrenches forward and yanks off the lower half of his leg. He raises it, boot and all, then brings it down hard upon the prone man's jaw, which breaks under the force. He raises it again . . .

'Enough, Wynn. He was right. I do have a girlish laugh. Leave the man alone. And do buy his friends a drink.'

Matheson is frozen in his chair. He wants to run. He wants to clamber down and help the fallen man. Yet he also wants what Ansell can offer him. And he knows he would be a hypocrite to chastise him for paying a more able man to protect him during his sojourns to inhospitable locations. Has he not done the same?

'This is Wynn,' says Ansell, brightly, as the giant tosses a coin to the publican and another to the stricken grave-digger's friends. 'He is my father's idea. He looks after me, you see, saves me from too much mischief and stops mischief finding me. He has been a boon, though his conversational skills are somewhat lacking. Quite the brute, isn't he? I've seen him take a cow's head off with a sword, if you can believe such a thing. I find myself surprised that your own protector is otherwise engaged this evening. You must be a benevolent employer.'

Matheson tries to unstick his tongue from the roof of his mouth. He has witnessed violence before, of course, but there was something so clinical and emotionless about the giant's beating of the grave-digger that he finds himself shivering, as though he had witnessed something otherworldly.

'Stone, yes,' says Matheson, trying to recover his voice. 'Meshach. Had business of his own tonight. A woman, I believe. He's been a tremendous asset . . .'

Ansell peers at him over his glasses. 'Meshach, you say? Meshach Stone?'

'Indeed, sir.'

Ansell gives a huge grin and slaps the table, causing the candle to spill wax and the tankards to jump. 'Good Lord!' he says, beaming. 'The Hero of Herat? I wept when I heard he was dead and laughed to the rafters when I heard he had survived that damnable march. Court-martialled, was he not? Turned his back on the whole damn lot of them. Gave up the diplomatic service and all that came with it. Became a mercenary, sir. And a dashed good chap.'

Matheson is taken aback. He had known that his protector had distinguished himself as a soldier and diplomat but has never heard him described with such enthusiasm and vigour.

'You know Meshach?'

'He was Major Stone at the time of our acquaintance. Still very much a member of the establishment. Handsome devil, too, though his temper was not something to provoke. Our paths crossed in some far-flung place north of Bombay. I'm something of an artist, Mr Matheson, even if my father finds the gift distasteful. Or, at the very least, I was trying to be. A handful of friends and I had the idea we could go somewhere exotic and paint some sunsets. Rather silly and infantile, looking back, but we believed we were adventurers and untouchable. We slipped away on a ship and made our way south. We had no notion we had caused such a commotion. One of my chums was the son of a general, you see, and the general had the ear of the prime minister. You see? A good man was sent to find us. That man was Major Stone.'

'My goodness,' says Matheson, and realises that the sweat has gone cold upon his body. He feels ill suddenly, as though there are spiders on his skin.

'He was a formidable man,' says Ansell, sucking his cheek. 'Our fathers were right to worry. We were hopeless. All we cared about were whores and sunsets and the horrible drink they serve out there. We got ourselves into so much trouble. He arrived none too late and escorted us safely home, though not before telling us quite what he thought of our over-privileged and selfish lifestyles. We were no strangers to a reprimand but there were those among my party who feared he would kill us. He could have, too. A fiend with a sword and, if not for his rifle, we would have starved on the march home. I followed his career after that. He acquitted himself damn well in Afghanistan. And then his name vanished from the presses. Killed, some said. Deserted, said others. It does me good to learn that he is well. Lives – and earns, too! A protector. A guard and guide. Good Lord, this settles it.'

Matheson is about to speak when a commotion causes him to turn. There is a thump against the wood and then the door bangs open. Meshach Stone tumbles on to the wooden floor. He has lost his hat and is bleeding from beneath his left eye. He reeks of whisky and opium and there is vomit on the lapel of his coat. His small axe tangles in the lining of his coat as he tries to stand and he gives a half-laugh as he attempts to retrieve it. He spots Matheson and nods, like a dog pleased to have followed its master's trail. He falls forward again, and snorts something between a guffaw and a sob as he lays his head in the blood that has oozed from the grave-digger's wounds. The scarf covering his head has come unknotted and the ruination of his scalp is visible as an ugly, painful mess of tenderised meat.

Matheson turns to Ansell, who is grinning widely as he stares at the figure on the floor.

'He is usually a sober, reliable confidant . . .'

Ansell quiets him with a wave, then extends his hand. 'Please, Mr Matheson, say no more. I insist you join me at the family home. You are welcome to examine the collection and my father be damned. I owe this man my life. I have never had much time for destiny but I see signs that encourage me to leave this city and take you and my old friend with me. Will you agree?'

Matheson looks through the glass at the slow-moving funeral train, smells the blood and rot, the burning tar and wet earth. He looks at the only man he trusts, sprawled upon the floor with blood on his face and tears spilling from his closed eyes. And he imagines the Ansell mausoleum. The family chapel and the treasures in its belly.

He takes Ansell's hand and shakes it warmly.

The Zealot can wait.

From Diligence Matheson, c/o The Vicarage, Limber Road,
Croxington, North Lincolnshire, England
29 August 1849

Dearest sister,

Yes, your forgetful, dithering and inattentive brother is indeed corresponding again. Will wonders never cease? Will blue rain fall and pink grass grow and horses ride their menfolk over fences? Truly, this must be an indication of a changing world!

You must forgive my silliness and high spirits but, sister, you would smile to look upon me as I write. My grin stretches almost to the back of my head and the intensity of my penmanship has already cost two nibs. The justification for such excessive passion? I am about to commence the next leg of my journey. I am invited to Randall Hall, the sprawling, magnificent home of the Ansell family. Lord Ansell's son, Phillip, has approved my request to view the extraordinary collection of artefacts within their reliquary and I sense I am just days away from discoveries that will alter my life and my view of the world.

Mr Ansell is a peculiar fellow but a delightful raconteur and I look forward to spending more time in his company. Upon our first meeting we talked long into the night and he was even good enough to show me some of his exquisite pencil sketches. His father disapproves of his artistic skill so Mr Ansell goes unrecognised. His portrait work should be in demand in the homes of the rich and influential, but he declares his painting to be a private joy. That said, I was at least able to purchase the attached work. Is it not glorious? I am sure the image requires no explanation from myself but you will see it shows Hypatia in the final throes of her martyrdom at the hands of the mob. It is a powerful depiction of a story that I know means much to you. I am relieved to live in an age when a woman's intellectual and mathematical prowess is not paid for in flesh, as it was by that beautiful and scholarly maiden. Truly I am calmed by the notion that such viciousness is now a relic of less enlightened times.

Doubtless you wish me to expand upon the health and wellbeing of the good Mr Stone. I wish I were able to report that his melancholy has lifted or that he shared my ardour for the coming days. Alas, he remains in a fearful malaise, with his dependency on his vices ever more pronounced. He seems freshly bereaved, and it pains me to see a man so formidable brought so low by loss. He has not shared any confidences with me but I sense our visit to the cholera-blighted city of Hull has taken his fight. Sister, these eyes have not looked upon a more frightful or saddening sight than those I witnessed in that cursed city. I will spare you any description of the torments endured by its citizens and pray to God that the suffering ceases before the whole landscape becomes an open grave.

Oh, do not fear for our friend Lazarus! I have written to the good Reverend Verinder who has vouchsafed to ensure that the crypt is not molested during our absence. I have requested that a parishioner be paid to stand guard, and another to say a nightly prayer in memory of the resurrected apostle.

I will cease my ramblings now. It brings me great joy to imagine you reading my words and perhaps sparing a moment's thought to the day of my return, when I can spill stories into your ear, like wine from a bottle.

With deep affection,
Diligence

5

It is a little after six p.m. when the carriage begins its slow ascent, pitching to the left upon loose stones and roiled, grooved earth. A watery light pours down from a sun the colour of buttermilk and illuminates a landscape of tall corn and evergreens.

Randall House is almost half a century old, though a manor house has stood on the spot for generations. The modern construction is little more than a façade hiding the ramshackle edifice within. It was completed in 1802 to the design of the celebrated architect Marmaduke Pycock of Wakefield and sits at the upper lip of a small valley. It looks out upon an immaculate green lawn that rolls down to a quiet road and up again through a wood, which is carpeted in bluebells each spring. The building itself is functional but attractive. From the front it seems little more than a rectangular slab of tallow-coloured brickwork, bookended by two smaller, boxy constructions. Only upon venturing closer to the property does its grandeur become apparent. This is a place of high ceilings and wrought iron, of great shuttered windows and doors hewn from ancient trees. It is at once forbidding, joyless and splendid, and Meshach Stone would happily watch it, and all others like it, turned to ash.

'Majestic, isn't it?' says Matheson, excitedly, as the carriage driver gives the horses some extra encouragement to get up the sloping approach. 'A proper country estate, Meshach. That's old England, right there. That's all the things I thought about when picturing the Motherland. Good Lord, it's a fine house.'

Stone turns his head away. He stares down at his boots and hopes he has shit on his shoes so he can traipse it through the house. He spent his childhood in a home like this and remembers

54

nothing majestic, only cold stairways and cobwebs, unlit rooms and the scent of emptiness. His reminiscences are painful. He cannot help but see himself alone in his grand bedroom, watching the cloud of lonely breath float upwards to the distant ceiling and evaporate into blessed nothingness.

'Do you not want to see?'

Stone could not care less. He hunkers down in his seat, scowls and wonders if it would be wrong to lift his window shutter and spit on to the neat stones of the drive.

'Please try to enjoy yourself,' says Matheson, with the closest he ever comes to reproach. 'This is an honour, sir. Surely you must be at least a little enthused by the prospect of some time in this magnificent building. If not because you wish to be here, then at least because it will get you away from the reverend's wife for a time.'

Stone turns angry eyes on Matheson but finds himself unable to scold his employer. The young Canadian is trying so damnably hard that Stone is softening. He almost gives in to a smile. And then he pictures her. His thoughts fill with Laura. And all he wants is a bottle and a pipe and a blade to carve himself open.

'I do wish you would perk up a little,' continues Matheson. 'You are not just my protector but companion too. At present I would get more conversation from a stone.' Matheson jumps in his seat as he realises he has made a neat pun. 'A stone, Mr Stone. Ha! Lord, but that is a fine jest. You are living up to your name, sir, and no mistake.'

Stone remains silent. He waits for the horses to stop, then opens his door to save himself the expense of tipping the driver. He climbs down from the carriage to an expanse of neat white stones, then turns back and begins to haul down his chest and rifle. He halts when a footman gives a reprimanding cough. 'I would be glad to assist you, sir.'

Stone gives the footman an appraising glance. He is perhaps sixty years old and dressed like an undertaker, a charcoal drawing against the whiteness of the stones. He has wet eyes and silver hair, a bulbous nose and ears so full of hair that it is a wonder he can hear his master's commands. He also has the knowing air of one who has seen and done much, while enjoying precious little.

'Help yourself,' says Stone, and reaches into a pocket for a bottle. He takes a swig of whisky and his spirits sink a little further. The last dozen measures of the spirit had done little to energise him, though he'd had high hopes for the thirteenth.

Matheson has crunched over from his side of the carriage and is attempting to treat the footman to conversation. The footman is being polite but is clearly unused to being engaged with such gusto. He whistles for two younger servants and they begin to carry Matheson's cases towards the house. Stone turns his back on the affair to stare out over the valley and loses his thoughts in the tangle of woodland beyond. He can see himself there: his back against a sycamore, drawing deep on Turkish resin and his wife's hair, praising his dead womenfolk with each lungful of pain.

'At last! At last! My word, it's good to see you!'

Stone turns at the sound of Phillip Ansell's voice. He is unsure how to feel about the young gentleman. Two nights ago he came to on the floor of the Golden Bear public house on Hull's Spring Bank. Three men were staring at him. He was not unhappy to see the worried round face of his employer. The others brought with them a flood of memories. He recalls Ansell from a rescue mission some years before. The boy had been arrogant, exuberant and charming, and Stone had taken to him despite himself. He was a talented artist, he remembers that much, and the only one in his group with the wisdom to realise that without Stone they would have been dead within the month. Through the drunken haze he had managed some pleasantries, though he could find no civil words to share with Ansell's great hairy mountain of an associate. The man had looked at him with undisguised contempt. There had been challenge in that gaze, a defiance and mockery that had angered Stone into sobriety. The Welshman was a fighter. A brute, paid to hurt. And Stone had found himself looking forward to the day when they could test their opinions of themselves against the other.

Ansell has dressed as if attending a carnival. He is a vision in greens and golds. His cane is topped with a silver unicorn head and his riding boots look as though they have been licked to a high shine with a cat's tongue. He holds his hands out wide and takes Matheson in a bear hug, as if the two are cousins or childhood friends.

'I've been pacing the floors, sir! Mrs Huggett has had devilled eggs and kidneys on a warm stone for the past three hours. I hope to goodness they are to your liking. They are a favourite of mine and no mistake, but I have resisted the temptation to help myself. I have so few friends to stay that this is a genuine treat for me, Mr Matheson. Indeed, it seems wrong to call you such. Could we be first-name friends? I am Phillip. Do shake my hand. And Diligence, yes? Please, do explain.'

Matheson looks a little shaken by the warmth of the greeting and the strength of the embrace but recovers himself, like a gentleman. 'My father is a believer in the Quaker tradition of naming one's children after virtues,' he says, shooting a look in Stone's direction. 'My sister is Constance. I have a younger brother named Worthy. My father is not similarly saddled, having been given the far less entertaining sobriquet of Henry by parents who clearly did not believe that childhood abuse improved character.'

Ansell gives his high-pitched laugh and clasps Matheson's shoulder. 'What would my father name me, were he again given the chance, eh? Disappointment? Fool?'

'What about Presumptuous, you impertinent popinjay?'

Stone and Matheson turn at the sound of the deep, commanding voice.

Lord Soulden Ansell is stamping across the gravel towards the carriage. He is a portly man of advanced years, who has been poured into the most sensible and sober of suits. His face is a desolate landscape of disapproving features, topped with hair that likely last advanced across his crown during Napoleon's final days. A few feeble wisps of silver have been slicked across his scalp but the vanity fools nobody. He looks belligerent and perennially displeased, as though he took a hasty meal some forty years before and has suffered indigestion ever since. He seems, to Matheson and Stone, about as welcoming as a portcullis studded with severed heads.

'Diligence, may I present my father . . .'

'No, you may damned well not,' barks Lord Ansell, as he stalks to the carriage. Up close, a physical deformity becomes more pronounced. His lower lip is distended and bulbous, stained purple as if he has been drinking ink. It is a tumour, of sorts, and serves as a shallow well for the frothing spittle that gathers as he spits angry words.

He gives Matheson a swift glance, then turns his attention to Stone. 'You, sir. Stone, is it not? Son of Arthur? My goodness but you let him down. Disappearing like some ha'penny magic act? By God, sir, you broke his heart.'

Stone opens his mouth to speak and closes it again. He feels childlike and weak, as though he is back on his first day in uniform, being reprimanded for his sloth by a sergeant-at-arms.

'And you. Mr Matheson, yes?' asks Lord Ansell, abruptly. 'My son has informed me you are to spend time with us. That he has agreed to your examination of my curiosities. Believe me, sir, he acted without authority when he gave you his consent. Had he taken the time to check with his father and benefactor he would have learned that the reliquary is a sacred and private place. But he has never been one to give a damn about the thoughts of his father. He remains an impulsive, weak and foolish man, and the only way I shall see him produce grandchildren is if I disguise a woman's cunny as a young man's backside! Did he tell you of the disaster of his first marriage? An affront to decency. She was but a girl who knew no better. Buggery, by God! It would have shamed the family had her father not seen the marriage annulled and found her a man willing to overlook her debasement. But good manners dictate I yield to his promises and I therefore extend the hand of welcome, even if I would rather chew it off than allow your companion to clutch it.'

Matheson's face is a picture of conflicting emotions, twisted into something between a grimace and a grin . . . Stone takes pity on him and manages a tight smile and shrug that suggests the rich man's opinion is of no consequence. He fixes his eyes on Lord Ansell and takes a noisy swig from his bottle.

'Mr Stone has proved an able and competent guide, Lord Ansell.'

Ansell's laugh reverberates off the high walls. 'Competent? My God, but he should be! The man had every chance. Every opportunity for advancement. And he treated it like a foot treats a shoe, sir! I have every sympathy with his father. I, too, know what it is to have an ungrateful and arrogant son. I only hope that, through our guidance, Mr Matheson, both our lost sheep find their way.'

Matheson smiles uncomfortably. He wants to take Stone aside and ask him what to do. He wants to tell Lord Ansell that his rudeness is unacceptable and that he no longer wishes to view his relics. But that would be a lie. Matheson has travelled halfway across the world for this opportunity. And Stone is well compensated for enduring such abuse. 'I found your son to be a capital fellow,' he says stiffly. 'His knowledge of the classics is impressive and his company enjoyable. It was he who explained the quality of your collection, sir, and he who must be thanked for our meeting. As for Mr Stone, I think of him as friend and brother, and would ask you to extend to him whatever courtesy you would extend to me.'

Lord Ansell pauses for a moment. His gaze swings in Stone's direction, then back to the short, fat Canadian in front of him. 'I will house him, but not as I would house a gentleman. We have constructed a hermitage, Mr Matheson. A folly, if you will. It stands not a mile from here and will ably keep your companion. There he can drink and smoke his time away. He can squat in the dark and think upon his manifold sins against his father. I will not have him within my walls, sir. I will not have him further drag my son into degeneracy!'

The distance between Stone and Ansell is the length of a fallen man, but Stone knows he could cross it in a heartbeat. He concentrates on breathing, forcing his expression to alter from one of furious hatred to a scornful half-smile. He can feel his nerves jangling and reminds himself it would be a hanging offence to pull out his axe and carve open the fat old bastard's chest. How dare he claim to know his father? Arthur Stone would have shared no confidences with this fool. They have not spoken in many years and Stone feels a bubbling anger inside himself whenever he considers his childhood home, the brothers and sisters who swan around its great rooms, but he knows his father to be a better man than himself, and also that he would consider Ansell to be the very worst kind of bigoted buffoon. Yet his lordship's words sting. They pin Stone's doubts and fears to the wall, like a pin through a butterfly. He wants to defend himself but can find nothing good about his personality to hang his defence upon.

'Don't worry about me,' says Stone, and hears his words as drunken and shrill. 'I can sleep on a laundry line, Mr Matheson. And, besides, I have heard that the mansion house is cold and damp. I would be better suited to the woods.'

The silence extends too long. It falls to Phillip Ansell to lighten the mood.

'Excellent, my friends! Perhaps Wynn can escort Mr Stone to his lodgings, while we install Mr Matheson in one of the guest rooms. We'll have brandy and devilled eggs, shall we, and talk of the past and the future? We shall talk of saints and zealots, bones bought and sold. Wynn! Please show Mr Stone to the hermitage.'

The giant Welshman appears from the portico. He is more smartly dressed than he was two nights ago, but no less imposing. The fading sunlight turns him into a long shadow, a tower of blackness that grows taller and more formidable as he approaches the carriage. He grunts in greeting, then turns his eyes on Stone. 'Shall we stock up on whisky, sir? It may be too far to stagger to the main house. Perhaps you should fill your mouth with spirits now and swallow increments as the night wears on.'

Lord Ansell's laughter sounds like artillery fire. He throws back his head and enjoys the mockery of the man who stands, unsure how to react, in the dying light. 'Very good, Wynn. We shall make a thinker of you yet. Do take Stone from my sight, sir. And, Phillip, for the Lord's sake, put your gloves back on before I shave those damned tattoos from your skin myself! Wynn, do carry Stone's case and pack. Mr Matheson and I shall be within, sharing some brandy and a cigar, and questioning the decisions that brought us into contact with such low characters.'

Matheson looks at Stone and is gratified to see a half-smile on his protector's face. It may be a defensive mechanism, but it appears genuine. He is giving his blessing to the accommodation arrangements, dispensing a benediction that forgives his own insult.

'Will I be seeing you at dawn, Mr Matheson?' asks Stone, looking deep into Wynn's eyes. 'Should I retire sober with a prayer and a blessing upon all here?'

Matheson looks at Stone and the giant and wonders how much damage would be done to his own calling were Stone to open the man's throat. 'A night of sobriety would be well compensated, my friend. As would a curtailment of certain thoughts . . .'

Stone smiles. He turns his attention to the Welshman, who holds his heavy case as if it were full of dead leaves. When he speaks, his voice is a perfect mimicry of Lord Ansell's brusque, upper-class bray. 'After you, my fine fellow. Let's try to make it through the woods.'

6

The heat of the day is fading, the blue sky putrefying to a purplish grey as the sun slides behind the tree line. A sharp wind has begun to blow from the east and the birds that nest in the high trees squawk and protest with each fresh gust.

The two men walk in silence.

Wynn trudges ahead, case held in his arms. Stone walks behind, plucking leaves and berries from the thickening woodland and hoping to God that the big man gives him reason to draw his dagger and carve a new smile into his throat.

'Good money?' asks Wynn, at length. 'Keeping the gentry comfortable?'

'You would know,' says Stone, who is pleased that his voice does not falter. 'You work for Lord Ansell, don't you?'

Wynn gives a snuffle of laughter and turns belligerent eyes upon his companion. Behind him, a crow takes off as a breath of wind startles it. It circles above Wynn: a dark spot of foreboding.

'The Ansells take no protecting. The name is enough to scare the shit out of any attacker. You? You're looking after an unknown. He cracks the wrong joke or insults the wrong woman and the next thing it's swords and pistols and blood, blood, blood.'

Stone pushes past some laurel berries and wishes he were sucking his pipe. At length, he comes up with a reply. 'You're saying that I work harder for my money than you do for yours.'

'What I'm saying, pretty boy, is that I work for somebody that matters. You don't. You work for a foreigner, see? You work for a weak man with no friends or influence. I win, boyo. I fuckin' win.'

Stone screws up his face and wonders if here, now, would be the right time to settle their philosophical differences. He knows a challenge when he hears one – he's read enough Walter Scott to consider himself a warrior. But to fight Wynn would be to risk his employer's welcome, and Stone is sober enough to know how much that would hurt his young benefactor. He vouchsafes to button his lip and to tolerate whatever insults may come his way, however much he would like to stamp on the man's throat. He has fought men bigger than Wynn and won. Were the two stripped to the waist and forced to fight as pugilists, Stone doubts he would keep his own head attached for more than a minute. But Stone does not fight like other men. When dispatched to Bombay, he was fortunate enough to employ a manservant who had trained for a time as a wrestler. He taught Stone how to turn a man's strength against him, how squeezing the right muscle or pressing the right joint could bring the biggest of men to their knees. Stone had embraced the knowledge, and trained until his own skills surpassed the other man's. He had sought further instruction at the temple, from men whose understanding of a practice called yoga had turned their bodies into living prayers. They worshipped their gods with their physique. They could break boards with the lightest of touches and bend themselves into positions that brought tears to the eyes of British observers. Stone had learned from them all. How to use his body as both weapon and tribute. How to throw a blade with deadly accuracy. To walk on his hands and arch his back into a bridge. He learned the art of belching fire from a pilgrim who had entertained at the court of emperors, and to slide pins into his flesh without drawing blood. He wishes that he had found the time to learn peace of mind. He remains free of any such blessing or skill.

'I'm to have the best guest bedroom, then?' he asks, ducking under a branch and taking care not to trip over the tangle of tree roots that twist upon the forest floor.

'We've enough room for an army, son,' says Wynn, without turning. 'We let the bloody rat-catcher stay in the big house. You've got to be a proper piece of shite to be relegated to this.'

Stone laughs. He finds himself almost admiring the Welshman for his commitment to being unpleasant. He imagines he would have made a decent sergeant, then wonders if he has ever served.

63

He's about to ask, then sighs and keeps quiet. His head is starting to hurt and his boots are rubbing. His clothes feel damp against his skin and his flesh itches. Suddenly he has a vision of himself being eaten from the inside out, sees ticks chewing upwards and spilling on to the surface of his ruined body, like ants from a mound. He physically recoils, throwing his hands to his face. He digs his nails into his scalp and lets the pain wipe his mind clear. When he opens his eyes, the evening has turned almost to night and Wynn is looking at him as if he were a specimen in a jar.

'Here we are,' says Wynn, with an expansive sweep of his hand. 'It's not warm, or comfortable, but it's good enough for a man such as you. You'll be happy here, Mr Stone. It'll remind you of your glorious past. Oh, yes, I've heard it all. You're a hero, right? "A man of proper fortitude and judgement" – isn't that what the citation said? I heard his lordship read it when he heard you were to stay. Long way to fall, I'm guessing. What was it? A woman? The dope? Ah, yes, that'd be it. I sees it in your eyes. From diplomat to drunkard, eh? I've never had those worries. I'm just a big fella. I'm just a tough. I don't need no rifle or sword, son. Fists is all I need. It'd be interesting to see how we did in the boxing ring, though. You and me! I'd pay to watch that.'

Stone is about to reply when he enters the small clearing in the darkening wood and takes in his accommodation. It is little more than a hovel, built from tree trunks and rough stone, covered with moss and bricks. It is a vaguely octagonal shape, with an open, pointed doorway.

'Hermitage,' says Wynn, by way of explanation. 'There used to be a real one, centuries back. People would come here to find wisdom. Had a real hermit, though they're the devil to find, these days. Her ladyship asked Lord Ansell to build a new one and, like a true gentleman, he obliged. It's cold and damp and you'll hear the animals until dawn, but I reckon a hero like you will love it, eh?'

Stone winces as Wynn throws his case on to the muddy floor. Does a quick mental examination of his possessions. Does he have a flame? A candle? Something to read? A bottle? He suddenly realises he is being dumped a mile from the main house, like a beggar too fetid to be allowed near the tapestries.

'It's lovely,' says Stone. His voice sounds thin and reedy and he hits himself in the chest until he sounds a little more like himself. 'Reminds me of Wales, actually. Your mother isn't here, though. Shame. Would be nice to take the edge off the day.'

Wynn gives a snort of laughter. 'You wouldn't like my mother. Teeth like tombstones, sir. She'd take the skin off it and no mistake. Your father now. He knows how to please a man.'

Stone breathes in damp earth and rotten leaves. He wonders how it would feel to slip his blade between the second and third rib of this huge, brutish bastard. Then he remembers his duty. His purpose. And he gives no more than a smile as he enters the dank cave.

'Sleep tight, sir,' says Wynn, as he turns his back. 'I'd hate you to fall asleep imagining your throat being cut.'

Stone smiles. He pulls the bottle from his pocket. 'It's not far to the pigsty, Wynn. I could find wherever it is you lay your head.'

They lock eyes. Issue a silent challenge in the dying light: two warriors determined to put the other on his arse. Outside, a vixen screams as a fox pins it fast. The crows in the trees seem to laugh at the spectacle, and the slap of branch on branch forms raucous, angry applause.

'I'll bid you a good night,' says Wynn, retreating.

'And I'll bid you fuck off,' says Stone.

The moment of defiance does not sustain him for long. As soon as he is certain that Wynn has departed he slumps against the wooden pillar that supports the low, muddy roof. With fumbling fingers he retrieves his tinder-box and manages to spark a flame. The pitiful light casts waving, dancing shadows on the uneven walls and Stone shivers as he watches them move upon the coarse brick. He presses his hands to the wall, which is cold and damp. He swigs from the bottle and closes his eyes. Wonders, again, at how far he has fallen. He has slept in worse places, of course, has spent nights under canvas with the bodies of his fellows as a pillow, the blood of enemies and friends drying upon his skin. But such nights were for duty. For England. For glory and for revenge. Tonight he sleeps in a midden while his employer eats fine food and drinks good wine in a mansion a mile away. Stone wishes he could feel angry. But this is the life he wanted. He turned his back on the military and went into the world as a mercenary. Drink, arrogance and games of chance brought him here and he almost revels in the humiliation.

Within moments, the bottle in Stone's hand is replaced with his pipe. He does not add the precious strands of his wife's hair, simply slices off a wedge of dark resin and wedges it inside, like wadding in a rifle pan. He holds the flame to the bowl, sucks deep and feels the thick, fatty smoke fill him. A moment later, he slithers down the wooden pole and flops on to the sludge and grime of the hermitage floor.

'If you could see me now . . .'

Stone might have spoken to any of the ghosts he carries within him. On this occasion, it is his father he pictures. He sees him in all his glory, looking down upon him as he sprawls at his feet. He knows his father's thoughts, knows what he thinks whenever he looks upon him or calls him to mind. Stone is the son of a common soldier. A rapist. A murderer. He is at least half evil and the rest of him is a fading memory. Stone knows his father's thoughts because they are the same as those he holds in his own breast.

Christ, how he wishes she were here. He was wrong to leave that place. He should have held her where she lay – should have wiped the dirt from her body with his own hands and massaged her dead limbs until she could be laid to rest in a proper coffin, in a proper grave. But he had fled, found more drink and more opium and numbed himself to the agony of reality. He feels like crying, and wishes he had some tears.

'A pox on trespassers! Damnation upon those who would steal a man's bed! The torments of Job upon you. Fight me, sir. I call you out!'

Stone raises his head and opens his eyes into fire. He smells burning fat and winces at the bright red flower that wavers in his vision. He feels hands grab at his clothes and instinctively pulls his curved dagger from his belt. He slices wildly, and feels the blade clink against metal. The hands drop him and he falls backwards into the dirt.

'By God, you could have sliced me through!'

Stone rolls sideways and tries to stand but the booze has dulled his wits and he finds himself unable to focus or support himself. He stumbles and crashes into the brick.

'You stink like a tinker and you have the honour of a Turk! You have marked my silvers, you ruffian! I'll box your ears for daring to insult the name of Wellesley Goodhand!'

Stone blinks until the figure comes into focus. Then he laughs and reaches for his bottle.

Wellesley Goodhand stands little taller than a child, though his large tricorn hat adds another foot to his height. Beneath golden, curly hair, his face is flat, square, and looks as if it has been assembled from misshapen rocks. His shape is vaguely rectangular, broad at the shoulders and thick at the thighs. He has the torso of an ape and the limbs of a prize sow. Stone fancies that if he were struck by a runaway coach, it would splinter around him. He may be the sturdiest creature that Stone has ever seen.

'My silvers,' wails Goodhand, holding his lantern to his waist and inspecting his belt buckle. 'You've made an enemy here today, you blackguard!'

Stone pulls himself into a sitting position and extends the bottle. 'My apologies,' he says drowsily. 'You woke me. I defended myself.'

'You invaded my home,' shouts Goodhand, angrily. 'I have slept here five nights past!'

Stone spreads his hands apologetically, and proffers the bottle once more. 'I'm a guest of Lord Ansell,' he says, then laughs at the nonsense of the statement. 'I was invited, after a fashion.'

Goodhand says nothing, then accepts the bottle. He uncorks it and takes a large pull. 'Strong stuff,' he says grudgingly. 'I will keep it for the insult and the damage.'

Stone is warming to the sturdy little man. 'What did I damage?'

'Belt buckles – see?' Goodhand holds the lantern nearer the crossbelt that runs across his green coat and scarlet waistcoat. 'Smelted them myself, I did. Rats, sir. My business. My trade.'

Stone leans forward and examines the workmanship. Two rats, cast in silver, chase across the leather of the belt. Stone's blade has cut the ear off one of the animals. 'The rat saved you,' he says. 'That dagger can cut the balls off a butterfly. If it weren't for your belt buckles we'd be slopping about in your innards.'

Goodhand seems to consider this. Eventually his face relaxes into a grin. The effect is transformative. Suddenly the little man seems unnaturally jolly and companionable. 'Never had a rat save me before,' he says, taking another drink. 'By Christ, they owe me no favours. I'm their nemesis, see. Mother rats tell their babies about me. I'm their nightmare. I've killed more of them than they've taken of us and I'll not be happy until I've put myself out of work.'

As he speaks, Goodhand reaches behind him and grabs a small metal cage in which a large white rat with angry pink eyes gnaws upon the body of a smaller, brown rat. Stone shudders and Goodhand seems to enjoy his discomfort.

'Never bothered me, see? Even as a boy I didn't mind the rats. Used to let them run over me, I did. Up my sleeves and trouser legs. Made a few pennies that way. Always had a rat in a pocket. Taught 'em a trick or two. But ain't no money in rat tricks. It's catching and killing that people want. And I weren't but ten afore I was in demand. Got the ear for it, see? Ear and nose, you might say. I knows a rat's ways. I knows what they like. And I knows how to kill 'em.'

Stone reaches across to his case and takes a fresh bottle from its depths. He fumbles on the floor and retrieves his pipe, knocking the resin from its base and replacing it with tobacco. He lights it and sucks the smoke into his lungs, blowing out a long plume, which coils around the central pillar, then drifts around Goodhand.

'You'll be making money, then,' says Stone, sitting upright. 'Rat-catchers are always popular when the cholera comes.'

Goodhand grins and sits down with his back to the pillar. He drops some crumbs into the rat's cage. There is a crunching sound coming from within. The white rat is grinding its way through its dead companion's skull.

'A pretty one,' says Goodhand, making himself comfortable and pointing at the rat. 'Make a fine pet for a lady. Shame to waste the pretty ones. I breeds them, see. Sometimes they fight, sometimes they're rutting before I've closed the cage door. This pretty one didn't like her mate. I'll try her on a blackie soon enough. See if we can't get a stripy one, eh?'

Stone extends a hand. 'Meshach Stone,' he says. 'I'm more of a rat than a catcher. And I'm sorry for taking your bed.'

Goodhand shrugs. 'Not much of a bed, is it? They said I can stay in the servants' quarters but I don't keep sociable hours. And, if I'm honest with you, I'd rather lie in a coffin with an angry terrier than stay in that great mausoleum. Gives me the chills. And her ladyship's not right in the head, I can tell you that much. Not that it puts her off her feed. Always a plate outside her door, that one, and a young lassie in the kitchen says she hasn't let her grieving put her off having a fiddle with herself. The noises coming from that room! Eating cakes and shoving her fingers in. That's the nobs for you. That's the life we all be wanting.'

Stone rubs his forehead and decides not to tell the little man about his family's name and holdings.

'Happier out here, I am,' says Goodhand, tickling the white rat behind the ear. 'Got to go where the work takes you, see? And, aye, you'd be right in saying it's a good time to do what I'm doing. Aren't many of us with a real taste for it. Me and that pretender Jack B. You'll have heard of him, no doubt. Loves the sound of his voice. Rat-catcher to the Queen, he calls himself. Well, he's welcome to her. Leaves the field open for the real professionals. Vision, that's what I got. I hear cholera and I think of all those worthies and wealthies worrying their poor heads about getting something nasty. So I comes up north, tells the toffs I can keep the rats from the door and, by Christ, I'm a man of my word. Lord Ansell's only the latest. Making enough to die a rich man, I am.'

Stone runs his tongue around his mouth, then sucks on his pipe. 'Anybody paying you to kill the little bastards in Hull? People are dying like it's a battlefield.'

Goodhand's smile drops. 'A bad business,' he says. 'From your eyes I'd say you've lost somebody that mattered, eh? My condolences. Plague comes and don't care where it lands, but it seems to have it in for the poor more than for the rich. I'd need an army to catch all the rats down by the river in that city, sir. They should condemn the place. Close it up and give it over to the rats, maybe.'

Stone turns away. He takes a sip of whisky and laudanum. His eyes are adjusting to the gloom now and he is making some sense of his surroundings. He can see what the hermitage used to be, the shape of a fireplace and hearth in the far wall, bricked up and mossed over some time before.

'A damn peculiar place, this,' says Goodhand, following his gaze. 'Got a feel to it, it has. Cold, like, but cold to the bones, if you follows me. You know when you venture into a church and you just know it's seen more burials than births? It's got that sense to it. And the mistress! She's a black cloud, that one. And the fop – wouldn't want to be left alone with that one, sir, not unless I were wearing a chastity belt and had swallowed the key. It's paying well but I'll be pleased to be gone. There's a nest somewhere near, I knows that much. Followed some of the biggest beauties you'll ever see. I can burn them out if it comes to it but they'd pay handsome at the terrier pits for a dozen of these monsters, I'll tell you that.'

Stone's gaze hasn't left the fireplace. He is staring at the twin holes in the brickwork. Deep and dark, they look as if they were left by musket balls or crucifixion nails. Slowly, he lets his stare travel upwards. It seems almost as if a shape is forming on the dark brick: a hallucination, like a face appearing in moving clouds or dancing flames.

'You'll be no stranger to the games, eh?'

Stone turns back to his new acquaintance. He lets out a laugh. 'You see before you a rich man brought low by games of chance, Mr Goodhand. Aye, I know the games – know them too well.'

Stone sees his own recent sins. He sees the small fortune he paid over to the bookmaker at Axl Pehmoeller's tavern, betting on terriers and vermin with money he had borrowed from the tavern-keeper himself. He'd been on a good run. The numbers had presented themselves in his mind without room for doubt. The white terrier with the stumpy tail had been on good form. Stone had said seventeen. The dog would kill seventeen of the squealing, biting vermin in the pit on the tavern floor. He'd been out by one.

And he'd lost more money than he'd ever had in his life. He'd borrowed to keep going. Lost that too. And within months he was fleeing creditors who wanted to take their payments from his flesh, but had taken it from his wife's instead.

'What brings you here?' asks Goodhand, quietly. 'Was it you I saw with the big man? Brute, isn't he? Word is, he has a wooden leg, though if he does it don't cause him to limp. He's a menace. Drinks in a hop-pole kind of place down Skidby. Hasn't paid for a drink as long as I've known him. Belongs to Lord Ansell, see? And Ansell dotes on Wynn. Lady Ansell, too, though it's hard to tell now with that one what she wants or likes. Funny family. Had their share of pain . . .' Goodhand tails off. He considers his companion. 'You'll be knowing about that, Mr Stone, unless I'm mistaken. Pain.'

Stone turns his gaze back to the chimneybreast and examines the two holes again. They stand some six feet apart. He starts forward, to look for matching holes lower down, but his energy is departing and he yearns for sleep. 'I've seen enough of it, aye,' he says quietly. 'I've no doubt I'll see more.'

Goodhand says nothing. Just sits expectantly, waiting for more.

Stone lays his head back and takes a swig. He lets his mind drift to his bereavements. 'She died,' he says softly. 'The one who could have made it better.'

'Your wife?' asks Goodhand. 'They're a rare find, a good wife. I hope for one some day.'

Stone scratches his head and enjoys the sting. He is surprised by the truth of his thoughts. 'My wife was too good, Mr Goodhand. I can't atone for that. I should never have brought myself into her life. No, I found something special in a woman I paid. A young girl paid to open her legs for the scum of the earth. And I convinced myself she could see my soul. She held me . . . kissed me. I found peace in her. She saw me as I am and didn't blink. I saw her, too, and glimpsed something that seemed to have been made just for me. I don't know. Maybe she could have fixed me. Maybe I could have saved her. I was too broken to take the chance and now I never can. The cholera took her. And all I did was fling money at her undertakers. I couldn't even bring myself to look at her. The girl who gave me more than she could ever have known, and I was too frightened by the smell of her to kiss her lips again.'

Stone's voice breaks and Goodhand covers the sound with a cough and a whistle.

'A goodbye's an important thing,' says the little man, at length. 'They've more bodies than minutes in the day down Hull right now. You should say your farewells. They'll not have nailed the lid down yet. You don't need another regret.'

Stone's breath comes out ragged and weak. Could he? Matheson doesn't need him. He's not welcome here. His presence is an insult to his host, and if he stays, he will smoke and drink and hate himself to death. He should have said his goodbyes. Should have kissed her brow and told her that she had helped him take the only breaths he can remember savouring. He wonders, briefly, whether to convince himself of Heaven – wonders if he were to confess his sins and find a way to get himself killed whether she might be waiting for him somewhere peaceful and beautiful. Just as quickly he shakes his head and spits on the floor of the folly. To believe in Heaven is to believe in Hell, and he knows that no amount of atonement will spare him the flames. He has missed his chance at redemption, allowed fear to push him away from the embrace of a girl who truly seemed to care if he lived or died.

'Do you know any songs?' asks Goodhand, suddenly. 'I like an Irish reel, so I do. I have an Irish father, though I don't tell everybody that. Great one for the reels, he was. I have a penny whistle, if you'd care to hum.'

Stone shakes himself from his thoughts. He manages a smile for his new friend and wonders, for a second, whether he's really there. 'I'm pleased to make your acquaintance, Mr Goodhand,' he says. He feels tiredness pulling its sackcloth over his head, muffling him with warmth and darkness. 'You are a credit to your profession.'

Goodhand smiles, then seems to blend with the darkness until there is only the sound of wind and soft rain. His voice is the last thing Stone hears before his eyes close and the night takes him.

'She needs you, Mr Stone. Still and for ever. Death has no answers, see? You need to ask questions. Nobody else will . . .'

7

Matheson feels shamefully comfortable. His belly is full of fine food, and the crystal glass in his hand seems to replenish itself with every sip of brandy. Even the cigar that smoulders between his fingers seems less abrasive to his sensitive lungs than those he has struggled through before. He is enjoying Lord Ansell's home. He keeps pushing the thought of Stone's humiliation and banishment to the back of his mind. He will deal with it later. Were he to give it his full attention, he knows he would begin to feel guilty, and to do so would be a disservice to the pickled eggs, potted pheasant and grilled turbot that sit so pleasantly in his stomach.

'Refill, man!' Lord Ansell barks at a tall, straight-backed servant. The man is clad in so much black that he has all but disappeared into the shelves of books that line the wall to Lord Ansell's rear. He appears smoothly at his master's side and pours another two inches of amber liquid into the proffered glass.

'Deaf as a loaf of bread, that one,' says Lord Ansell, as the servant resumes his position in the darkness at the back of the library. 'Artillery, so he tells me. Cannon blew up three feet from him. Blew his friends to bits and left him half dead and three-quarters deaf. Still, the Lord preaches charity and he can fill my glass as well as anybody. Moreover, we don't need to worry about him loosening his lips and sharing our secrets, eh? Not like those bitches in the kitchen. Gossips, the lot of them. I'd take the whip to their backs were it not that it costs the earth to get new servants. And they do run off with tedious regularity. Always whelping a new litter. Can't keep their damn knees together. Were I a younger man I'd have them sewn shut! You see, Mr Matheson? Not a flicker on his face. I told you, deaf as a brick.'

Matheson gives a courteous nod in the general direction of the servant and takes another sip of brandy. Despite his host's spirited invective about the failings of the fairer sex, he can feel a warm, comfortable tiredness beginning to wash over him and does not want to give in to it. He has yet to do much to advance his cause or satisfy his curiosity regarding the crypt. He is trying to be polite and let the conversation flow but it is all he can do not to sit forward in his chair, and eagerly beg for a lantern, a key and a map. He forces himself to sit back in the plush, high-backed chair, and turns his gaze towards the small fire that crackles in the large, rectangular hearth. He takes in his surroundings afresh. There are gas lamps on each of the hardwood tables that sit beside the trio of leather armchairs facing the fire. Two of the walls are stocked head to toe in books and the remaining walls have been given over to Lord Ansell's hunting trophies. The light of the fire flickers in the cold glass eyes of the dead beasts and Matheson has quickly learned not to let his gaze travel in their direction. It feels a little too much like being watched. Instead, he looks at Phillip Ansell, sprawled languorously in the opposite chair. He has pulled a robe over his clothes and is smoking a long, thin cigar that he has screwed into the end of a slender black tube. He has thrown one leg over the arm of the chair and is petting a small lapdog that sits on his knee behind a folded copy of *Punch*. He has a smirk on his face, made harder to read by the red-wine smile upon his lips.

'A fine likeness, Father,' says Ansell, sucking in his lips to mime the suppression of a laugh. 'We should commission him, don't you think? A family portrait on the chimney breast in the great hall, perhaps.'

Lord Ansell stares right through his son. The pair have either bickered or ignored one another throughout the evening meal. The younger man's behaviour puts Matheson in mind of a petulant child, deliberately misbehaving to win attention of any kind. He has been poking at his father's temper ever since their arrival, though the elder man has yet to give in to the explosion of rage that clearly simmers in his blood.

'What do you think, Mr Matheson? Like holding up a mirror, is it not?'

Phillip Ansell holds up the periodical. The cartoon plainly shows Lord Ansell in all his bulbous, buttoned-up and constipated majesty. The expression upon his face is of a man dealing with a prolonged episode of trapped wind and the colouring across his cheeks indicates that his fondness for drink is no secret. Matheson cannot make out the wording beneath the image but does not expect it to be flattering.

Lord Ansell clears his throat. It is a habit of his and sounds to Matheson's ears like the warning growl of a battle-scarred old hound.

'It seems my son is attempting to embarrass or anger me with the grubby rag he holds in his girlish grasp, Mr Matheson. Forgive him. He has embraced many of the feminine virtues. He is a spiteful butterfly, spewing poison even as he flutters so prettily among us. I should put him in a dress and lash him bloody, as I would any such young woman who dared speak to me thus. But I will resist the temptation out of deference to our guest. Forgiveness is the most Christian of solicitudes, is it not?'

'You will forgive the cartoonist, then, Father?' asks Ansell, in a voice that could sidle under doors and slither through keyholes. 'You harbour no festering resentment?'

'When a fool acts as a fool, it should cause no surprise,' says Lord Ansell, coolly. He turns to Matheson. 'I beg your pardon, Mr Matheson. You must be confused by this exchange. To explain, I am currently the subject of some gentle merry-making in such infantile publications as a result of a misinterpretation of a speech I gave in the House . . .'

'He said the poor should eat curry powder instead of bread,' says Ansell, gleefully. 'Said that with potatoes or bacon it could warm a man through. That the poor were simply not trying to solve the problem.'

'That is not what I said,' hisses Lord Ansell, turning furious eyes on his son. 'I simply advocated a hitherto untested method of keeping the poor warm and fed. I intend to try it on the servants this winter. We will see who is laughing then!'

'The testimonials are a treat, Father,' continues the younger Ansell, pretending to read. 'A letter here from a grateful work-house master. Apparently, at your suggestion, he has cut costs to an extent he never imagined – and with only a few dozen deaths. Moreover, having thinner patrons means he can put four more people into each bed . . .'

'Enough!' Lord Ansell slams a hand down on the arm of the chair. He glares into his son's eyes and something passes between them. At length, the younger man gives a nod and a shrug. 'My apologies, Mr Matheson. My father and I have always enjoyed a relationship built on barbs and jest. Sometimes I overstep. If I caused you discomfort, please do forgive me.'

Matheson waves his hands, scattering ash and splashing brandy. 'No apology necessary. This is your home and I am a mere inter-loper. Please, proceed as you would were you alone.'

Phillip Ansell scoffs and looks as though he wants to spit into the fire. 'Were we alone we would be in different rooms, sir.'

'Phillip,' says Lord Ansell, in a warning tone. For a moment, the younger man seems about to throw a minor tantrum but instead he flashes a smile and dismisses the tension with a barked laugh.

Matheson looks up inadvertently at the stuffed foxes and mounted stag-heads that line the wall behind the young man. A petal of red flame dances on the lenses of the creatures' glass eyes. He has a sudden memory of scripture, a passage about the fall of the angels. Cast from Heaven, tumbling into the abyss and damna-tion, the vista of a fading Paradise was burned into their eyes so that they would be forever reminded of what they had lost through their treachery. Matheson wonders if such a thing could be true. Whether he will ever see the flicker of eternity wink at him in the eyes of a stranger.

'You saw the city, I understand,' says Lord Ansell, with a sneer. 'It would be a mercy to give it over to the sea, though I fear it would poison the fish.'

Matheson looks at his host. 'Hull displeases you?' he asks.

'Hull is paying the price for its gluttony and lust,' says Lord Ansell, emphatically. 'It is a pit of devilment and debauchery. A rat grown fat through cannibalism and the devouring of filth and faeces. Do you hear me, sir? I have warned of the reckoning that awaited that city and now we see it for ourselves.'

Matheson's face betrays his disapproval. 'You do not believe, my lord, that the cholera is simply a disease? A vile and cruel thing that brings misery to those already suffering poverty and hardship? You do not believe, as many do, that simple improvements to the sanitation of the slums would put an end to what you see as the wrath of God?'

In his chair, Phillip Ansell raises his eyebrows and allows himself a smile. He is unused to seeing his father challenged and seems curious to discover what effect it will have on him.

Lord Ansell's face turns cold. His eyebrows knit together so thunderously that for a moment he seems to be growing another fist in his forehead. 'We almost certainly disagree on many things, Mr Matheson,' he says, with a low growl. 'I, for example, do not need proof of the glory of God. You search for him with candle and spade. I follow His teachings, and you ask Him for evidence that He deserves our devotion. I take possession of artefacts and relics so that I may protect them and glory in their proximity to the Lord. You look for the bones of the apostles so you may subject them to analysis and determine their provenance. I see devilment at work in Hull. You see something to pity.'

A small, exasperated laugh escapes Matheson's lips before he can bite it back. Its incongruity causes Phillip Ansell to giggle, and Lord Ansell's expression suggests that he is unused to being laughed at in his own house.

'I'm sorry, my lord,' says Matheson, sincerely. 'The charge you level at me is nothing I have not heard before. Indeed, my father could have written your script. I say to you what I say to him: a questioning mind has been bestowed upon me for a reason, and I glory God by following its whims. I do believe in the Lord. I also believe in the arrogance and duplicity of man. The Bible cannot be seen as conclusive proof, sir, not when it has passed through the hands and minds of so many clerics and scholars. Did you know there were conferences, centuries ago, to choose which of the books to leave in the gospels and which to remove? Does each story and parable not fill you with a desire for more? I seek my own path to God, my lord. I envy you your conviction.'

Without being asked, the footman emerges from the darkness and fills Lord Ansell's glass. Ansell has not taken his eyes off Matheson. His countenance speaks of a desire to do bloody murder.

'The gold, for example,' says Matheson, warming to his theme. 'Do you not question its whereabouts?'

'The gold?' asks Lord Ansell, through gritted teeth.

'The gifts brought to Christ's crib by the wise men. The gold handed to the infant Christ. Gold would be a handsome gift for the family of a carpenter, a life-changing endowment. And yet Christ was raised within a humble family. His father continued in his work. Would Christ's gold not be a remarkable find, Lord Ansell? Do you not at least want to know where it went?'

For a moment, Lord Ansell says nothing. He seems to be ruminating, or trying to dislodge something unpleasant from a rear tooth. Eventually he gives a nod and drains his glass. 'You will forgive me, Mr Matheson,' he says. 'I am suddenly overcome by tiredness. We will doubtless continue our conversation at another time. For now, I shall retire and pray that God sees only youthful folly and not dangerous malice in your nonsensical words. Good night to you both.'

Without another word, Lord Ansell stalks from the room. Matheson does not have time to begin an apology or to rise from his chair. He is left wide-eyed, his mouth open like an uncorked bottle. He turns worried eyes on Phillip Ansell. 'I'm sorry, my friend. I wished only to . . .'

Ansell gives his girlish laugh, then makes a complicated lapping gesture with his tongue, like a cat enjoying a shallow saucer of milk. 'My father has always taken disagreement as insult,' he says, placing a pinch of snuff upon the delicate inkwork at his knuckles. 'I have never decided whether or not he is suited for politics. Is it better to have conviction or the capacity for

78

changing one's mind? Certainly he was a fine soldier. I imagine that utter conviction is crucial in such work. That is why I struggle to see Mr Stone being at home on the battlefield. He is a man of many fathoms, is he not? I question whether he truly believes in anything.'

The mention of Stone sends a ripple of guilt through Matheson and he gulps at his brandy, wondering whether his companion even made it through the woods with the giant Welshman. He makes to stand – suddenly aware that he has acted shamefully. He feels a sudden compulsion to run to his friend's side and make earnest apologies. He has been blinded in his duty to the living by his pursuit of the dead. He pushes himself forward in his chair and opens his mouth to speak when a sudden chill wind ruffles the hair at the back of his neck and causes goose-pimples to rise upon his forearms. Instinctively he shivers and turns his eyes to Ansell.

The young man is standing, his gaunt, jointy body bent in a deep bow. 'Mother,' he says theatrically. 'You herald the winter, do you not?'

Matheson stares at the figure that has appeared. Lady Claribel Ansell looks like a pot of ink. She is squat, rotund and clad entirely in black. A lace veil obscures her face; her black dress is buttoned to the throat and fastened with a cameo brooch carved of some raven-hued material. She trembles slightly as she stands in the open doorway, and reaches out a wavering hand. 'Please,' she says, softly. 'Another . . .'

Matheson pushes himself to his feet. He is about to introduce himself but his gaze is drawn to the glass eyes of the stag. The woman seems to have little or no reflection. She is a blob of blackness, bereft of life and colour. He feels himself growing cold and wonders whether the firelight dancing in his eyes could be mistaken for the pure light of Heaven or the flames of Hell.

'A moment, Mother,' says Ansell. 'Will you sit? This is my friend Mr Matheson. He is Canadian and a fine fellow. He has shown interest in our crypt. Father is to grant him access to the relics, unless his mood has been damaged irreparably . . .'

'Another,' says Lady Ansell, again, in a voice so hoarse it sounds as though there is a boot on her throat.

Ansell nods dutifully, and reaches beneath the seat on which he has been lounging. He retrieves a thick pad of papers and hurriedly turns to a fresh page. He crosses to the fire and selects a smouldering twig. Then, with swift, deft strokes, he attacks the blank page. His eyes take on a ferocious intensity as he works and Matheson sees, for the briefest of moments, a similarity between the cold gaze of the dead animals and the young man's deep inky pupils.

'Here,' he says, sounding breathless. 'She is smiling, do you see? At peace, Mother. Always at peace . . .'

Lady Ansell totters uncertainly forward and Matheson sees that she wears nothing upon her feet. She has pink, fleshy toes, with untrimmed nails and a ring of hair at her briefly exposed ankle. He turns away, embarrassed at the glimpse of flesh, then back at the sound of paper crumpling against the woman's chest. She has taken the picture from her stepson's hand and crushed it in an embrace. Now she holds it at arm's length and stares, adoringly, into the eyes of the child that has been hastily sketched in black upon the perfect white of the page. 'My darling,' she says tremulously. 'My poor, poor angel.'

Ansell seems to want to hug the woman, yet something within him keeps him from doing so. He seems ill at ease with the proximity of her grief. Instead he clears his throat, the sound reedy, pitiful, compared to the bass gruffness of his father's authoritative growl. 'Wynn!'

Within moments, the giant has appeared in the doorway. He takes in the lamentable figure of the lady of the house and something like tenderness crosses the scarred cliff of his face. He starts forward and gently takes the woman's elbow. She does not resist. Indeed, she seems to fall against him as he turns her, slowly, back towards the door. As she passes the fire, the flames seem to shrink. To Matheson, she is a woman so crushed by grief that she carries winter in her heart. He thinks of the myths and curious tales he has heard in his travels: of people able to move things with their

80

mind; of crying statues and weeping walls; speaking skulls and teeth continuing to grow in the heads of decapitated priests. Can it be true? Might grief bestow an almost supernatural power? Might she truly be causing the fire to die, purely with her nearness? Matheson finds himself shivering and unable to speak as she passes him, clutching the drawing of her dead child against her chest.

'My apologies,' says Phillip Ansell, quietly, when Lady Ansell and the big man have passed from the room. 'She does not always attend me of an evening. Sometimes the daubs I give her last her for weeks. Others she devours in days. I hope it will bring her comfort. Lord knows, naught else has lifted her from the despair that consumes her.'

Matheson looks at his empty glass. Wordless, he waves it in the air. The deaf servant emerges from the gloom and fills it. Matheson takes a gulp. 'I have never seen anyone so broken,' he says, sitting back down. 'Truly. She honours your sister's memory with her grief, though I fear such mourning may be almost a sickness. Is there nothing I can do? It pains me to see one so shattered.'

Ansell gives a small, tight smile and a nod of gratitude. 'She is not my mother but has been a good guardian to me,' he says, leafing through the pages in his pad. 'I ache to see her grieve. But, believe me, we have tried all that we can. Her grief is a bitter, hungry thing. It sucks the heat from her and the life from this house. She cannot see her in Heaven, do you understand? My poor, fragile sister. Mother needs to see her face. Needs to picture her somewhere safe and happy. For so long she believed her soul to be in torment. Now she fears the fading of her image from her memory. I have no such fears. My mind stores faces like books in a library. I can conjure my sister's without effort so I sketch her. I give her smile and bright eyes to my stepmother in the hope of bringing her back to the light, though I fear my efforts are to no avail. My father has already banished her from his heart. He grieves as men like him have always grieved – silently and angrily. He has lost patience with his wife. I wonder if I was right to bring you here. This is a home of secrets and shadows, and a grief that seeps into the soul. You came here to see bones, Mr Matheson. Instead I offer you the vision of a splintered heart.'

Matheson stares into the fire, trying to absorb its warmth into his suddenly cold bones. 'She thought your sister was in Hell?' he asks softly. 'Had she sinned? Did she die unredeemed?'

Ansell turns the sketch book to face his companion and points at the image scratched savagely into the tattered page. It shows a young girl, naked save for a dirty cotton smock. There are hands upon her. Serpentine tongues and curving grey claws slithering and tearing at her, red welts and streaks of crimson lashed deep into her pale flesh. A vicious hand has sketched agony and ecstasy upon her twisted features, lost in pained climax upon a bed of flame. 'This is what she saw,' he says, closing his eyes. 'What she still sees in her dreams. She drew this while asleep, Mr Matheson. Please, tell me, how does one heal a mind and soul that has descended so far as to tunnel into Hell?'

Matheson does not speak. He just stares at the picture until he feels his gorge rise. He swings his gaze away, focuses on the fire and watches the flames close in on themselves, like petals at night-time.

Tomorrow he will petition Lord Ansell to examine the relics of the dead. But, first, he must sleep in a house that feels like a doorway into something unfathomable, dark and deep.

8

It has been some time since Rose Davey thought of herself as a whore. Those days seem to belong to another life. When her mind wanders she can almost forget that time. She can pretend that her memories were put there as flights of imagination, pictures created by storybooks and gossip. In the village she now calls home, few would see anything in her appearance that would betray her brief flirtation with depravity. She is an apprentice washerwoman and lives with her aunt in one of the small but comfortable cottages next to the church. She should have come straight here a year ago, holding the letter her aunt had written and thanking her humbly for extending the offer of companionship and accommodation. But Rose had broken the journey from her native Sheffield with a night in Hull. She had allowed a fat man in green silk to buy her dinner and carry her bag. She had been charmed, had allowed the devil to drip honey into her ear. And she had opened her legs and allowed men to enter her until she felt as dead below the waist as she did within her heart.

Here, now, she thanks the good Lord that she was able to pull herself back from the edge. She fell to the very brink of Hell, but God yanked her back with His grace and forgiveness. She bears the marks of the descent. Still aches some mornings from what the man in the shadows made Natalie do to her. Still doesn't let herself touch the scars at the base of her spine and on the back of her legs. Perhaps some day she will invent a story of their origins that she can herself believe. Tell some credulous husband that she was whipped by a cruel uncle or dragged behind a horse. For now, she has to hope that her suitors are so overcome with desire for what lies at the delta of her thighs that they will resist the temptation to touch her anywhere else.

Rose shivers as she looks up at the purple black night, and marvels again at the clarity and perfection of the stars. There is little light here and she has never seen the heavens look so crisp and perfect. Each dot is a diamond scattered upon dark velvet. The moon seems twice as big as it should. She fancies that if she reached up, she would be able to prick her hand on its pointed edge.

Rose giggles. Tonight she has had her first swig of gin in an age. She dropped the bundle of laundry off at the vicarage and made friends with one of the younger maids. They shared some nettle wine together, then gossiped their way through a bottle of best gin that the vicar's wife had hidden behind a loose brick in the downstairs privy. Rose had enjoyed talking with a girl of her own age. She likes her aunt, but Rose is not yet eighteen. While she was working for Barrelman she had company, girls her own age. She had people to hold her and wipe her eyes. She made the right decision when she fled his employ but she wishes she could have brought some of the others with her. Laura, perhaps. She was too pretty for such work. Too sweet and tender. She should have come with her.

It's a pretty place, Patrington. She's perhaps fifteen miles from Hull but it feels like a different world. It's a rural community that makes its money from farming, and where the village church is a place of pilgrimage so grand it is known across Yorkshire as the Queen of Holderness. A whore could make good money here, should she so choose, though Rose is not tempted. She has real silver in her purse, and her life has taken on a pinkish hue.

She leans back against the willow tree, enjoying the cool shadow. She shivers, with cold and anticipation, as she looks at the note again, and traces the letters with short, pale fingers, rendered spotlessly white by their immersion in cold washing water.

Rose has fallen in love with words since she changed her life. The vicar's wife has been a patient and kindly teacher. Rose and the other young woman who showed an interest in becoming more proficient at her letters have learned to love their lessons in the parlour at the vicarage. She has become a devotee of romance

84

novels. Her heart flutters at descriptions of trembling caresses and the poetry of courtship. Her head has been turned by the notion of love. Not so long ago she would have been unable to read even the simple note she holds. Now she has allowed it to strip her of the most basic defences. She has cast off her wariness, as if it were a cloak.

Will he want more than a kiss? Will she let him? It feels strange to Rose to ask herself such questions. She knows how to please a man.

She wonders why she is so nervous, then realises it is because the thought of kissing frightens her. She has not kissed a man before – she has done unspeakable things with all manner of bastards, but her soft lips have never parted for the kiss of a gentleman.

The thought frightens her. Frightens and exhilarates.

'Oh, Rose, you silly fool . . .'

She feels girlish and high. Like a character in one of the stories her auntie reads to her from the periodicals or in a book by that trouble-causer Dickens. She is a heroine. A woman to be wooed. A strong, independent spirit making her own way, humble and determined, in a place populated by people with less noble hearts.

'Rose,' comes a voice, from the pitch dark. 'You came . . .'

Rose fights to hold in the squeal of excitement. The letter left in her laundry basket had been signed with a kiss. It had said a time and a place and had given instructions that she not tell a soul. She had never felt so adrift in romance. Had never felt so desirable and womanly.

'And who might you be?' she asks quietly.

The darkness remains silent. Rose shudders, squinting through the leaves of the weeping willow. She is only a few hundred yards from the centre of Patrington, next to the barn that Frank Cornwell fills with turnips each autumn and where her suitor instructed she wait for him in her best white gown. Where he had insisted – his quill tearing the page – that she be barefoot, her long, brown hair unfettered by ribbon or cap.

'You are a beauty,' comes the voice, quietly. 'Truly. Come towards the light.'

Rose squints again. 'What light?'

With that, a tinder-box is sparked. A small jewel of dancing orange flame seems to hover in the darkness. Rose moves forward, wondering if she wants to see the man who has so fallen for her, or whether identifying him will lead to disappointment. Perhaps she should just part her lips and allow the romance to dictate what happens next.

She watches the flame. Moves to meet it. Opens her eyes and lets the face come into focus.

Her expression betrays her. There is no glance of recognition. She does not know the man who stands in the shimmering flame. All she recognises is the intent in his expression. She has seen it before in the gaze of countless men, all intent on taking their pleasure in a way she cannot fathom.

'I'm sorry. I should go in,' stammers Rose, taking small steps backwards. Her feet suddenly feel cold on the damp grass; her shoulders goose-pimple in the cold breeze.

The man smiles as he moves forward, a grin that a demon would call beautiful. And then he raises his club.

Rose comes to in the gloom of the barn. A small fire flickers amid the damp straw. She has a pain by her left eye, her breasts have been exposed and her best dress is slashed from floor to thigh.

'Please,' she says, shivering. 'Please . . .'

She tries to move her arms and feels a rope bite into her wrist. She attempts to lever her legs free and feels nothing but burning heat at her ankles.

The man is watching her, standing just beyond the perimeter of her vision. Rose has a sudden flicker of memory. She recalls that room. That night. The sting of the lash. The warmth of Natalie's kisses and the drip-drip-drip of blood down her thighs.

'I don't do that any more,' she blurts, into the darkness. 'Barrelman can find you a girl—'

Her words are cut off by a sudden crushing blow to her left

forearm. Another. Another. The blows pulverise the bone between elbow and wrist. Her scream is stopped with a swatch of silk, stuffed into her throat with rough hands.

'You're going to be broken,' says the man, calmly. 'Broken on the wheel. Look behind you and you'll see. It won't take me long. I'll break your limbs and thread them through the spokes in the wood. And then we'll begin . . .'

Rose is gripped by an agony so ferocious that she feels as though she is holding a hot coal. Suddenly she knows she is going to die. She squints and makes out the man's face. Wishes she saw something comforting there. Wishes she knew why this was happening.

'I'll make you beautiful,' he says, coming closer. He hefts the long, tarred club and looks down at her pale, bare knee. 'I'll make you sublime.'

The man in the shadows brings down the club.

And begins . . .

9

An unwashed light, dribbling in through a gaping troll's mouth; the scent of rotting vegetation and nibbled bones . . .

Stone wakes with an aching head and sickness in his throat. He feels as though somebody is kneeling on his windpipe and it takes a good five minutes of frenzied coughing before he can breathe without a whistle or wheeze.

'You sound like you've been gargling with pebbles, my friend. Please forgive me for being the worst kind of companion.'

Stone looks up through watery eyes. A cold, bright sunlight casts a faint, whisky-coloured halo around the unmistakable shape of Diligence Matheson. He is hovering in the entrance to the hermitage, turning his hat between his fingers, like the wheel of a great ship. Stone smells last night's brandy and cigars upon the younger man's clothes and skin, and instantly gives a half-awake grin of approval. 'You partook of his lordship's hospitality,' he says, pulling himself to his feet and brushing the mud and leaves from his clothes. 'I hope you drank the place dry.'

'It's not a job I'm well equipped for,' says Matheson, entering the folly and looking with fascination upon the peculiar construction. 'But I did purloin this for a friend more suited to the task . . .'

From beneath his blue coat, Matheson reveals a green bottle full of best Spanish brandy, alongside a small china plate. 'Brandy and potted pigeon. I am reliably informed there is no better breakfast, if you happen to be a drunkard, warrior and disgraced diplomat. It was warm when I left the house but the footman's directions were a little vague and I have found myself making progress towards you in loops, circles and criss-crosses. Viewed from above, I may have written my signature in footsteps.'

Stone rubs his face and smells the earth upon his flesh. A tiny hair tickles at his skin and he plucks it from the back of his hand. He recalls white rats and the sound of crunching bones, a small man and a promise to the dead . . .

'I have to go back to Hull,' says Stone, suddenly, and hearing the words spoken aloud gives credence and power to the previously unarticulated thought. He takes the drink and plate from his employer. 'I'm sorry, Diligence, it's just going to eat at me if I don't . . .'

Matheson nods. He seems so grateful to be forgiven for having abandoned him the previous night that he would happily allow Stone a night in his sister's bed were it to lead to reconciliation.

'There was a little fellow here last night,' says Stone, thoughtfully, as he scoops a mouthful of pigeon into his mouth and grunts appreciatively at the rich, deep flavour. 'Rat-catcher. Reckons her ladyship has been touched in her mind by the angels. Your friend Phillip tell you that when he invited you to the castle?'

Stone watches as Matheson registers the mild note of reproof. He looks ashamed of himself as he glances around at the damp, unwelcoming cave where Stone spent the night and pulls a face as he notices the peculiar holes and striations in the supporting wall.

'I met her ladyship last night,' says Matheson, leaning against the wall and inserting a finger into one of the cavities. 'After an exchange of views with his lordship. The poor woman seems eviscerated by grief, Meshach. Truly, I have seen mourning. I have witnessed pain. She has been dragged so low by misery that I see her as little more than a puddle of ink.'

Stone takes in the whiteness of his round face and the bags beneath wide, troubled eyes. 'You didn't sleep? Not even in a big soft bed?'

'Nightmares,' says Matheson, miming a shudder. He looks at his hand, as if seeing it for the first time. 'Chicken-skin! I pimple at the mere memory. I dreamed of a storm so ferocious that to catch the hail was to grab a musket ball from the air. I watched my skin perforate beneath its assault. I woke fearing I had been turned inside out by Nature. And the sweat that dried upon me tasted more of charcoal than of salt. For all its drapes and linens, that house is as cold as an unfilled grave.'

Stone stretches elaborately. He unwinds the scarf from his skull and begins to refasten it.

Matheson stares at the ruin of his head. 'We've never spoken of your injuries, Meshach,' he says quietly.

Stone is trying to work some life into limbs made heavy and dead by the unforgiving ground. 'Not much to tell,' he says, shrugging and refastening his weapons inside his coat. 'They wanted information. I had none to give. They treated me like a Christmas pudding and left me looking like a trampled turd.'

Matheson moves back into the sunlight so that the warmth of the day can help suppress the chill that threatens to overpower him. 'I cannot imagine anybody having the physical abilities to render you so helpless,' he says loyally. 'Were you betrayed? Drugged?'

Stone gives an indulgent laugh as he stoops to retrieve his hat from the floor. 'I'm no Hercules,' he says. 'If you had been in the tent when they hurt me . . .' He tails off, his mind suddenly awash with memories. It was maybe a year after he emerged from the mountain of bodies and walked away from all he had known. He had been in battle-scarred Lahore for only a few days when he crossed paths with the group of British deserters. It was a dangerous place for anybody with an English accent, and it was only Stone's mastery of the local dialect that had allowed him to remain unmolested during his stay in the city. The deserters had no such skills. They were private soldiers. Thugs. They were half mad with dehydration and hunger when they staggered into the brothel, demanding girls and arrack. Stone was sitting in the dark, shielded from the rectangle of yellow light that speared in from the high window. The men were jittery. They had their muskets trained on the brothel-keeper and their swords in their hands. They drained the bottles of arrack and brandy that he brought for them. He tried to claim that there were no women, that it was a mere tavern. So they began to hurt him. And when Stone stood up, drunk and half helpless, one of the men recognised him as an officer. The fight was brief. He took a beating that half killed him. Each time he passed out they woke him and began to hurt him afresh. They seemed confused over their motives. Half of them wanted information about whether they were being pursued. The others just wanted to hurt an officer. It was a broad-shouldered, red-haired Irishman who both saved his life and marked him for ever. He burst into the brothel to warn the men that soldiers were coming. One drew a blade and prepared to cut Stone's throat. The Irishman held him back, telling them death was too good for an officer. He said he wanted to leave his mark instead. He dragged Stone outside into the hot, damp air, where a group of natives were boiling pitch to make repairs to the city walls. There was no fanfare. No devilish grin or smart remark. The Irishman simply plunged Stone's head into the pot and held him there. It had felt like being swallowed by molten lava. Pain galvanised him. He kicked out and felt the grip loosen. He pushed himself backwards, pulled his curved dagger from inside the folds of his robes and opened the Irishman's belly.

By the time the deserters had been caught, Stone's screams had ceased. The brothel-keeper's daughters picked the cooled pitch from his skin and held him close each time his flesh came away from the bone. When the bandages and ointments were removed he no longer recognised himself. Stone found himself strangely disinterested in the loss of his good looks. He felt that his reflection better suited the man he knew himself to be.

'Meshach?'

Stone pulls himself back to the present and tries to put his feelings into words. 'When you've seen battle you'll know that even the strongest of men can be brought low,' he says, and sighs. 'And I am not a strong man. My heroics were invention and good fortune. I made my name on a mission synonymous with tragedy and disgrace. Please drop this notion of me as some mighty warrior poet. I am a fool and a reprobate. I have protected you because I have been equal to the threats. But do not believe yourself invulnerable.'

Matheson waves a hand, as though his friend is being modest. 'Wynn will learn the error of his ways, I'm sure of that,' he says. 'And should you wish it I have no doubt that Lord Ansell's sword would be cleaved in two by your Indian blade. You may dislike yourself, Meshach, but you will not convince me you are anything other than a good man laid temporarily low by happenstance.'

Stone examines the tubby man, and feels an unnatural impulse to take him in his embrace. Instead, he uncorks the brandy and takes a deep, purposeful swallow. 'I need to see her properly put to rest,' he says. 'Laura. It's a persistent itch. A painful thing. I left without seeing her body. I shirked and shrank. I have abandoned all notions of duty, Diligence, but this is something deeper. Something that matters. I can't explain it. I wish I had a poet's words . . .'

Matheson steps forward and puts a warm hand upon the wiry muscles of Stone's shoulder. 'You seek redemption. Don't be afraid to say the word.'

For a moment, Stone stares into the soft blue of the other man's eyes, seeing his reflection float in the wide, tranquil pools. He likes the quiet innocence of the view. 'I won't be more than a day or so,' he says, turning away. 'I hope Ansell lets you in. If not, kick him in the balls and go to the reliquary anyway. You're in no danger here. Well, maybe from Phillip . . .'

The two share a grin as Matheson shoots him a reproving glance. 'You do not truly believe he has committed those sins, do you?'

Stone manages to stifle a smile. 'I've seen men request permission to marry a goose, Diligence. I've seen men touch themselves while under siege and officers request their drummer boys based on the shapeliness of their arse. I've given up guessing what mankind will do, but I know what a man, an individual, is capable of. And I warn you – keep your door locked while I'm gone.' He gives his friend a sly wink. 'Unless you fancy doing otherwise . . .'

'Are you in funds?' asks Matheson, colouring and changing the subject. 'You have provisions? Food? Drink? Lord Ansell placed a horse at my disposal. He's stabled at the house, if you wish to make use of him. I'm not one for riding, as you have witnessed. I look like a closet wobbling about . . .'

Stone takes his friend's hand and shakes it warmly. 'Take care, Diligence. And, please, try not to express any opinions that will lead to upset. Not until I'm back, at least.'

Matheson grins and salutes. 'I will bite my tongue. I will be a gracious guest. And, by God, I'll get into that reliquary.'

Stone enjoys the earnest zeal on the younger man's countenance, and wishes he shared a passion other than doing right by the dead. He takes a gulp of drink, and prepares to gaze upon the corpse of a woman he now knows he loved.

IO

It is a little after ten when Stone disembarks the carriage on Hull's Spring Bank. His fellow passengers this past hour have numbered a drunken lawyer being carried home after a night in a Cottingham tavern, and the grieving uncle of a butcher's apprentice who has succumbed to the cholera.

Stone wishes he were better suited to conversation, that he had done more to comfort the grey, barrel-chested man than turn his back and stare out of the window at the soft rain. He wishes he could find it in himself to give a damn.

'We can come back the same way,' says the driver, as Stone puts a boot on to the muddy cobbles of the thoroughfare. 'A coin or two will always change the route.'

He says nothing, just stares past the driver at the dying city: all of the flame and cloud and stench.

'As you wish, sir,' says the driver, in response to Stone's silence. 'Not everybody will take you, is all. Some say you can carry the plague on your person. I don't worry about such things. Not when compensated . . .'

Stone breathes in, absorbing the scent of the tar in the great burning barrels that spew noxious black clouds across the wide, dirty street. He coughs as he takes in the stink and sea spray of the docks. Above, half a dozen birds squawk and caw, throwing unnatural patterns on to the blurry son. Stone squints against the glare as he tries to find his bearings. He turns and takes in the tall, terraced properties that stand as sentries in front of the sprawling cemetery that has been swallowing the city's dead since this terror began.

'You have lost someone, my son?'

94

Stone has swallowed no more than half a dozen decent lugs of brandy and should not feel as woozy or drunk as he currently does. His belly is empty and his mind spinning. He smells Laura, smells the sweat of her skin. The sensation is dizzying, debilitating. He feels an urge to fall, as if a cannon shell has burst within earshot and his senses are scrambled.

'My son? Are you well? I have brandy about my person . . .'

Stone blinks hard and lets his eyes focus. Before him stands a tall, handsome vicar in his early middle-years. He speaks with an accent that Stone does not recognise but which seems to originate a long way from this diseased port. 'I'm sorry, Father,' he says, without intending to, and the double-meaning almost makes him vomit on his boots. 'I am quite well, I assure you. Perhaps the stench of tar has made me nauseous . . .'

The vicar nods, as though acknowledging the possible truth in his words. 'I have grown accustomed to it,' he says quietly. 'At first I would wash my clothes and hair each night. Now I endure it. People bear much worse, do they not? I can tolerate the smell of the dying.'

Stone straightens. He adjusts his hat and takes a deep breath. As he stares up at the blue sky, patterns and images swim in his vision. The smell of Laura has vanished to be replaced by the sizzling skin of his dead bride. For a moment, he accepts his own madness, consents to lunacy. Surely he must be mad. Here, on this wide, shit-streaked thoroughfare, standing before this cemetery transformed to a vision of damnation of interment, he sees no place for sanity.

'James Sibree,' says the vicar, taking Stone's hand. 'Forgive my appearance. The nights and days run into one.'

Stone considers the man before him. His black cassock is stained and dirty and his beard has grown in a way that suggests the careful grooming of a month before has been set aside for the sake of expediency. 'Stone,' he answers, extending a hand. 'Meshach. Once of the Bombay Artillery and Her Majesty's Government.'

'Once?' asks Sibree, intrigued.

'I am a fallen man,' says Stone, trying to keep his balance and wishing that the scent of tar and death would leave his nostrils.

'We are all imperfect,' says Sibree, absently. 'Meshach, you say. And how has the fiery furnace treated you?'

Despite himself, Stone smiles. 'I cannot complain to be as holy a man as my namesake. When the trumpets of Nebuchadnezzar sounded, I would no doubt have bowed down.'

'We do not know whom we are until God tests us,' says Sibree, warmly. 'You are the first Meshach I have known. I hope, at Judgement Day, to meet another.'

'I hope, at Judgement Day, to be allowed eternal rest,' says Stone, and is overcome by the sincerity of the statement. He feels tears prick at his eyes and cuffs them away. 'You bury the cholera victims? You deliver the last rites to the damned?'

Sibree frowns. 'Why do you believe the victims of this plague to be damned?' he asks.

'Do you not?' asks Stone, reaching into a pocket for brandy and his pipe.

'I have seen misery and sadness,' says Sibree. 'I do not question God's wisdom. But I do not see His hand in this plague. I see a result of bad sanitation and decision-makers too greedy to provide help for the poor.'

Stone says nothing for a time. He sees a soft wisdom in the other man's eyes. Feels a desire to learn. To weep and be consoled. He is about to speak when a sudden dreadful ululation pierces the air. It is at once song and scream and it makes the hairs upon his arms rise like sails.

'Irish,' says Sibree, sadly. 'The "death wail", it is called. The womenfolk cry out in their native tongue and no amount of persuasion will make them cease. I have few words of comfort. The cholera plot has become a quarry. Worse, a ploughed field. Each time we dig we disturb those recently interred. Each time I shake a mourner's hand it is in the full and certain knowledge that I will be burying them within days. I fear I am growing hardened to the horror. I barely hear the cries now.'

96

Stone listens to the alien, terrible sound, then turns his head and finds himself staring into the flames that smoulder in the heart of the tar pits. He wishes he could drain his laudanum, that he could see Laura dance in the flickering light. 'I lost somebody,' he says quietly. 'I don't know why I speak of her. I don't know if she was mine to lose. But she mattered. Mattered more than me . . .'

Sibree stands silently. He seems to consider the man before him. To see one who has suffered. He looks for a moment like a man who thought he had used up his last reserves of pity, only to be proved wrong. 'I was going home,' he says. 'Would you perhaps walk with me?'

Stone sniffs deeply. He screws up his face and remembers his sins. Wonders what he would first confess, were he given to Papist apology. He nods, grateful.

'I was here for the ground-breaking,' says Sibree, as Stone falls silently into step beside him. 'It will be twenty years next July since I arrived. A hundred and seventy miles on an express four-horse coach that brought me to Barton-upon-Humber. Do you know the town? A handsome place, though that day I was too tired and dirty to appreciate it. A steamboat brought me to Hull. I see myself now, young and afraid, trying to soothe my aching bones before my first foray into the pulpit. I can tell you I had no instant fondness for the city, Mr Stone. It seemed to come from the end of the earth. It was the flatness, you see. I missed the hills and dales, the glades and forest of my native Somerset. I was tempted to take another position at Deptford, offered me by my friend and tutor, but God blessed me with a sense that Hull was where I should make my home. I felt a sense of purpose and duty. They offered me a hundred pounds to stay, Mr Stone, and I am pleased to say I accepted.'

Stone has been fumbling with both pipe and bottle. As the pair walk down the dirty brown cobbles, he gives up on both vices. He cocks his head and pays attention.

'Two years ago, I was among a select group of guests who were invited to attend the official opening of the Hull General Cemetery,' says Sibree, with the air of a man who has talked of naught but death for weeks and is enjoying the chance for an alternative to reminiscence. 'One should not think fondly of such a place but it seemed a handsome, even beautiful place in which to be laid to rest. Truly, it was a real and great blessing for a city that had for too long endured woefully insufficient cemeteries. Before the opening, it was scarce possible to dig one grave without encroaching on another. We recoiled at such horrors, Mr Stone, but we made it our business to mend the situation.'

Stone blinks, and hurries to catch up with his eloquent new companion. "You tried to make it beautiful?'

'Under the guidance of Superintendent John Shields, it became a place befitting eternal rest. Rare moths and butterflies were attracted to the colours and splendour of the flowers that grew beside the graves. Birds of the sweetest song abounded. If it were not for the undesirability of shuffling off the mortal coil, one would almost long to call it home.'

Stone swallows. He can still taste her. Can still recall the mixed pleasures on his tongue as he pushed inside her and felt the welts upon her flesh . . . 'You sound as though you speak of a different age,' he says feebly, and manages to cough some strength into his voice. The mixture of phlegm and acid that shoots up from his gullet makes him shudder.

'This summer has destroyed all thoughts of gentle death, Mr Stone. This last month has taken parts of me that I did not know were ripe for taking. I have been nothing but an undertaker, a foreman, overseeing the one duty shirked by all others. I have worked twelve hours a day. I have been sole witness to the wearied trials of our good superintendent. Morning and night I have witnessed the digging of graves for the dead – only to witness the burial of those who only days before had been mourners. Most oppressive, most trying, have been the burials when the sun has gone down and there is only the moon to lighten the darkness at the grave and a solitary lantern burning to help in the dreary work. I feel I am burying a city.'

Stone stops, pressing his hand to his face. 'You are a man of God,' he says. 'This must fit into your understanding of His plans.'

Sibree smiles gently, as if chiding a tired child. 'I serve God because I love God,' he says, taking a handful of his beard and staring through the trees at the most recent grave. 'It is not love of His plans that keeps me at the graveside. It is a duty to man. A duty to those who have fallen because of poverty. Look at the houses yonder. For a month their inhabitants have seen nothing but funeral processions. They have not witnessed God's wrath – they have seen the result of man's lack of charity for his neighbours. In the light of the burning tar barrels they have seen the product of ungiving hearts. These are the poor, Mr Stone, and I have a duty to show them that this is not the work of God, or of the devil, but of sloth and greed. I hope, despite the tiredness within me, that I can continue such work, even in the face of overstuffed graves and mud that gives up flesh and bone with each new insertion of the spade.'

Stone feels something prick at his eyes. He feels drunk and cold and worthless. He suddenly wants this man to take him by the chin, look into his eyes and tell him that he is forgiven.

'Your friend,' says Sibree, stopping short. 'You said you sought answers?'

Stone swallows. He reminds himself of whom he once was. He has seen buzzards pecking at the eyeballs of fallen men, sacrificed lives for the good of the many and slipped his blade between the ribs of those who opposed the diplomacy of Queen Victoria's empire. He should not be so disturbed by horror, should welcome grief and misery as lifelong friends.

'She died,' he says, and feels dampness at his throat. 'A whore. We spent one night together but I sensed that she could heal me. If not her, I fear nobody could.'

Sibree looks upwards, as though talking to God. 'She succumbed? Succumbed to the cholera?'

Stone nods. Blinks back a tear, then presses the heel of his hand against his face.

'Her name, my son,' says Sibree, quietly. 'I may have helped her into Paradise.'

Stone looks at the ground. He studies the outline of a bootprint in the churned mud and wonders if it belonged to a mourner, head bowed and damp beneath a patina of sorrow. Whether its owner is puking their life away in a hovel by the river, or is already turning to gas and bone beneath the soil. 'Laura,' he says, and as he does so, he fancies he has coughed up a sluice gate. Tears fall from his eyes unconstrained. Without seeking approval, he clutches at Sibree, pulls the man close and sobs into his black lapels.

'I have known many of that name,' says Sibree. 'I fear there is no name I have not spoken at a graveside and I make no judgement upon how she lived her life. Her soul is in God's hands now. Only last week I laid to rest a seamstress of ill-repute. She had been brutalised, sir. I believe her brother languishes even now in a gaol cell, though it would be more charitable to find a hospital bed for one so horribly touched by the angels. And, in a time of plague, I fear that few care about the butchery done to the damned in the moments before their passing . . .'

Stone can barely hear his words over the sound of rushing blood in his head. He turns and heaves a breakfast of brandy into the gutter. 'Please, my son, if you would join me in prayer, perhaps we could find a way to fathom the madnesses of this most terrible of times . . .'

Sibree is talking to empty air. Stone has turned his back. His mind is full of her now, drunken hallucinations and imaginings. He is consumed by a need to see her, to breathe her in, even if all he inhales is the scent of death.

He stumbles towards the city, feet churning up dust and mud and horse-shit as the crows and gulls squawk and caw and scrap in the sky above.

'Will no one buy? Will no one buy?'

Stone's feverish sprint has slowed to a painful, haphazard jog when the sudden shout gives him an excuse to pause and catch his breath. He takes a gulp of cold, damp air and looks up into a sky that seems to be closing over the city, like a gloved hand.

A fruit-seller with greasy hair and a drooping left eye is rubbing a dirty cuff over a face the same colour as the drifts of burning tar smoke that float in front of and behind him. His beard is a straggly, stained affair, which makes it hard to guess his age. He could be anything from his middle-years to seventy. He looks as though he has not slept for days, and in the pale grey air, it seems to Stone that he could easily come apart, like damp paper, disintegrating on the breeze to become clouds and steam.

'You, sir,' says the man, seeing Stone pause. 'An orange? It's good for the bones. Good for the skin. We need sustenance in these hellish times and it's cheaper than strong ale.'

Stone looks at the man's goods. Apples, oranges, plums and berries sit in woven baskets on the back of his small cart. Nobody has bought his wares in days. 'You should go home,' he says, between gasps. He is inexplicably angry at the fool's attempts to sell good health to a city squeezed by a great mortality. 'Nobody's going to buy. Eat it yourself. Give it to your loved ones. Do what you must do.'

The man looks reluctant to give up his chance of a sale. 'Meat's the ticket, sir,' he says, as though imparting great wisdom. 'Meat and ale. And I can't buy it unless somebody buys from me, can I? Would you take an apple, perhaps? Freshpicked. I do have flowers, should you have a liking to impress a lady. Tulips. Bought the last bunch from the last boat that came from Amsterdam, I did. Been saving them for the right man. I'll put them on a grave, should I need to, though how could one bunch of blooms commemorate all this, eh?'

Stone looks about him. The street sign declares him to be in St Thomas's Place, off Portland Street, in the heart of the city. The properties are tall but their white frontages have taken on the same unhealthy pallor as their residents. A squat red-brick factory stands mute to his rear, its great double-doors shuttered and locked. Further up the street, an alehouse, its sign a scrawl of illegible red paint, gives away no sign of life. On its front step, a bag of rags and white hair mumbles to herself, face pressed into the coarse brick.

'Anderson's,' says Stone, suddenly, turning his attention back to the man. 'Undertaker. Round here, yes?'

Casually, the fruit-seller extends a hand and clears his throat. Stone rolls his eyes and bares his teeth but still produces a coin, which he places on the man's palm. He takes an apple from the cart. As he turns it in his hand he exposes the rotten, maggot-chewed corruption at its base, hidden beneath the shining red and green succulence of the face that had been pointed at the weak sun. Stone drops it. It bursts on impact with the earth.

'Anderson's cart's at the cemetery,' says the man, ignoring the look on Stone's face. 'Apprentice lad should be in the back of the yard, catching up on sleep. Worked round-the-clock they have. Been harder for them than most.'

'Friends of yours?' asks Stone.

'The very best,' says the fruit-seller, nodding. 'I don't envy them what they've been through. Only helped them out once or twice and it's got into me dreams. They live and breathe all this. There's some reckon they've got dispensation from the Almighty. Reckon they won't die until the last body is buried.'

Stone tries to look as interested as he can. He spent years flattering great men and generals of all races and intellects as he sought to better the lot of the empire. He has smoked with shahs and slit the throats of radicals and traitors. He knows how to talk to a simpleton like this, even if a voice inside him is telling him to pin the trader against the brickwork and threaten to take his eyes.

The fruit-seller leans forward, his smile suddenly lascivious. He leers as he begins his tale. 'We had some mad old bitch down here trying to touch them the other day,' he says, and spit gathers in the corners of his mouth. 'Reckoned they had something miraculous about them to have been spared. Wanted them inside of her. Lifted her skirts and wailed and cried like a stabbed animal, she did. Took a constable giving her a hiding to move her on, though she didn't get no further than the pub there. She got what she wanted in the end.'

Stone raises his hand to his nose and wipes away the bead of moisture that has run from his eyes. He wants to overturn the fruit cart and stamp every berry beneath his boot. He snatches off his hat and rubs his hand against one of the scars upon his skull. The movement causes his coat to fall open so that the small axe and curved blade gleam in the dying light. Stone watches the fruit-seller's expression change.

'I keep a rich man safe,' says Stone. 'Safe as any can be in a place like this.'

The fruit-seller gives a nervous grin. 'The young apprentice,' he says. 'He's not a bad lad. You won't be wanting him for any trouble, will you? Only we've all had a bellyful of that . . .' The man stops talking. Stone wonders whether his friends have told him of the wild-eyed, drug-addled madman who emerged from the darkness and gave them coins to disentangle a dead whore. Whether they spoke of scars and foreign weapons, and the cloud of malevolence that emanated from within.

'I mean nobody any harm,' says Stone, though he wonders at the truth of it. 'A friend of mine. A girl. They've been preparing her. Making her fit . . .'

The fruit-seller babbles, his eyes flickering back to the blade, 'We've all lost somebody. Did they tell you a day for the service? Only things have got a bit disordered. She may be in the ground already, sir, begging your pardon.'

Stone reaches into his pocket and pulls out the whisky. He takes a deep swallow, then hands it to the fruit-seller. He has found no better example of diplomacy than the sharing of a bottle. 'I paid them,' he says. 'She was . . . contorted. She'd been left. The stiffness had got in her bones, y'see. They couldn't have put her in a coffin without hurting her. And if you'd seen her, you'd not have been able to bring yourself to . . .'

Something in the fruit-seller's expression changes. He turns away, raises the bottle to his lips and pours the liquid into his mouth without letting the glass touch his skin.

Stone stares at the side of the man's face. His lip curls and he feels chill fingers upon his neck. 'They talked of her?' he asks. 'You know who I'm speaking of?'

The fruit seller sucks at his cheek, picks an apple from the pile and buffs it with his cuff, smearing rotten juice upon cloth and skin. 'Tam needed a drink after seeing her,' he says, not meeting Stone's gaze. 'They'd bathed her, like you'd said. Warm water and vinegar. Cared for her as you would your own wife, have no fear on that. They're good people, the Andersons. Run their business the right way, if you follow. Tam didn't deserve to see that, sir. You'll be the one who paid them, are you? They did have questions. Wondered if you knew . . .'

The fruit-seller's eyes dart again to the weapons in Stone's coat. Something flickers in his eyes: a question and an accusation.

Stone hears the rushing of blood in his head and smells something metallic and thick. For an instant he hears battle. Remembers, suddenly, the first cry of danger as the Persians attacked Herat. The recollection hits him like a fist. He has little time to wonder at its origin or meaning as he is sucked into memory. A younger man, hopelessly out of his depth, weakened by scurvy and starvation, trying to repel an attack by trained troops while commanding a straggle of helpless, siege-weary Afghans. The stench that came from the west . . .

He grabs the bottle as if he is drowning, takes a long swallow and pushes down the memories. He breathes hard, like a horse pulling up mid-gallop. 'Tell me,' he says, through gritted teeth, 'what they saw. Where is she? What did they see?'

The fruit-seller backs away, half undone by the sudden madness in Stone's eyes. He reaches for the length of knotted wood he keeps below the stall and raises it, with a wavering growl of fear and defiance. The cholera may take his trade and his life but he will not allow some drunken, plum-voiced gargoyle to open his belly as if he's gutting an eel . . .

Stone's body does not move. But his hands twist in a blur. The Indian blade is out of his coat and spinning through the cold air before anything in either man's expression has time to alter.

There is a yelp, then the clatter of wood on cobbles.

An instant later the fruit-seller is staring, wide-eyed and unbelieving, at the lethal-looking blade stuck deep in the very centre of his club.

'Tell me,' says Stone, in a whisper. 'I don't want to harm anybody. I don't want to, but I can. I need to know what they saw.'

The fruit-seller tears his eyes from the blade and appears to wonder, for an instant, whether he is looking upon the knife that did the things to the poor dead whore that Tam Anderson had been paid to disentangle.

'They didn't see it when they found her,' he stammers, and his drooping eyelid becomes a funnel for a sudden torrent of red-seamed tears. 'Begging your pardon, sir, but she'd been left, you see. Had been days without discovery. And when they were called to take her away they thought she were like all the others. They thought the stains were the same damn shit that makes paupers of princes and ensures we all die humble and penitent. She were caked in it, sir. Nowt they hadn't seen before and no worse than any of the other poor bastards they've seen to these past weeks. They told me it all over an ale. Said this fearsome soldier-type had given them coin to see her proper buried. And I swears to you they did what you bid. Washed her. Cleaned her. Bought her a good cotton dress to be laid out in . . .'

'You saw her?' growls Stone, through the gristle in his throat. 'Came in to gawp, did you?'

The fruit-seller considers his options. Considers the blade. 'Tam said he could tell she'd been a beauty,' he says, shaking. 'A peach, he said. Could see it in the shape of her. It weren't nothing mucky. He massaged her skin, like he was instructed, rubbed in the oils. It took a good heave-ho but we disentangled her. And then we saw . . .'

Stone raises his eyes to the sky. Spots the last necklace of golden light. Stares at it and watches the clouds take it into their possession. The sky turns grey.

His mind fills with Laura. With the fire and sadness and compassion in her gaze. With the heat of her embrace and the sour, salty softness of her kisses. He feels again the poor-quality lace of her smock beneath his fingers and wonders, for an instant, why he had allowed her to keep it on when he wanted her nakedness more than he had ever desired anything. Had she insisted? He was too drunk and doped that night to remember. Yes! She'd tugged at the hem, made a joke about preserving her modesty, then taken him inside her and shushed his protestations with a warm tongue. Good God but she had been beautiful. Pure, somehow, despite the things she had endured and the misery of her situation.

'Where is she?' he demands, stepping forward. 'Tell me what you saw!'

'They called the constables, sir. Sergeant Cook came. He took a statement. Told them to put her in the ground.'

Stone reels. He'd known that she would be buried, that the churned earth of Spring Bank Cemetery would close over her. But that she has already been devoured, that she lies among strangers, beyond his reach, beyond his embrace . . . He feels robbed. Freshly bereaved. Damned afresh by her absence.

'What did you see?' asks Stone, again, and he feels his right hand quiver itself into a trembling fist as the certainty of the answer screams above the blood in his brain.

'She'd been sliced, sir,' says the fruit-seller, grimacing at the memory. 'Across, upside down. From her tits to her slit and from hip to hip. It weren't shit, it were blood. Blood gone brown from the heat and from being left so long, like. It were bad, sir. Bad enough to call the peelers. Nobody were to know. So many dead, she were just another. But that had been done with a blade.'

Both men look down at the shining streak of silver that protrudes from the gnarled black wood at their feet.

'Who?' says Stone, though the sound is barely audible. He coughs. Spits. Tastes blood. 'Who?' he demands again. 'Who would do it? Why? Why did they bury her? There would be questions . . .'

The fruit-seller gives the most tactful shrug he can manage. 'Anderson's did what they had to. They did right by you and by her. They called the peelers and then they did what Sergeant Cook told them to. They still put the dress on her, sir. Still made her as pretty as they could. These are hard times. Who knows why madmen do what they do? Maybe in another time there would have been an outcry. But when so many people are dying every day, the sound of one death won't be heard over the multitude.'

Stone feels a pain at the centre of his chest. Unbidden, an image arrives in his head. He retches as he pictures a sharp silver blade carving her skin like ripe fruit.

'She'd felt pain before, sir,' says the fruit-seller, and panic swims in his eyes as he tries to make himself clear. 'I don't mean owt bad by that, just that the wounds we saw on her weren't all fresh, like. She'd been hurt. Perhaps it were a blessing. The cholera kills quick but not as quick as a knife, eh? Perhaps she got more mercy than all of us.'

A chill wind gusts in from the west. It carries with it the smell of turned earth and rotting skin. It catches the flames in the tar barrel and fills Stone's nostrils with a bitter, acrid tang.

And then his mind is full of her again. Of the lace smock. *Lace.* Where would she have bought such a garment? And why would she have refused to undrape? What had she been hiding?

'Wounds?' asks Stone, pressing his sleeve over his mouth. 'Tell me.'

'She'd been whipped, sir. Stripes on her back like a tiger's. White on white. Like the bristles of a broom. Clustered, above her backside. A mess, it were. Mangled. Who'd do that, eh? To such a beauty . . .'

Stone can barely hear the man. He looks up at the sudden cawing of a gull but the skies are empty, save for the shifting patterns in the clouds. The noises are all inside him, the screeches and cries manifestations of the pain that pulses through him; the rage from which he has numbed himself for too long.

'Why?' asks Stone. 'How deep? How long ago?'

'Forgive me,' says the fruit-seller, again. 'Don't make me think on it again. It was hard enough saying it to the man who came round Sabbath day. Had Anderson's buried a whore? Had she been whipped? What did she look like? He weren't no gentleman . . .'

'What man?' asks Stone. 'Speak plain.'

'The big man,' says the fruit-seller, backing away as far as the wall. 'I told all this to Cookie and Barrelman. They've done their asking all over, so I hear. Please, sir, don't hurt an old man . . .'

Stone stoops and pulls his blade from the wood. He has tired of diplomacy. He steps forward and raises steel to trembling flesh. 'Name. Place. Everything. Now.'

The gulls take off from every building as the scream pierces the air. Stone does not hear. His head is filled with rushing blood, galloping hoofs and the babbled pleading of the man whose throat he wants to open.

It takes an effort of will not to hurt the fruit-seller too badly after he has told him what he needs to hear. It takes every last drop of self-restraint not to add another name to the list of lives he has ended. For just a moment, he has risen above the darkness. He had the chance to do violence, and chose not to.

He feels the breeze upon his scarred face, the salty kiss of sea-spray upon his dead flesh. He shivers at the sensation.

For a moment, he feels them. Feels Claudia. Feels Laura.

Shakes it away.

Begins to run.

12

It is mid-afternoon and the sun has yet to win its battle with the blanket of cloud that smothers the sky. Within Randall Hall, what little heat can be coaxed from the embers of last night's fires seems to die in the damp embrace of the air before it can warm the breath that emerges, ghost-like, from the men and women who huddle in the kitchen by the dead hearth.

Diligence Matheson looks again at his pocket watch.

Come on, come on . . .

He pushes his tongue into a rear tooth, dislodges a raspberry seed and stifles a burp. He brushes soil from the knees of his thick moleskin trousers. It falls to the tiled floor, and before he can reach down to retrieve it, one of the kitchen-maids has brushed it away with an efficiency that Matheson wishes her employers would emulate.

Don't do this to me, Phillip. I'm so close to something . . .

Matheson has been waiting for hours. Waiting and growing impatient. Growing cross. Growing hungry and thirsty and maddeningly warm in his ridiculous working clothes. He is sweating and itchy despite the chill of the draughty house.

After he had said goodbye to Stone, he trudged back towards the house, criss-crossing his earlier route but only losing his way a couple of times. Breakfast was a lonely affair. Lord Ansell had left for London before the sun rose and there was no sign of Phillip Ansell at the long, gleaming table in the hall. Matheson had breakfasted on calf's liver and poached eggs, then half a jar of fig jam with freshly baked bread. By the time he dabbed his lips with an expensively textured napkin and sifted the last of the tea leaves through his front teeth, the heavy head that he had woken with was much repaired. He felt a surge of enthusiasm for the possibilities of the day. He crossed to the long windows and stared across a landscape that looked freshly painted. A drab drizzle fell from a sky the colour of drowned flesh, but it rejuvenated the green of the sloping fields and the daubs of colour in the flowerbeds. Not for the first time, Matheson wished he could paint. He wondered whether to ask his young host to scribble him something commemorative and personal that he could post home to his sister. He had seen no reluctance in Ansell when it came to making something fetching in his pad, and the artwork he has already shown Matheson verged on the sublime.

Matheson considers his watch again, picking at a crumb of the delicious berry pudding that had been scaldingly hot and magnificently enticing when he followed its aroma to the vast kitchen an hour before. He had charmed the cook without intending to. He had called her 'madam' and complimented her on creating a scent that, were it to suffuse a woman, would see her enjoying the amorous attentions of more suitors than Helen of Troy. The cook had not understood half of what he said and declared his accent to be 'awful queer' but she enjoyed his fancy words and saw in his round face the appetites of a man who would appreciate a slice of her summer berry pudding. She had cut him a wedge so generous that it could have been used to halt the wheels of a carriage. Matheson had not let a burned tongue slow him down and had devoured it. He has now found friends for life in the cook and her helpers, and has enjoyed regaling them with stories of his life in Toronto. He likes the cosy, bustling kitchen. The rest of the house has the feel of a mausoleum. Last night's sleep was restless. Despite the brandy and the full belly, he had wriggled and fidgeted his way through a fitful few hours, thrashing the blankets into an unruly mess and shivering as the sweat of his nightmares dried upon his skin. He is still unsure whether he should have told Stone of his dreams. Still unsure whether he should have let his protector leave him alone in this unwelcoming place, with its living ghosts and eerie shadows.

'We can't serve it to him now, Mr Matheson,' says the cook, pouring another drop of tea into his cup. 'Take another slice. His lordship don't like no pudding that he's not cut himself, you see. And as for her ladyship . . .'

There is a titter from one of the maids as the cook, who enjoys the way Matheson pronounces the 'H' at the start of her surname, puffs out her cheeks to demonstrate that Lady Ansell has partaken of sufficient cake and pastry to turn the stomach of a sow.

'Mrs Hugget, if I eat another crumb I fear I will be good for nothing but sleep and snoring until breakfast,' says Matheson, warmly. 'Though I guarantee to wake with appetite if I know that your delicious potted pigeon is among the treats on offer.'

Mrs Hugget shoots her younger assistants a glance and revels in the attention of the charming young man. She has been a widow for more than a decade, but even before her husband's death, her life had not been full of compliments or pretty words. She is now almost fifty and does not expect to turn any young man's head. For one so adept at fashioning fine dinners and confections, she has a bony and ungainly frame. She has a little hump upon her left shoulder and walks with a lopsided gait, having broken her leg as a child and had the joint unsatisfactorily re-set. Her face, too, seems slightly crooked, like a drinking straw half-submerged in water. Her jaw does not move properly as she talks, though she opens her mouth to its full capacity when she throws her head back to laugh at her guest's witticisms. Each time she does, she exposes the gap in her top teeth: the result of biting down hard upon the coin in the Christmas pudding at a previous place of employment.

'I met her ladyship last evening,' says Matheson, turning past the large cooking range and the row of gleaming pans to stare at the wooden doorway in the hope of Phillip Ansell's sudden emergence. 'Consumed by grief, is she not? My heart quite trembled at the thought of being so overcome.'

Mrs Hugget sniffs haughtily. It is clear that there are plenty of things she would like to say about Lord Ansell's wife but knows that she would be better served if she held her loose tongue. She picks at a spot of jam on the long table, scratching at it with a short, hard nail, then absent-mindedly sucking the finger.

'The house has been cold without the little one,' says Mrs Hugget, at last. 'The mister and I were never blessed with children. Not that we didn't keep hoping, right up to the last. But some are meant to have children and others ain't and it's a blessing that it's the good Lord who makes that decision and not tainted mortals like me, sir. How He does so is beyond me, I must confess. I thank Him every day for His infinite wisdom, and hope only that He finds His reserves of mercy and ceases trying to teach us all so strict a lesson.'

Her voice takes on a sombre tone as she speaks and there is a tearful sniff from beside the sink, where a young, dark-haired maid is shelling peas.

'Fears for her brother,' says Mrs Hugget, quietly. 'She's from a good family in Vauxhall Gardens. She's been a great helper to me since she were taken on. Hasn't been home since the cholera came. We got word, days back, that a family known to her was stricken with the illness. We've written her father but heard nothing in return. She's close with her brother. Sickly boy. Always got a runny nose, so she tells us. It's the weak that the cholera takes first, ain't it? He's in our prayers but there's naught can be done except hope and ask for mercy.'

Matheson can think of nothing to do but nod. Each mention of the cholera humbles him. He has come from privilege and wealth. Though he has made his bed in haystacks and ditches, taverns and bordellos, he has never truly suffered and never felt at risk of succumbing to the cholera's fetid embrace. He cannot imagine such a life. Cannot comprehend how it would feel to wake in filth and fall asleep in filth and wade through filth all the hours in between.

'The young master's moving about,' says Mrs Hugget, cocking her head and listening to the faint thump of a boot on a wooden floor. 'Never one to rise before noon, as I told you. Rare to put himself abed before the sun is beginning to rise. Not that he ever looks like he's had a hard night of it. Sprightly and light on his feet every morning, colour in his cheeks and fresh as daisies and dew.'

This last prompts a snigger from one of the maids and Mrs Hugget shoots her a fierce look. Then she turns back to Matheson and again refreshes his cup. 'Apple of his mother's eye, was Master Phillip. Lady Ansell should be grateful to have inherited a son like him as well as a house like this. He dotes on her, he does, though we get no thanks. Indulges her every whim, even though his father has long since lost interest in pressing himself behind her. Probably reminds him of his days as local inspector of slaughterhouses, if you ask me!'

Mrs Hugget presses a hand to her mouth as the maids give a gasp of surprise. She pulls a face and rubs her hands together. 'You'll forgive me, Mr Matheson,' she says, sitting forward. 'Sometimes my mouth do run away with me in the presence of a gentleman who knows how to catch a humble servant unawares. I mean no ill. And Lady Ansell were once a fine woman . . .'

'Have no fear,' says Matheson, gallantly, turning his head to the window and peering into the mist for evidence of life beyond the glass. 'I am a repository of secrets. But I am also an inquisitive man. An inspector of slaughterhouses, you say? That sounds almost like honest toil!'

Mrs Hugget decides she is safe to share confidences. 'Don't be too impressed by the big house,' she says quietly. 'It were the first Lady Ansell as brought the money to the pot. Lord Ansell were from money but not wealth, if you understands me. He were a soldier first, then came back home and went to work. Inspector of slaughterhouses, he were. It's a national job, now, all regulated and the like. Back then, it were paid for by a few farmers who formed a guild. Keeping standards up, is the way I understand it. That were my meaning. Saw many a big pink pig going off to its death, he did. Doubt it upset him, though – not after all that butchery overseas with musket and sword. The first Lady Ansell were the daughter of a baronet. Man who lived here.'

Matheson turns away from the glass. 'I'm sorry,' he says, confused. 'This is a new house, is it not? It cannot be more than three decades old.'

Mrs Hugget, who has spotted some error in the way one of her maids is peeling carrots, stands up from the table and takes the bowl and blade from the underling's hands. Expertly, deftly, she begins to skin and slice the vegetable, talking over her shoulder at her fascinated guest. 'Never lucky enough to see the house as it was,' she says wistfully. 'They say it were a splendid place. Been here nigh on five hundred years. Same family for most of it, though there were mischief and trouble during the Civil War. One of the plotters called it home. Guy Fawkes. You've heard of him, have you, over in your Toronto? Aye, he knew how to make his point. Would have cost us king and Parliament were it not for chance and God's mercy. One of the plotters was pulled from hiding on this very spot. Taken away and treated like I treats a pig's trotter. Trussed up, sliced and salted, he was. But Lady Ansell's family were naught if not determined and they hung on to their lands. The baronet were killed in India. Malaria, so I'm told, though it sounds enough like cholera to call the disease its twin. Left the family with money worries. And when his daughter fell in love with a dashing blue hero, well, it didn't matter he were an inspector of slaughterhouses. What mattered was that he had a little money to keep the family's head above water. Shrewd man. Invested wisely and used his new wife's name to impress people. Soon had enough to buy the Crown Jewels, or so they say. Advised the prime minister, and made friends at the Horse Guards. Was made a lord lieutenant twenty years ago. Lord Lieutenant of Holderness. But you asks anybody, he's called Lord Ansell. He pulled down the grand front of the old place and had this thing built around what were left. Bloody labyrinth it is, if you pardon my Saxon. But it were a happy place, so they tell me. I've only been here a few year and it's been cold as the grave since the little princess died. Nothing but wailing and banging doors since then, Mr Matheson. You may have come to see cups and nails and the like but you won't need to dig. Not when this whole house feels like such a tomb . . .'

Mrs Hugget turns in the face of sudden silence. Nobody heard Phillip Ansell enter the room. He is dressed in a flamboyant crimson waistcoat over a gaudily patterned shirt and breeches woven of a silk that seems to shimmer in the candlelight of the long, silent room. The cigar at his mouth is wedged between lips twisted in a smirk and he wears spectacles of smoked glass perched upon his nose, between his tall hat and neatly trimmed moustache.

'Entertaining my guest, Mrs Hugget?' he asks. 'I see you have fed him sufficiently well that such titbits might be considered an indulgence. But, please, do continue. Talk as if I were not here. Indeed, talk as if you were not in the employ of this house. You may think of it as practice.'

Matheson lets out a nervous laugh that hushes Mrs Hugget before she can speak. He gets to his feet and brushes the crumbs from his shirt, pulling out his watch and pointing at it theatrically in a bid to distract the young master's attention from the slanderous words he has overheard. 'An early start, my friend? My goodness, the best part of the day has been and gone! Were it not for my new acquaintance here I would have considered myself quite unwelcome in the Ansell home. Indeed, I would have considered that the man who invited me here had done so out of spite and malice rather than in an attempt to better my understanding of the good Lord's works. I have much to thank Mrs Hugget for, and it would seem that the same may be said of you. She has had much to say about your fine character and gentlemanly ways, as well as your ability to look exceptionally handsome when compared to a muddy and meddlesome boor such as I.'

Phillip Ansell looks between Matheson and the cook. He seems to be deciding whether to behave like his father or be true to himself. Eventually his face splits in a grin and he waves away Mrs Hugget's worries with a snorted laugh. 'Pay no heed, Mrs Hugget,' he says, sitting down heavily at the table and scooping up some berry pudding from the dish with his dainty, tattooed hands. 'I am an unfortunate combination of my father and mother. Today my father spoke through me. Believe me when I say it was an unfortunate and unpleasant experience. And, my dear Mr Matheson, please do forgive the lateness of the hour. I had hoped to rise early but I was awake until the small hours in a flurry of imagination. Please, examine this and tell me if you think it worthy of my tardiness.'

With a flourish, Ansell pulls a roll of paper from inside his waistcoat and lays it upon the table before Matheson, then looks down upon it, like a father bending over the crib of a newborn. 'Your Zealot,' he says softly. 'I hope you do not think that I mock you or the object of your attentions. When I paint, it is a prayer.'

Matheson stares into the extraordinary jumble of colours. The image is of an elderly man. He is grey-haired, dirty, and has been stripped to absolute nakedness. His hands and feet are nailed to pieces of timber so exquisitely drawn that Matheson fancies he can feel the splinters and wood grain against his fingertips as he reaches out, reverentially, and touches the damp work of art. 'Is that . . .?'

'You recognise it?' Ansell gleefully claps his hands. 'Yes! Caistor, as it was. As I imagine it, at least. This is how it could have been, Diligence. I hope you like it. Truly, I hope you do.'

Matheson's chest feels tight. He is amazed to find tears in his eyes. He is staring into the face of Simon the Zealot, crucified two millennia before for preaching Christ's word in the garrison town. The nails have been pounded through the old man's hands and the blood runs down his wrist. His feet have been nailed to the cross together; three great nails thumped through beneath the ankle bone in a puddle of dark blood.

'I am right, aren't I?' asks Ansell, excitedly. 'Did you not tell me that you had encountered a text that said the first two nails snapped and it took a third to secure him to the wood? Have I imagined such gory detail? Such images come to my head unbidden. This came to me in a fury.'

Matheson is still looking at the painting. A fat Roman officer, his feet unsullied by the mud or blood of the thoroughfare, is staring up into Simon's face and at the darkening sky beyond. Matheson, too, is transfixed by the blissful agony upon the martyr's countenance. He peers closer, drinks in the precision, the ferocity of the brush-strokes, winces as he sees the tooth trapped in the old man's beard as he struggles against his bonds and tries to remember a prayer that will end his suffering before his wits are too dull to resist screaming. 'There's no beauty there,' he says, without thinking, then turns, suddenly, to look into Phillip Ansell's crest-fallen face. 'No, you misunderstand. I have only looked upon the paintings of those who would convince us that martyrdom is peaceful. Beautiful. Reverential. This is something else, Phillip. This is like nothing I have ever looked upon. Like nothing any eyes have looked upon since the moment his martyrdom occurred. You have painted a window into a world we cannot ever truly know again.'

Ansell grins childishly, and clasps an arm around Matheson's shoulders. He tenses and returns his attention to the picture. He looks into the faces of the crowd. Peasants. Farmers. Britons aghast and enraptured by the agony of the old man's dying moments. He sees a face. A splash of pink and brown. Eyes that he saw last night, chiselled on to paper with a still-warm stick of charcoal.

'Your sister?' he asks, pointing.

Ansell's smile fades. He looks again at his own work, as if for the first time, reaches out to touch it, then draws away. 'It is a gift,' he says, shrugging. 'Where my thoughts come from is anybody's guess. I have no choice in what I paint. I hope you like it. My father calls my work blasphemy. I call my pictures presents for my friends. Come, shall we see where this old family stores its relics and bones?'

Matheson considers the image for a moment longer, entranced. If he stares at it long enough, he feels he will be sucked into the painting. For an instant, he feels trapped, as if pinned behind glass.

13

Stone tips the green bottle to his mouth and lets the fierce combination of rum, brandy and laudanum scald his tongue and trickle down his gullet. He breathes in deep, then raises his pipe to his lips, takes a short, harsh puff on tobacco, resin and human hair, then pushes it all out in a cloud so thick it could have been drawn in pencil.

For once he is drinking to remember and not to forget.

His hands shake and his fingers curl inwards. A sensation of wooziness invades his skull. For a moment he imagines a wave breaking against the inside of his crown and spilling out of his ear to drench his coat. He gives a little giggle at the silliness and raises the bottle again . . .

He is leaning against the brick wall of a fruit warehouse on Humber Street, watching the soft rain fall gently on the shit-streaked cobbles. It should be a bustling, chaotic scene. Men should be hauling boxes and haggling over prices. Clerks should be ticking off deliveries in journals. Windows should be opening and closing as messages are bellowed over the bustling sound of commerce. The street-gangs should be playing chase with the blue-coated constables, filching from pockets and timing their thefts against the fifteen-minute circuits of the local constable.

Last time Stone came here, he had seen a ripening city. Seen possibility and life. He takes another swig and tries to become the man he was that night. 'Think, Stone. Think.'

There is a madness within him. The knowledge of Laura's murder is clawing at the edges of his sanity. He feels manic with the need to understand. To avenge. And yet he recalls so little of their brief union that he wonders if he has any right to feel anything at all. The fruit-seller had said the same, as Stone pressed his boot beneath his jawbone and demanded answers he could not give. He had snotted and whined beneath Stone's fists. *Why?* That was what he had demanded as he bled. Why did she matter so much? Was she a lover? A sister? A favoured whore? And why confer significance amid this surging ocean of death? Stone had not answered. Just kept the pressure on the fruit-seller's windpipe and insisted the poor bastard describe her wounds with a detail that had turned both their stomachs to bile and ice.

He had got answers, of course. The fruit-seller had given him more than he'd thought he knew. He had told the fevered soldier just what had been done to Laura's guts. 'Like opening stale bread,' he had said, through bleeding lips. 'As if a hand had reached in and torn her open. Not clean cuts. As if a small hole had been ripped . . .'

Stone had not known he was crying until he saw the water running from his nose and on to the dirty pink cheeks of the man he had come so close to throttling.

Here, now, he needs to remember. To know why she mattered so much. He must become the man he was that night in the hope that his memory will hand him a fuller picture.

He raises the bottle again, takes another draw on the pipe and tries to remember . . .

It had been a hot night. Damnably hot. His clothes had felt lousy and damp against his skin. He had been drinking since the moment he and Matheson had separated on the outskirts of the city. Matheson had had an appointment to discuss theology with some young student. Stone had come along for no other reason than to drink and dip his prick in something warm. He had woken that morning even more bitter and full of self-loathing than he had been when he staggered into bed. His dead wife had visited him in his dreams, her face melted to the bone on one side, her dress ripped. He had tormented himself with images of her final moments, had imagined himself bursting in and preventing the final assault. Had seen himself a hero, blade in hand, their bodies at his feet – hers pressed gratefully against his own. He had known, in his gut, that in her final moments she had entertained such a notion. She had expected him to come home to save her. To be her warrior and protector. Instead he had been in a distant tavern, licking brandy from a fat *señorita*'s back.

Stone had breakfasted on brandy and laudanum, and had continued the repast in a dozen boisterous gin houses. He was barely able to stand or see by the time he staggered on to Humber Street and started his slow, tottering descent into Hell.

There was blood on his knuckles, he remembers that. He had aimed a swing at a sailor who had looked at him in a way he took as threat. The swing had been high and wild, and he had heard something break in his finger as he struck the wall. He had found himself laughing at the swelling joint, had grinned even as the sailor pulled out a cudgel and threatened him with dire retribution if he did not go on his way.

Here, now, Stone grimaces with the effort of recollection. He shudders with revulsion as he pictures himself and recoils at the demon he sees. 'Particular tastes,' he mutters, pressing his face into the damp brick and screwing up his face. 'That's what he said . . .'

He had been pissing up against a warehouse wall when the man in green approached him. Stone had thought him a rifleman at first, clad in the bottle-green of the celebrated 95th Rifle Regiment. Stone's father had seen service with it. Arthur had smiled fondly as he told his son that the Green Jackets were always the first into battle and the last remaining in the fray. Marksmen. Crackshots. Skirmishers, who turned the wars in Lord Wellington's favour and sent Bonaparte on his way. Stone had been raising a hand in greeting when the image became clearer. This was no soldier: he was a whoremonger, clad in dirty shimmering silk.

'I'll reckon you to be a gentleman of particular tastes,' said the man, as he leaned against the wall and looked down at Stone's prick. 'And one blessed by Adonis, I see. Neither shrivelled nor poxed. We should all pray for such blessings. Might I enquire what a man of such sanctification is doing in the gutter among the plebeians? I see from your clothes you are a gentleman and, though your hands have done harm, you have not known too much shovel work or cold. The hat and scarf disguise an injury, that is clear, and the bulge in your coat betrays your weapons. I smell gin, brandy and a resin I have not enjoyed since I made the journey to this cursed place. I conclude, then, you are an interesting gentleman and one whom I would wish to know, serve and assist. I am Tam Cooper, though there are those who would have me introduce myself by a different name. They call me Barrelman, and though the reason is slander, I do not object to its use.'

Stone had been unable to control his vision and turn the shifting, swimming images into one picture. Only with an effort of will and the support of the wall had he gained a clear picture of his new companion. And the sight had all but turned him sober.

Tam 'Barrelman' Cooper was well named. Short and monstrously fat, his chest and gut swelled his gaudy green coat to such an extent that he might have been carrying a barrel within its folds. He was completely bald and his fat round head poked out from the swell of his trunk like a coin pressed into an apple. His face was all leer and intelligence, sharp eyes peering out from a face that had seen violence and cold. Effort had been made to twist the ends of his red moustache into a Hanoverian curl but the heat of the day had melted the wax and now they stuck out erratically to give his face a lopsided look. In one fleshy hand he held the silver knob of his walking cane and in the other a carpet bag that jingled and clinked, like coins and glass, when he settled it by his booted feet. He smelt of cigars and sweat. In his drunken state Stone wondered if this was a devil sent to test him. His voice was soft and persuasive, dripping charm and empathy. It was the voice of the instant friend. The voice of somebody who understood and did not judge. Stone could barely find the strength to answer, and had none to resist.

'You'll have seen it all, I wager,' said Barrelman. 'Seen the best and worst of man. No stranger to the battlefield, I fancy. I'll warrant that you indulged in all manner of adventures of the flesh before finding what pleased you. Now, you tell me, sir, how Tam Cooper can make your evening feel as it ought. Tell me what you're hungry for. Would it be a boy, sir? I have them, fresh and firm, and they don't make a sound as you goes in. Not unless you asks. Or would you like a young lassie? I has one with the face of an angel and a body like a china doll. I've had customers tell me they like the way they reflects on her eyes, sir. She don't move, see? Stiff as a dead 'un and her eyes wide and staring as dinner plates. You want one with meat on her? I can get you a girl so fat you can rub yourself between the folds of her gut and swear it was a cunny. Tell me, what can Tam Cooper do for you?'

The gin was turning sour in Stone's belly. He could smell his own sweat and his skin felt as though the hairs were being brushed the wrong way. He wanted to murder this man – to slit his stomach and watch his guts spill. Could do it, too. Even through the drunken fog he could have done it. Instead he found himself listening. He allowed himself to imagine a warm body beneath his own and soft hands upon his scarred skin.

'Comfort,' he had said, in reply to Cooper's query. And when that did not seem enough, pushed out the words 'pretty' and 'dark'.

'You'll be wanting our Lady L,' said Cooper, clapping his new customer on the back. 'A beauty like no other. Dark and soft and tender. These will be the most comforting legs that have been around you since you slithered from your mother, my friend. Warm as toast, she is. Slim, with skin the colour of almonds, and lips and eyes that should be looking down from a church wall. And inexpensive, to one who appreciates true value. You could, of course, navigate your own way through this warren of iniquity. But if you will allow me to be your guide you can avoid disappointment. You will get what you pay for and the object of your affection will be content to permit it . . .'

Now, as he lounges against the wall and lets the alcohol and opiates charge through his system, Stone finds himself disgusted. He wishes he could reach into the mental picture and slit his own throat. He had allowed himself to be manipulated by a guttersnipe. He, the one-time toast of Her Majesty's Government, cooed and coaxed and tempted to foulness by a man who could read his needs the way Stone could read a battlefield.

Stone drops the glass bottle. It cracks on the cobbles, splashing a spurt of liquid up his leg. The noise is loud against the silence of the evening and serves him a moment of sober thought. He remembers Cooper's arm upon his, remembers being steered, unsteadily, through the darkening, narrowing streets, remembers the foul stench of Cooper's breath on his ear.

'. . . I've a Calvinist minister comes four hours out of his way to have her piss on him, sir. Would you credit that? A man of the cloth? Best customers, they are. You can devote your soul to God but only when your prick is in the hands of the Barrelman's whores, that's as I say . . .'

And then he was leaning back against damp timber, chasing the ends of his shirt as he tried to tuck himself into his breeches and ended up spinning like a dog seeking its tail. Cooper was entering a tall, narrow building that looked to Stone as if it were built from shadows. It drifted in and out of his focus as the day died and the distant gaslights flared into life, giving the darkening sky a sickly glow.

Stone tries to focus on the man in his memory. What was he seeking? Why in God's name had he allowed the base nature of his blood to overrule the counsel of his conscience?

And then he sees himself pressing coins into Cooper's fat hands and being led, like a child, down a corridor dark as the grave.

'Go in. Do as you will. She'll only cry out if you asks her to, sir.'

And then he was inside. In her pitiable chambers. Alone with her in a room that stank of desire and damp and rotting hay . . .

The only furniture was a straw mattress and broken chair. There were holes in the roof where the tiles had been torn away by gales or stolen by the other scroungers, beggars and whores who crowded into this rat's-nest of interconnected rooms and corridors. The only window, high up on the far wall, had been stuffed with a dirty rag to keep out flies and prying eyes.

'Tam tells me you seek comfort.'

He could not make her out at first, not in the claustrophobic gloom. And then she stepped forward, into a patch of soft light, and he felt all the breath leave his body in a rush.

She was dressed in a white shift, elegant lace embroidery at its throat and hem. She was barefooted, her feet pale. Dark hair fell to her small, pointed breasts, pushing against the material of her gown. A pulse beat in her elegant neck. She took a step towards him, offered a smile that showed healthy white teeth and pinched at her cheeks until she gave off what could almost be called a glow. She lifted her shift to reveal dirty knees and thighs.

Stone had seen something beautiful and broken and had not known whether to protect or brutalise her. He wanted to see her cry, he remembers that. He had grabbed her hair, throat and breasts in questing, rough hands, and pushed her back on the straw mattress, as if she was an enemy soldier.

She fell back without struggle, helped him to push down his trousers, then turned her head away so he could better find her throat with finger and thumb. She raised her arms above her head to emphasise her helplessness. He had been a monster. A vile, bestial half-thing. He had pressed his face and mouth into her armpits, gagged at the stench of her, turned her face to his and opened his eyes . . .

Stone cannot allow himself to remember more. He is shaking. He feels sick and cannot get his breath. It is as though some giant is holding him in an unyielding grip and squashing him, moment by moment. He wants to fall to his knees and beg for forgiveness – to tear off his clothes and lash his skin until repentance runs from his flesh in crimson waves.

The whip . . . the skin . . . the scars . . .

Stone remembers the moment he ran his fingers across the mess of risen flesh at the base of her spine. It had felt like a fistful of straw. She had manoeuvred herself away from his hand, pulled down her slip and placed his hands back on her breasts. She had looked up at him with eyes like those of an orphaned calf. Something inside him had broken and the blackness had taken him. He had fallen asleep with his mouth against her neck and his breeches around his knees. The last thing he remembers is her fingers stroking the scars upon his back as he drifted into oblivion.

Stone cannot stomach the memories any longer. He knows now why he must find out who killed her. It is not just because she gave him comfort, holding him in a way that made things feel better for a time. It is because she was somehow unsullied by the life she led. Even in the filth and the darkness, there was sunlight inside her. He should have plucked her from that place, but to do so would have been to suggest that she'd somehow be better off with him. Such a thought would have been impossible at that time and in that place. But he could have given her coin – he could have taken her from the city and established her somewhere else. He could have done so many things differently if he had not been saturated with his own misery. When she had held him, stroking his bare skin and softly quieting his drunken apologies, he had been given a chance at some form of redemption. Had he not seen true affection in her eyes? Even in the moments when he despises himself most, he cannot shake the look of genuine desire that seemed to fill her in the half-light of the following morning. She had reached out for him in the dark, pulled him close to her, opened her mouth and slipped her small, warm tongue between his dry lips. She had pressed her forehead to his and breathed into his mouth as though trying to push her soul inside him. They had made love among the rags, softly and tenderly, never once taking their lips from one another. Afterwards he had slept, blessedly dreamless, for the first time he could remember.

And he had thrown it away, through fear and selfishness, just as he had with the wife he could not save.

Stone throws the broken bottle at the wall and stares at the hovel she called home. He sees the fleeting smudge of bobbing, curious faces as they peer out from behind grubby rags and smashed windows to glimpse the well-dressed apparition that stands in the teeming rain.

Stone knows hatred the way others know love and finds himself utterly detestable. And yet he knows he has skills not shared by many. He is intelligent. He knows how to manipulate and persuade. Above all, he knows how to snap a limb and squeeze a throat. He knows that, of all the men in this dying city, the only one who cares about what happened to Laura is him.

He looks up at the rain and wishes that it had the capacity to wash him clean. But he is beyond redemption. His soul is already damned. He seeks justice for Laura not in the hope of earning himself a place in Paradise but in the sure and certain knowledge that he is already in Hell.

He pushes himself away from the wall and marches up the

creaking stairs to the rotting double-doors that mark the entrance to the chaotic assortment of rooms. He puts his boot to it and is satisfied to see the wood splinter. He kicks again and goes through.

'Tam!' he shouts, pushing open doors and squinting into the gloom as the scents of shit and death close their fingers round his throat. 'Tam Cooper! I'm a man of particular tastes, you degenerate bastard. I have money to share with those who do not judge. Come, whoremonger. Charm me. Tempt me now, you bastard!'

Stone hears footsteps behind a door to his right. He tries the handle, then boots it when it refuses to give. He pushes himself into a room even smaller than Laura's. Inside, a family cower in the darkness. Two dark-haired girls, a red-headed boy and a father whose face is so under-nourished and scrawny that his family would know him if presented with just his skull.

'Tam Cooper,' says Stone, angrily. 'I want answers.'

The man stammers and stutters as he moves into the light. He has teeth missing at the front and a rash of spots at both temples. He nods and repeats the name.

'Yes – Cooper. Where?' demands Stone.

The man speaks and Stone curses as a flurry of Gaelic assails his ears. He has no understanding of the language, though he is able to see in the man's frantic gestures that while the name of the pimp is known to him his whereabouts are not.

Stone turns and stamps further down the corridor. He tries to remember which room was hers, and pushes open a door that hangs loose on one hinge. A flood of emotion almost has him on his knees.

Her bed. Her blood . . .

The room is so pitiful that it is all he can do not to wail. The broken chair. The straw mattress. The rag stuffed into the broken pane. He starts forward, losing strength, and looks down upon her bed.

He wishes he could not see it. He wishes his mind was that of a simpler man. But there is no denying the outline of the brown and red patches. He can make out her shape, curled up like a baby, arms hugging knees.

Stone puts his hand out to touch the bed. It is trembling.

'She's gone,' comes a voice from the far wall. 'There are others, though you'll have to work hard to find them.'

Stone spins in the direction of the voice. Its owner is a short-haired woman in a ragged brown skirt and man's shirt. There is a bucket by her feet and a cloth in her hand, dripping water on to the hard floor.

'Cooper's not here. Building don't belong to him, mind. Owner of this here hovel's upped and left. Tam's taking care of it. I helps him when he needs it. What you after? Lady L's gone to stay with an uncle but there's an Irish girl lifts her skirts without complaint . . .'

Stone clamps his jaws shut. Has to fight not to let the tears spill. 'An uncle,' he says. 'She's in the ground, miss. Split from her neck to her knees and tipped into a new Golgotha by people who never saw the light in her eyes.'

The woman gives him a quizzical look. She screws up her face and comes closer. She's perhaps a little shy of her thirtieth birthday, though the ages of people this poor are nearly impossible to discern. There is bruising on her left eye and marks on her bare wrist. As she stoops to put the cloth into the bucket, the buttonless shirt falls down and he sees breasts swollen painfully with milk.

'My child,' says the woman, matter-of-factly, as she follows his gaze and covers up. 'Taken by the plague not two weeks since. I'm swollen like a cow, I am. Another time, Tam would have sold me as a speciality of the house . . .'

Stone wants to grab her jaw and close her mouth by force. It sickens him to think that people see him thus, appals him that, upon first sight, he seems like the kind of man who would pay to suckle a whore on a mattress of dried blood and rotten straw. Yet he knows that he has paid to do worse. Men like him have contributed to the truth of this woman's life. For her and so many others, the world is a charnel house of misery and depravity. He wonders where he would appear on a scale of vileness. How many people are worse than himself?

'She meant something to me,' says Stone, feebly. 'Weeks since. I hoped to see her again. Maybe to help her. To take her away, if she could stomach me. When I came she had already died. Cholera, they told me. I paid for her to be taken care of. I came today to see her laid out and was told she had been ripped. As if she were a side of meat . . .'

Stone falls on to the bed. Feels instantly damp as the rotten straw soaks into his trousers. He looks up to see her standing over him.

'I'm Natalie,' she says quietly. 'And you'll be Mr Stone.'

Stone is startled at the sound of his own name. 'Yes, but . . .'

'She spoke of you,' says Natalie, and something like a smile is playing around the sooty lines at the corner of her eyes. 'Said you was different.'

Stone scoffs. He feels the urge to spit.

'She hoped you'd come back,' says Natalie, sucking at her cheek and pursing dry, split lips. 'Not many of us dares to think of a life after this. You gave her that, soldier-boy. Don't ask me how but you put a smile in her. That were Lady L, though. Heart big as a ship, she had. Saw something in you that I don't see. Must have liked how you rutted, eh? Silly cow, you ask me. Shouldn't have believed you'd be back. Not that it matters now. Pain's over, though she experienced enough of it in those last days.'

Stone feels his chest constricting. He tries to focus on her words. 'You knew she had been killed?' he asks.

'One of my gentlemen is a bobby,' says Natalie. 'I left the game when my baby came along but I ain't got no other way to make the rent so I've been on my back again. Weren't more than a day and a night after the death of our wee James before I was on one of Tam's mattresses with Constable Cosgrave taking his commission. He told me her ladyship had been split. Made me come over queer, it did, and I'm one who's seen it all.'

'Cosgrave,' says Stone, as if committing it to memory. 'He viewed her body?'

'Said she were purple. Stiff as a board. But there were no doubting the holes in her belly. Crying shame she weren't found earlier but the plague's changed things. Weren't the same comings and goings here over the past few weeks. Nobody checked. Nobody saw. Even Tam were staying away. When he came to check on her he saw a body and a load of what he took for her leavings, if you'll pardon me. It shook him up, but he was going to do right by her. Wasn't going to have her dumped in the river like old potato peelings. He cares for us, in his way. Then you came and paid for some sort of state bloody funeral. Made a right fool of him. Took it out on his girls, he did, but I reckon it upset him to lose one as valuable as Laura. Bloody shame.'

Stone realises he is rocking. His hands are shaking and his need for a drink is all-consuming. 'There have been others,' he says. 'A girl cut up by her brother . . .'

Natalie scoffs. 'Alice. Poor cow. And daft Jamie wouldn't step on an ant without crying about it,' she says dismissively. 'No, his sister got herself a mister with particular tastes. Tam's a speciality man, see, gets people what they want. No complaints and decent coin. The risk is higher but so's the reward. Alice weren't a special one, like Laura, but she made her misters happy. Jamie found her body cut up so bad he didn't know if she were herself or butchered pork. Daft lad thought calling Cookie was the right thing to do.'

'Cookie?'

'Bearded bastard. Peeler. Brute and bully – and a rich man, thanks to what he takes from those who've got it and those who ain't. It was him said Laura should go in the ground, like as not. Him who don't want Chief Constable McManus sending for detectives from London or asking questions that Cookie don't want us answering.'

Stone's mouth is dry. His throat feels squeezed shut, as though a boot is being pushed against it. He sniffs deeply, and finds an ember glowing in his chest. He takes a breath. 'Cookie knew her?'

'Knew her and ploughed her,' says Natalie, callously. 'One of his perks, she was. Alice too. He's a vicious bastard, that one. I've seen him open a man's head like a boiled egg. Shouldn't have turned his stomach the way it did when he saw her, all opened up and rotting, like. Not like him. Aye, like as not it were him ordered her put in the ground. He wouldn't want the stink she'd cause him. Doesn't want prying eyes on his turf or anybody questioning his reputation. He'd want her out of sight – and do the same with Alice if it were up to him, but she's still at Dr Easter's rooms, waiting for Jamie's trial, if he ain't found strung up in the madhouse first. Cookie's got a long reach . . .'

'This is Alice . . . she hasn't been buried?'

'Dr Easter's a clever man,' says Natalie. 'Likes to poke around and see what we've got in our insides. Used to pay a girl I knew to spread her legs and let him peer in with a candle. Black lady, she were. He'd scribble down pictures and words, though what he saw in there is anybody's guess. He never did nothing improper, or more improper than writing about her cunny.'

Suddenly Stone is standing. His breath comes in short bursts, as if through laughter. He wipes a hand over his face and is surprised to see it bloody. He crosses to Natalie and holds out a coin, then empties the last of his money into her palm.

'I know I let her down,' he says, and winces at the insufficiency of the statement. 'Somebody did this to her. Maybe to others too. I don't think anybody cares. Maybe I wouldn't have cared if I hadn't felt something come to life in me the night we held each other. But I want to help. To stop it happening again. I want it to matter . . .'

Up close, he can see the burst blood vessels in Natalie's eyes and the swelling above her cheeks from the tears that have fallen since she lost her son. She looks into him as if studying his soul, gives the curtest of nods and blinks back a sniff.

'Cookie won't like you,' she says, with a faint smile. 'You ask him about Tam's special client. You ask him about the fortune he's had off Tam. Ask him about the parties.'

'Parties?'

'One of Tam's specialists. Had plenty of coin and kept his fingers in a lot of pies. Liked the shadows. He had a temper but paid handsome to be allowed to use it. Had a few of us, over the weeks and months he were feeling flush. Alice. Me, though Tam stopped me going when my belly started to swell. Had me slapping fifty shades out of poor Rose, just cos he liked to watch. Still, Laura were his favourite, though that's no blessing. They came back sore but they could eat well for a week or two. Even got a few presents. You saw her lace gown? Beautiful it were. Meant a lot to her . . .'

Stone has a knuckle pressed to his head. His other hand is inside his coat, wrapped around the hilt of his blade.

'Tell me everything,' he says. 'Tell me who liked to hurt her.'

PART TWO

From Diligence Matheson, c/o Randall Hall, Skidby,
Kingston-Upon-Hull
30 August 1849

Dear sister,
I pray this correspondence does not carry the contagion of my
mood. I confess to finding myself in a gloom that I cannot fully
explain or fathom. In my last letter I detailed my plans for the
coming days and spoke with great glee at the opportunities that
would be afforded me. And in that regard I have not been disap-
pointed. I am indeed a welcome guest at the splendid and princely
Randall Hall, and if rotundity and heartiness be proof of health,
then I am in fine fettle. I eat magnificently and sleep in sheets so
rich and comfortable that I sometimes wonder if I have drifted into
the clouds. More than anything else, my young friend Phillip Ansell
has made good on his promise and secured me access to his family's
inner sanctum. I have been permitted only the briefest of glimpses
but am promised that tomorrow I shall have light and time and the
freedom to study and digest.
You would find the reliquary remarkable, sister. I find my
thoughts returning to our lessons in the company of the thoroughly
estimable Dr Bruen. Forgive me if I babble but those lessons are
ever in my mind at present and may be what set me on the path
that I have chosen to follow. He told us of the terror unleashed by
that corpulent maniac King Henry when he split with the Catholic
Church so as to be rid of the wife of whom he had tired. Under the
authority of the wily Thomas Cromwell, the monasteries and
churches were dissolved and those found practising Papist ways

were hunted down and butchered. There were many in the realm who declined to abandon the religion of their heart and gave assistance to those good fellows still intent on preaching Catholic sermons. Great houses such as this were ingeniously altered to make space for tiny chapels. These were known as 'priest-holes' and for decades they were places of concealment for Catholics fleeing persecution. Some were even used to celebrate Mass in secret! Though the mansion that once stood here has been dismantled and replaced with a more modern and splendid construction, some of the old internal walls have been maintained, and within the tower at the rear of the Hall, one such priest-hole remains. Its construction, dreamed up some three hundred years ago, is a work of astounding intricacy and guile. I would have walked past that fireplace a thousand times and never known of the trapdoor behind the hearth, were it not for the expert guidance of my young associate. With a push of two stones and the careful removal of some ancient and weathered planks, I found myself in a tiny room as tall as man and twice as long. Inside stood a humble wooden altar, a silver cross and a shining Communion cup. These lay before a display case, carved of local wood, containing skulls, bones, rags and trinkets.

It was all I could do not to gather them to my chest and hold them close, but the light was too poor for proper study and Phillip was keen we curtail our investigations until the morrow, when I hope he will make good his promise to rise early and offer me all assistance. I do enjoy his company, though he is a peculiar fellow. His artwork, which I have already shared with you, is like nothing I have seen before. He captures the truth of what it is to be a person in pain.

Does that sound pretentious, sister? I must confess myself disquieted by the image he has created as a gift for me. He has turned the Zealot's martyrdom into something gruesome. Beautiful, but tangibly horrific. I have never seen its like and cannot help but wonder how one with such dark imaginings in his heart can be such a frivolous man. Perhaps much of what he displays is pretence. Certainly his father does not seem proud to call him 'son'. There is little joy within Phillip. Perhaps he grieves still for the loss of his dear daughter, though upon considering it, I would consider him twice bereaved. His wife is little more than a husk. She has been consumed by her mourning clothes. She is a blob of ink, shuffling and sliding through the great draughty corridors of a home that seems to shudder with her wails.

Do not think me unhappy, but I must confess to being troubled. There is a sickness here that leaves me unfathomably afraid. I know there is naught to fear, or else I would not have permitted dear Meshach to attend to his personal business, but I confess myself goose-pimpled at the thought of solitude. I wish I had requested his continuance at my side but I treated him abominably in the matter of our accommodation and he appears to be suffering from a malady of the soul for which I have no cure. I anticipate and long for his swift return.

I will halt, now, sister, for fear of causing you distress. Perhaps my concerns are just indigestion and heavy head. I have dined and drunk too well for one of my delicate constitution.

I hope my next correspondence offers more in the way of high spirits and jocularity.

Your loving brother,
Diligence

14

It cost Stone a silk scarf and his pocket-watch to be allowed to use the grand bathroom at the Royal Hotel. He bathed, shaved and chiselled the dirt from beneath his nails. He scrubbed his clothes in his bathwater and sent them to the kitchens to be dried over the oven. They returned crisp, clean and smelling slightly of suet. As he had lain in the tepid water and stared at the ceiling rose, he had felt somehow as though he were returning to his own skin after an absence. His mind had sharpened; his thoughts seemed somehow more under his control.

The drink left his system. The hate, too. He filled his pipe with tobacco and found the smoke's gentle passage into his lungs to be comforting. By the time he had dressed himself and pulled on his boots, his reflection in the ornate mirror looked a little more presentable. Though there was no disguising his wounds or the shading beneath his eyes, he looked plausibly like a former army major, and while he still resembled a pirate, it was a pirate who could read, write, organise siege defences and converse fluently in Persian.

It is dark when he walks through the gates of the asylum. He no longer has a watch to tell time but fancies from the position of the moon that it must be nearing midnight. It is an uncivilised hour to call upon a medical man, but it is a time when even the best of men can be off-guard: either half asleep or sliding into drunkenness. He has won diplomatic battles because his opponents have felt embarrassed to be seen in their night-clothes.

Stone visited an alehouse on the way but tonight it was for information, not liquor. Cautiously, charmingly, he questioned the ragged handful of patrons about the asylum and its owners. He now feels suitably armed to knock on its door.

The asylum opened a couple of years earlier. It has the look of a manor house and pains have been taken to prevent the premises seeming as bleak and nightmarish as its predecessor on Southcoates Lane. That was a place of horror, of lunatics tied to chairs, where the morning porridge was served in troughs to men and women who bore the scars of abuse at the hands of their warders and themselves. It stank of a foulness few could comprehend, and only those patients whose families could afford to pay were afforded any kind of human decency. The new premises did not come cheap. The new asylum is home to more than a hundred lunatics but each is at least afforded some degree of privacy and care. Male and female patients are kept apart and soothing activities are provided to keep them as calm as their conditions allow. A board of overseers visits regularly to ensure good sanitation, and two doctors work on rotation, aside from the orderlies and nurses, who have been hired because of a kindness in their souls rather than their ability to restrain the patients.

Stone bangs on the door. He stands in the soft rain and enjoys the quiet. He can hear hoofsteps and the trundle of carriage wheels, the sound of his own breathing and the thump, thump, thump of dirty boots being banged against the wall of one of the tall, handsome properties that overlook this small courtyard, with its well-tended bushes and clipped lawn . . .

The door is opened by a young woman in a long blue dress and old-fashioned bonnet. She has large teeth and a lazy eye, and puts Stone instantly in mind of a concussed rabbit. She holds up a lamp and peers at the unexpected visitor, then drops an unpolished curtsy when she sees his fine clothes.

'Good evening, madam. I am Major Mesach Stone and I ask that you forgive the lateness of the hour. I would speak with Dr Easter about a matter of some urgency, if you would permit me to cross the threshold of an establishment that does you both great credit. My compliments, ma'am.'

The mixture of bluster, lies and charm works immediately. Moments later, he is being led past an impressive double staircase and down a wood-panelled corridor. A bust of some bearded patron stands atop a plinth beneath some large, colourful land-scapes and daubs of tranquil animals. The whole place smells of paint and sawdust, with only the slightest hint of the chemical smell Stone associates with medical establishments.

'In there, sir,' says the young woman, nervously, pointing at a closed door. 'He won't be sleeping. He don't sleep – be playing with his instruments, like as not. Can I bring you refreshment? Tea, or a drop of something stronger?'

Stone smiles at the woman, appreciating her good manners, and hoping that his presence does not cause her trouble. He asks for coffee, knowing it will take longer to make, and gives her his most fulsome thanks. As she scurries away he takes a deep breath and raps efficiently on the wood. He enters without waiting for reply.

Dr Easter is seated behind a long, cluttered desk in the centre of a square room. A small fire smoulders in the grate beneath an impressive blue-tiled fireplace and the walls have been painted a soft yellow. It would be a warm, comfortable room were it not for the anatomical pictures on the chimneybreast, the cabinet of glass jars and textbooks against the far wall, and the strange, grainy images that look out from behind glass to his left.

The medical practitioner looks up but does not seem unduly troubled at being disturbed. He is a slender man, a little younger than Stone, with a thick moustache that reaches his chin; he has not shaved the rest of his face for at least a day and a night. He holds a magnifying-glass in his right hand and has been peering at an open book upon the desk. The room smells of a chemical that seems vaguely familiar, but which is masked by the deeper aroma of damp dog. Stone notes the huge, ungainly paws of a wolfhound poking out from beneath the desk, alongside its master's slippered feet.

'Dr Easter,' says Stone, in the voice he reserves for dealing with professionals. 'Do forgive me for intruding upon you at such an hour. My name is Meshach Stone, formerly of the Bombay Artillery and latterly attached to the diplomatic corps of Her Majesty's Government.'

Easter sticks out a lip and pulls a face that stops Stone in his tracks. 'Stone, you say? My goodness, you're not the one who got away, are you? I'm an associate of Bill Brydon. The good doctor and I trained together. Are you still in contact? And what brings you here, my resilient fellow?'

Stone is momentarily wrong-footed by the warmth of the greeting. It takes an effort of will not to twitch at the mention of his former colleague. He feels heat upon his back, the dryness in his throat, and remembers the ghastly trickle of blood upon his skin. He sees himself clinging to life and sanity as the musket balls bit into the hard rock and his fellows fell around him. He remembers the flies, black as night, descending as a swarm to feast on men and women not yet dead, then feels again the pistol ball penetrate his thigh. Remembers knowing that he would die. Remembers anger and resentment and a burning desire to fight until his lungs gave out. Remembers the sun in his eyes and the sand in his throat, then firing and reloading, firing and reloading, until they were upon him and all he had left was his blade. Remembers seeing Brydon's horse bolt, the doctor still clinging to the pommel. Remembers falling beneath the rifle butts and crying out in Persian: an unintelligible mixture of pleas and curses, and lashing out at the unfairness of it all as he saw himself left for the birds on that damnable road, a thousand miles from anybody who would mourn his passing . . .

Dr Easter seems invigorated by the unexpected arrival. He stands and beckons him in. 'My goodness, yes, I see it in your face, sir. You are recovered? I see not all of the injuries have healed. But, by God, you were treated shabbily. Elphinstone's Folly, is that not what the newspapers christened the mission? You were never afforded the credit that went Brydon's way, were you? Or the ignominy of your commanders. No doubt the court-martial cut you deep but at least history won't remember you as the cause of the whole damn debacle! To see you here is a dashed honour, sir. Tell me, what brings you?'

Stone presses his cuff to his face and gathers himself, concentrating on his breathing. He wishes he had a drink to hand, though he knows that if he took a sip to calm his nerves, he would drain the bottle and fight until he got another. He forces himself to smile, and extends a hand. It closes on warm, thin fingers.

'Dr Brydon, yes,' says Stone, as affectionately as he can manage. 'No, we haven't spoken since the battlefield, though I was delighted to hear of his escape. There was not much good fortune to be found in that place, and if there were, Bill drank the well dry. Not that he couldn't have done with a little more.'

'Indeed, indeed,' says Dr Easter, looking serious. He returns to his chair, puts his slippered feet up on his desk, leans back and encourages Stone to sit. 'I've seen the wound. Ghastly. Fascinating, but ghastly. Nearly made a boiled egg of him. Saved by *Blackwood's Magazine*, did you hear?'

Stone is about to reply when Dr Easter gives a huge snort of laughter. He reaches down beside him and tickles the dog at his feet, then shakes his head. 'Stuffed his hat with it to keep out the cold,' says the doctor, marvelling at his old friend's audacity. 'When the Afghan went to scalp him it took the worst of the blow. Still sliced him, of course, but not enough to take him down. The horse took off like a greyhound, did it not? The poor beast dropped dead the moment they reached Jalalabad. The newspapers lapped it up. The only one of four and a half thousand men and women to make it back from that hellish place. Not that there was truth in that story. Your good self, for instance. The Greek merchant. A sepoy, I believe? And those poor souls taken into captivity and treated like so many vermin. But I fear it will always be Bill Brydon people think of when they recall that dreadful time. He wishes it were not so – told me so himself. Said your own survival was all the more remarkable. "A capital fellow", he called you, and he's no fool. "A mysterious man", too, though I see no shame in that. Privately employed now, are you? If I can help you, I should be honoured.'

Stone makes himself comfortable in the low-backed chair. From his new vantage point he can better study the peculiar images on the wall. He recalls seeing something similar, months before, during a brief sojourn in Paris. Remembers the word and snaps his fingers. 'You are a student of this marvellous new device, are you?' he asks, grateful for a chance to change the subject. 'Daguerreotype –is that the word? The diplomatic service is keenly interested in its uses, though there are those who believe it an invention to be feared rather than embraced. I see you have mastered the art.'

Dr Easter looks delighted to be given the chance to discuss his passion. 'I am a mere student,' he says, waving his hand in the direction of the images. 'But, by God, I am enthralled by the device. The possibilities, sir. Can you imagine how it will be when all moments can be captured? When an expression can be immortalised? Imagine holding a duplicate of the moment your true love smiled or the sheer magical joy in a child's face as they see something that enchants them. And, medically, are you not fascinated by the possibilities? Imagine being able to preserve the image of a healthy organ and a sick one! Would we not advance our understanding at a miraculous rate?'

Stone points at the pictures again. 'Your own work?'

'Indeed, indeed,' says Dr Easter, smiling. 'Patients, Major Stone. Those troubled by hysteria and sleeping sickness, malady and lunacy. I have endeavoured to imprison their likenesses – though, as you will see, the exposure and the stillness required by the subjects were not masterfully managed, and we are left with the rather odd images you see. Still, they do hold a certain charm, do they not? I would hope that my next attempts are clearer, though the apparatus required remains an expense beyond the purse of a humble doctor. The camera designed by Levitsky was my pride and joy. I shed tears as one would for a child when it was broken, though I confess I was to blame. I left the office door unlocked, you understand. The attraction was too much for one so blighted. That poor soul was proof to me that illness of the mind can strike both high-born and low with equal viciousness.'

Stone feels confused. He stands, crosses to the images and stares into eerily distorted faces, their mouths and eyes blurred and twisted, like faces forming in fire and cloud. 'Your apparatus was damaged?' he asks, over his shoulder.

'There are those who despise progress,' the doctor says, sighing. 'Even those who benefit from such developments. One of our patients was unhappy at the idea of an image being kept for ever – felt discomfort at the very concept. So he destroyed my means to do so. Such is the lot of a man who devotes his time to the betterment of conditions for those afflicted by problems of the mind. It took an effort of Herculean proportions not to lose my temper with the poor misguided soul. Do you have time to look at a print I have here of an image made some ten years ago by the American Robert Cornelius? It shows his sister, and she is a beauty by any standards. Soon I imagine us all carrying photographs of the people we love and admire. Someone will make money from it, I am sure, though what that means for artists of palette and brush is anyone's guess . . .'

As Easter returns to the desk, Stone smiles tightly and nods at the picture being held out for inspection. He makes the right noises, getting close enough to the man to see his hands and note their coarseness. He has not spent his life by a warm fireside. He has lived and endured. Stone makes the face of one impressed by another's cleverness, then decides he has spent enough time earning the doctor's confidence. He turns to the matter at hand.

'Dr Easter, I am investigating the death of a young woman found in a low part of the city. Her body was left undiscovered for some days, and by the time she was found, the wounds that cost her her life were hidden and her demise was ascribed to cholera. I have since discovered that her belly was slashed and that she was left to die from injuries nobody should have been forced to endure. In the course of my enquiries I have learned of crimes that may be linked. I understand you to have in your keeping the corpse of another woman who suffered death by a blade . . .'

Dr Easter has steepled his fingers. He has stopped shuffling in his chair and seems suddenly aware of his appearance. He slowly removes his slippered feet from the desk and straightens his clothing.

'Alice' he says quietly. 'Yes, her poor bewildered brother would no doubt have got the rope for her murder in a time not so troubled as this. He was found by a member of Hull Police, cradling her body and soaked in her blood. He is now in my care and I hope the magistrates continue to allow me to provide a safe place for him. He remembers little of the incident and I have not pressed him. Obviously one cannot doubt the word of Sergeant Cooke, though I find it hard to imagine such an evil act being carried out by such a gentle soul. The victim you speak of, was she employed in a similar profession to poor Alice?'

Stone swallows, then nods. He tries to keep his face from betraying his feelings.

'A grim life, cut short,' says Easter, sadly. 'I was asked to examine Alice's body, you are correct. And we did secure it for study, as is common practice. I specialise in the difficulties of the mind but I am a surgeon and physician and have written two volumes on anatomy. I was allowed to view what had been done to her. It was almost Biblical in its ugliness, Major Stone. In a different time, and were it not for the quick discovery of a culprit, it would have scared this city out of its wits.'

'You still have the body?' asks Stone, though he is unsure he can view the murdered woman without drink in his system. 'I would compare wounds . . .'

Easter grimaces and shakes his head. 'There is a limited time one can keep a corpse usable,' he says. 'She has been interred in our private cemetery, at the back of this fine building.'

Stone does not allow his disappointment to show. He is about to speak again when Dr Easter interrupts him.

'I made sketches,' he says, eager to help. 'I have little skill as an artist, but they may be of use. I warn you, they are difficult to see, despite the grimness your eyes have grown accustomed to.'

Stone says nothing. His eyes roam along the bottles and jars, books and labels at the rear of the room. He makes out a small winged lizard in a jar, a tiny rat-like foetus, still encased in its mother's womb, suspended in clear liquid, the skull of an otter and myriad glass plates, each with a drop of blood at the centre and labelled in a neat, sloping script.

'Here,' says Dr Easter, who has been rummaging in his desk. 'I apologise for their crudity.'

Stone turns his attention away from the peculiarities to focus on something horrible. He tries not to shudder. 'They think he did that?' he asks quietly. 'Her brother? Cut them off?'

Easter nods. 'They weren't found. A search was made. She was buried without them.'

'Jesus,' says Stone, and breathes out, slowly.

'Indeed,' mutters Easter. 'I thought I had seen the worst of what humans will do not a month before. Turn the pages, sir. You will see.'

Stone does as he is bidden. His throat feels as though it is being pressed between finger and thumb and he tries not to let his gorge rise.

'Cooked,' says Easter. 'She was pulled from the river. It was devilish difficult to tell whether she was even female. Harder still to determine who she was. Just another poor soul, I suppose.'

Stone looks at the pencil sketch. The woman is almost inhuman. Her skin has been peeled off almost to the bone. The flesh that clings to her skeleton is putrid and blistered.

'I would fancy she was roasted,' says Easter, trying not to let emotion enter his voice. 'Cooked on a spit, then dumped in the river, where she bloated and drifted. Those who found her thought she was a dead pig. She was brought to me by a constable who knows of my interest in such things.'

'She was murdered?' asks Stone.

Dr Easter strokes his dog, as if for reassurance. 'Chief Constable McManus has accepted my findings that she died as a result of a fire. But he has also accepted the hypothesis that she set herself ablaze and threw herself into the Hull. Who am I to question it?'

Stone's left leg is jiggling and he makes an effort to stop it. He says nothing, even as the nurse knocks on the door and brings him his coffee. He cannot find any words until he has drained it and is nursing a scalded tongue.

Dr Easter gives an excited yelp and all but runs to the row of shelves. He retrieves a vial, stoppered and neatly labelled. He hands it to Stone, who holds it up to the light.

'I'm sorry, Doctor, I'm not sure . . .'

'Beneath her fingernails,' says Dr Easter. 'A scrap of what could be vellum, or the rind from her last side of bacon. Who can tell? It would appear to show lettering but I would not be able to say so with certainty. Does it seem like the letter x to you? Sinister, if so. One could almost scare oneself to imagine its connotations. Have you any thoughts?'

Stone considers the vial. He is about to pocket it when Dr Easter holds out a hand and he reluctantly gives it back. Stone stares about him, wondering at the absence of sound. He has visited asylums before where he heard screams and wails, shrieks and the sounds of many troubled minds.

'You are employed privately?' asks Easter, to break the silence. 'I have heard that the Metropolitan Police is establishing a unit of detectives, and that there are those in private practice whose skills of analysis and insight are very much in demand. One such as you could earn a good income. A soldier. A hero. A diplomat. What is your connection to this grimness?'

Stone is only half listening. He watches the fire die in the hearth, the light flicker on the blurred images, and loses himself in the depiction of a human being, stripped down to muscle and bone. He wonders what sort of man could cut off a woman's breasts for his own amusement. 'I would speak to Alice's brother,' he says. 'I wish I could tell you more about my employment. Alas, I am sworn to remain tight-lipped. But, believe me, access to Jamie would assist me immeasurably.'

Easter looks momentarily concerned, and seems about to demand to see a signed order or some form of authority. Then he half smiles, nods and pushes his hand through his hair. 'This way, please.'

A grandfather clock is chiming midnight as Stone and Dr Easter make their way upstairs and down a long corridor. Dr Easter unlocks a white-painted set of double-doors and nods to a sallow-faced, lugubrious man who dozes on a chair at the end of a hallway. Stone says nothing. Just breathes in the scent of the dozens of men and women asleep nearby.

'We have ninety-four patients,' says Easter, as they pass a large oil painting of the Madonna holding a plump, golden Jesus to her breast. 'Many are privately paid for. We make space for paupers where we can. Jamie is paid for from my own purse. The borough authorities are generous with time and money, and I thank God that the building has modern sanitation or I fear the cholera would have torn through here like fire. Many of the patients sleep in dormitories but those too troubled for company have private rooms. Jamie is sedated the majority of the time. It spares him nightmares—'

Dr Easter stops short as a sudden stream of sound screeches out from behind a locked door. He winces. 'One of our paupers,' he says. 'I fear she is beyond saving, Major Stone. Irish, as you hear. She has not a word of English and it saddens me that there is nothing to be done for her but force sedatives down her throat and dress her wounds when she hurts herself. Would you care to see?'

Stone looks at the doctor with disgust. Why would he wish to see such suffering and insanity? But he is here at the doctor's pleasure and must not offend. He is a diplomat, after all. 'Certainly,' he says. 'Though I would not wish to set back any treatment . . .'

The doctor reaches up to open a rectangular window in the door. He beckons Stone forward. As he moves closer to the viewing window, his heart is jolted by the sudden appearance of an adolescent girl. She leaps at the open flap as if it is a passageway to freedom, then screeches in her native language as she finds her way still barred. A dirty, pale, freckled hand pushes through into the corridor, grasping, tendons straining, as if trying to grab fistfuls of liberty from the air.

'She was arrested for vagrancy,' says Dr Easter, sadly. 'We do not even know her name. Her visions are worse than any poor Jamie suffers. We know she has witnessed something vile but we have no idea what. And after what was done to her . . .'

Stone recoils from the sight of the desperate hand and turns questioning eyes on the doctor.

'Whether by her own hand or that of another, I cannot say. But her tongue has been split, sir. Like a snake's.'

Easter sticks out his own tongue and mimes slicing it from tip to epiglottis. 'Even if we were to speak her language we would have no idea what she tries to say. And the poor girl can neither read nor write. She has no way of making herself understood.'

Stone watches the hand withdraw. Slowly, silently, he moves back to the viewing pane, takes the lantern from the wall and raises it. He looks at the girl within, crouched on the floor like a wild creature, rocking back and forth in a white shift so similar to what Laura had worn that he feels himself about to weep. She raises her eyes in the direction of the light. He sees white skin and freckles. High cheekbones and red hair. He sees something at once familiar and alien, and is about to speak when she opens her mouth, like a wounded beast, and he sees the ruin of her tongue.

'My God,' says Stone, withdrawing. He will never forget what he has seen.

'The world is full of cruel men. I do not know how to find out more about her or discover her loved ones. A physical examination would at least reveal if she were a working girl but I am unsure if such enquiry would cause more distress. She was discovered by Sergeant Cooke, and when she is allowed paper and paints, she draws things that we cannot make out. She has seen blood, we know that. When given red paint she does naught but daub it on her belly and screech her half-words . . .'

Suddenly Stone remembers the face of the man in the dark. The fear and the red hair. The family peering out from the darkness as he smashed his way from room to room in the hovel where Laura lifted her skirts.

'Dr Easter,' he says, as calmly as he can, 'is it possible that this girl was witness to one of the atrocities I speak of? Has she met Alice's brother, perhaps? Is she familiar with Pig Alley?'

At the mention of the address, the girl leaps forward and begins hammering at the door. She yells, screams and bares her teeth. Her eyes fill with tears that she makes no effort to wipe away.

'Laura,' says Stone, urgently, his face to the gap in the door. 'She was hurt . . .' He mimes stabbing. He locks eyes with hers and sees her skip back from the door as if he has thrown hot fat upon her skin.

'Laura,' he says again.

Stone turns back to Dr Easter but he has already moved on. He is unlocking another door and urging Stone to follow him. He steps inside and just as quickly returns to the corridor.

'As I feared. He is sedated beyond understanding. Perhaps if you came back in the morning . . .'

Stone waves a hand, no longer caring. He presses his face back to the Irish girl's viewing pane. She is lying on the bed, feet drawn up in a foetal position, shivering despite the muggy heat of the room.

'Tam Cooper,' he says. 'Sergeant Cooke. Barrelman . . .'

At that, she puts her hands over her head and begins to stutter, wetly, into the blankets. He can't make out any true words amid the sound of her distress. And then, suddenly, a word he recognises.

'Laura,' says the girl. 'Laura . . .'

Stone spins to Dr Easter. 'We must make her understood,' he says, and the madness is back in his heart. He needs drink. Laudanum. His pipe and blade. 'Doctor, this girl is a witness!'

Dr Easter looks at him with pity and concern. Stone can feel himself being deconstructed and sees Dr Easter's sudden realisation that he has allowed a crazy man into his asylum.

'Could I trouble you for an address where you can be contacted?' says Dr Easter, politely gesturing back down the corridor. 'Perhaps at this hour we are neither of us well placed to make good decisions. If we find a way to make her understood we can contact you . . .'

'Who was there?' shouts Stone, through the hole in the door. 'Who sliced her? Who cut her belly?' He forces Dr Easter aside and presses his face to the gap. She is sitting up in the light from one high window, half illuminated by a beam of silvery moonlight. She makes the sign of the cross. Makes it again. Then extends a finger and draws it from her throat to her genitals. Slices again, from hip to hip. She makes a gesture that Stone cannot comprehend. He watches as she holds up her hands and sees the frustration in her eyes as she fails to make herself clear. And then she is pointing at him, lying back and opening her legs. Bucking, obscenely, to mime violent intercourse. Pointing, again, and clawing at her hands . . .

'Please, Major Stone, I must ask that you stop disturbing our patients.'

Stone hears footsteps. He sees the sallow-faced man coming towards him, a club at his side.

Despairing, angry, Stone pulls a piece of paper and a pencil from a pocket and scrawls the address of Randall Hall upon it. He stuffs it into Easter's shirt. When he pushes a hand over his face he feels the fresh wounds in his scalp tear. He stamps away, failure and frustration in his soul.

He knows what he needs. He knows that he cannot be the man he used to be.

He knows that he needs to find comfort in Laura's room, then beat answers from the bastards who cut an Irish girl's tongue so they would not have to slash her throat.

15

Matheson looks longingly at the empty fireplace and wonders if it would be an unforgivable breach of etiquette to chop up the furniture and start a blaze. There are pine cones and dried bog-cotton in a basket by the cold hearth and he believes himself more than capable of the task. But manners dictate that he leave such jobs to either the host or a member of the household, and he would rather freeze to death than offend his absent host any further.

He shivers and realises there is at least a half-chance of this eventuality coming to pass. A chill has crept into his bones. Sleep did not come easily last night and when it did finally take him in its grasp, the embrace was an uncomfortable, feverish thing. He dreamed of dirt-streaked girls in fine linens and silks, pawing at his skin and clothes as if trying to get at the organs beneath. He saw a young girl with flaming hair smiling obscenely as she chewed on his kidneys, and gagged as brittle, rotten teeth clamped down upon his tongue and chewed it in half. He had woken drenched in sweat to a sky made of dust and wondered if he had slept through summer and fall, to wake in a house suffused with winter.

It is mid-morning and Phillip Ansell has not made good on his promise to wake with the lark and escort him to the secret room in the tower. Breakfast was once again a solitary affair and Matheson had no appetite for the cold meat and warm bread laid on the long, mahogany table by the high windows. He had settled for coffee and a few dried fruits, though seeds have lodged themselves in his back teeth; he worries at them with his tongue, pulling faces that make him look like a baby licking lemons.

He is toying with the idea of slipping away. He remains entranced by the idea of poring over the family's relics and artefacts but that cannot silence the voice within him that suggests he leave this place. It is not doing him any good. He was happy in Lincolnshire. He came to Britain to find the bones of the Zealot and he has allowed himself to be distracted. Could this be a test? Could the Lord be assessing his own zeal for the task He has chosen him for? Matheson wishes he had answers, that life were less full of riddles. More than anything, he wishes Stone were here to make him laugh and feel safe, and to lift his spirits with some good-natured teasing.

He looks around him. He is not quite sure what the room is called but he has come to think of it as the Pink Room. The walls are papered in a soft salmon colour and the high-backed chairs are covered with a fabric patterned in pink, peach and gold. To his right, a peculiar shadow is cast upon the russet carpet by a golden statue of a palm tree, while the walls contain more of the stern, stiff-backed patricians who stare down from frames in every room in the house. They are interspersed with huge oil paintings of religious scenes. Above him, a naked Madonna holds a soft-faced and serene Jesus to her breast. By the fireplace, Mary Magdalene looks upon the wounds of Christ in humble awe, her face perfect and unsullied, her clothes smooth and chaste.

Behind the floor-length curtains, a light rain is falling in diagonal sheets across the courtyard and lawns. From his position he can see the edge of the woods that lead down to the folly where Stone spent such an undignified and solitary night. The sight makes him catch his breath. He remains consumed with guilt over his treatment of his friend. Matheson wonders what appalling memories the experience would have brought back. Stone has shared few confidences about his time in Afghanistan but Matheson has read several books about the hellish conflict – Stone was mentioned by name in some of them. He survived where others fell, dragged himself through the rocks and snow of that terrible land as thousands of men and women perished at his side. Stone's escape was miraculous. Matheson scolds himself for the times he has lost patience with his friend for his bouts of drunken melancholy. Has the man not endured more than any soul should be subjected to?

A loud bang wakes him from his brooding introspection. He turns in the direction of the double-doors that lead to one of the house's impressive libraries. He swings his feet off the couch and cautiously hurries into the next room. The books are encased behind glass and line every wall. There is a circular table in the centre and desks by each of the windows. A chandelier of unlit candles is suspended from an ornate ceiling rose, but there is no sign of what caused the sound. Matheson wonders if he should call out. The room is half dark and it is possible that one of the servants heard him approach and concealed themselves.

'Hello? Please don't feel compelled to hide . . .'

The noise comes again. Sharp and loud, like a boot banging on a hard surface. Matheson spins in its direction and realises that it is coming from an area of bare wall between two tall bookcases. He moves closer, frowns and peers forward.

A panel in the wall swings open. What once was bare yellow-painted brick is now a black rectangle of cold air. Matheson steps back, too surprised to cry out, then retreats so swiftly that his feet tangle together and he stumbles backwards on to the hard wooden floor. When he looks up, he is staring into the face of a man so small and misshapen that he has to bite his own cheek not to yell in alarm. Curly-haired, flat-faced and grimy from head to toe, he seems like something from one of Matheson's nightmares, but the grin the man gives him is not an ugly leer, but a warm, apologetic smile.

'Begging your pardon, sir, did I frighten ye? Bloody rabbit warren, see. Tunnels and holes and all manner of places for the buggers to hide, though I'll give you my word that they ain't found a hiding place I can't track. Would you care for a hand? It's a dirty one but it's got a good arm behind it.'

Despite himself, Matheson allows the little man to help him to his feet. He stands and brushes himself down, blushing and embarrassed. This must be the rat-catcher with whom Stone spent a difficult evening and whom he only half remembered the following day. He, too, had wondered if Goodhand was a hallucination.

'Diligence Matheson,' he stammers, extending his other hand.

The rat-catcher pumps it, then turns back to the hole in the wall. He reaches inside and produces a small, long-haired terrier, and a birdcage containing a white-furred, pink-eyed rat of extraordinary malevolence. 'Tools of my trade, see. My goodness, they'll not have me foxed for long.'

'You're employed to rid the house of rats, is that correct?' asks Matheson, with all of the good manners he can muster.

'Yes and no, yes and no,' says Goodhand, distractedly, looking around at the grand surroundings into which he has stumbled. 'I'm following a trail, you might say, should you be so inclined. His lordship wanted the numbers keeping down so as the plague might not upset him in his grand house. Paid me handsome to kill the buggers in the outbuildings. But the outbuildings lead to the big house and the big house has got more rats in it than a whore's drawers has fleas, sir, if you'll forgive my coarseness. There's a nest, I'll promise you that, but with the tunnels and passages all dead ends and sudden openings and having more holes than a flute, I'm chasing my own tail. I'll be pleased to leave, no matter how much they pay. Professional pride, though. Won't let the sods beat me. I'll burn them out if I needs to . . .'

'How dare you?'

Matheson and Goodhand turn at the low rumble from the doorway. They see Wynn, grim-faced, turning an expression of pure fury on the smaller man.

'Ah, Mr Wynn, I was just engaged in a fascinating discourse with this fine fellow who had the misfortune of taking a wrong turn in his travails . . .'

Matheson stops when he realises the Welshman is not listening. Wynn is snorting through flared nostrils, like an exhausted horse, and Goodhand's face pales as he realises he is the subject of the giant's fury.

'You were told,' says Wynn, 'where to occupy yourself. How many keyholes have you spied at, runt? How many secrets you going to spill?'

Wynn is wearing a dirty blue coat over a loose white shirt, which hangs open at the neck. Matheson is appalled to see him reach inside it and produce a huge, tarred club.

'You will not spread your lies, rat-catcher. You will not!'

Matheson looks down at the dwarf and sees him glance in the direction of the door through which he had emerged. Despite his obvious temptation to run, he stands his ground.

'You want me to kill rats, I kill rats. I don't give a fig for no secrets unless they're about my beauties. And I'll have words with anyone who questions my good name. You may be a big man but I'll warrant you haven't got muscles on your bollocks and I'll have them cleaved off before you've even swung that club.'

Wynn lets out a low growl, then sucks in a breath so deep that Matheson fancies it may pluck one of the candles from the chandeliers.

'Mr Wynn, please, I'm sure there is no need for any unpleasantness . . .'

Wynn looks at Matheson for the first time. He weighs him up, as if inspecting a hunting trophy, then dismisses him with a snort of contempt. 'The man who employs a coward to fight his battles has the neck to challenge me? By God, you would do well to turn away. I intend to wring this little peeper's neck and I'm sure the blood will offend a fine gentleman like yourself.'

Matheson bristles. He knows he is hopelessly outmatched but he will not allow himself to be insulted. He draws himself up to his full height and frantically tries to think what Stone would do. Kick him in the kneecap, then break his nose, he supposes. But Matheson doubts his ability to do either. He feels a tremble at his feet as his hands begin to shake.

'Wynn, are you making a nuisance of yourself?'

The heads of all three men snap left as a voice emerges from the door in the wall. A moment later, the tall, slim figure of Phillip Ansell emerges from the darkness.

'Phillip,' splutters Matheson, relieved beyond words. 'I must protest, my friend, but your man here has caused great offence . . .'

Ansell turns bright eyes on Matheson, steps forward and takes him in a huge embrace. Matheson smells lavender water and eau-de-Cologne.

'Stand down, Wynn,' says Ansell, still pressing his pale, powdered face to Matheson's cheek. 'And, Goodhand, you will confine yourself to outbuildings and servants' quarters, no matter how great the temptation to do otherwise.'

Ansell releases Matheson, who finds himself blushing and embarrassed. He glances at Wynn, who remains stony-faced and ready for violence, then sees Goodhand reach down to pick up his rat. At this, the terrier emits a low, throaty growl, and the rat begins to scurry around his cage.

'They've got the scent,' says Goodhand, excitedly. 'Begging your pardon, could I be getting past your lordship? There's a nest, see, and I'll wager it's back the way your lordship came . . .'

Without taking his eyes from Matheson, Ansell waves a hand, then moves to the side. Goodhand is about to make his exit when he seems to remember something important. He reaches into his clothing and withdraws what looks to be, on first inspection, a branch stripped of some of its bark. It is only when he looks closer that Matheson realises its true nature. 'Beggin' your pardon, sir, but I thought this may be something important,' he says, to Ansell. 'Didn't like to leave it where it were. You've got a room for thon bones, yes? The dog came back with this one and I don't want it on my conscience he's been gnawing on one of the saints, see. Can I leave it with you?'

Smoothly, Ansell reaches out and takes the bone in his pale, tattooed hand. As he does so, Matheson is again astounded by the quality of the artwork. The image is all branches and twigs, disappearing in a cluster into the cuff of his splendid green coat. Ansell looks at the bone and shudders, turns to Wynn and hands it to him. He takes a handkerchief from his shirt-front and begins wiping his hands. He has grown pale and seems truly nauseated by the presence of the human remains. Behind him, Wynn holds the bone without any such disquiet. He looks as though he would gnaw upon it, if so instructed.

'Rest assured, Goodhand,' says Ansell, quietly, through his teeth. 'The relics are all where they should be. I fear you have stumbled upon the bones of one of the priests who perished here during their persecution. I will see it given a Christian burial, though I doubt I have the stomach to touch it again. We have Wynn for such things, do we not?'

Goodhand seems relieved. 'I gave the dog a clip, sir. Don't know where he finds these things but if it's got the smell of blood on it, he'll root it out.' He reaches down and scratches the dog behind the ear, then turns his eyes on Wynn. 'I'll be seeing you,' he says. 'And believe me, I sees a lot.'

In his haste to exit the room, the rat-catcher ignores Ansell's instructions and hurries back into the dark passage. Ansell, distracted and unnoticing, kicks the door shut behind him. Now he has seen it, Matheson knows the wall to contain a secret door and can see the join but doubts he would have found it, were he not privy to Goodhand's surprising emergence.

'Wynn, I shan't demean you by demanding apology, but I will insist upon you excusing yourself from our company,' says Ansell, without looking in the big man's direction.

Behind him, Wynn remains motionless. He has not taken his eyes off the wall. He looks ready to do something brutal. At length, he seems to remember the bone in his hand and gives it his attention. For the merest instant, something flickers in his expression. He raises the bone to his face and gives it the briefest of sniffs. He seems transfixed . . .

'Wynn! Be gone, man!' The spell seems to break with Ansell's warning. Wynn secretes the bone in the pocket of his coat then turns on his heel and marches away through the Pink Room. As soon as he is out of earshot, Ansell turns back to Matheson with a huge smile. 'Scare you, did he? He would me if not that Father would have him horse-whipped and skinned should he ever do more than growl. He's a fine man to have at your side when you've said the wrong thing to some damn fool but he has the manners of a pig and the same deportment at dinner. I say, you have gone pale, my friend. Did you not sleep well?'

Matheson licks his lips, aware that his throat has gone dry. 'That bone,' he says. 'It seemed . . .'

'Yes, yes, a great shame,' says Ansell, pursing his lips. 'These old houses are notorious. One never knows just how many skulls one is stepping on as one makes one's way to breakfast. I have always been a little unnerved by such finds. Grisly, is it not? The thought of what is inside us? I am not made for the battlefield, I don't think.' Ansell closes his eyes, then claps his hands and seems to become himself again. 'Now, I know I promised you my full attention today but would it be dreadful of me to ask for a brief delay in our return to the reliquary? I received a note from Father this morning and, despite my hopes, he is refusing permission. I am sure I will change his mind but in the meantime I would ask for a little patience.'

Matheson is barely listening. Distractedly, he runs his eyes along the books on the shelves. He wonders how many of the huge Latin tomes have even been read, then again, whether God is weighing his soul. 'I understand,' he says, and feels strangely relieved. He suddenly wants to quit this place, to put miles between himself and this castle of tunnels and bones.

'That's the spirit,' says Ansell, warmly. 'I guarantee the artefacts to be worth a brief delay. Chief among them is the finger joint of the Magdalene herself. Bitten off by St Hugh, you know! Imagine!'

Despite himself, Matheson is intrigued. 'Bitten off?'

'St Hugh of Lincoln, yes,' says Ansell, grinning. 'He bent to venerate the holy relic of the Magdalene's arm and bit off her finger to take back to his own church. One wonders how many other orifices it passed through before it made its way to us for safe-keeping!'

Matheson returns Ansell's smile, but he cannot force it to reach his eyes. He is cold and damp, hungry and sick. He feels very much alone and a long way from home.

'My dear Diligence, you look quite green,' says Ansell, concerned. 'Should I call to the kitchen for a restorative? Or would you care to walk with me in the grounds? The weather is foul but the Yorkshire air is said to be a true tonic.'

Matheson screws up his eyes, then opens them again before the vision in his mind fills his whole consciousness. He feels more than disquieted. Suddenly, he is afraid. 'Thank you, Phillip. I will withdraw, I think. A rest may do me good.'

Ansell looks upon him for a moment longer than is comfortable. Then he offers the crook of his arm, and walks him slowly back through the Pink Room, as though they are bride and groom.

Matheson allows himself to be led. He feels woozy and uncertain. He does not consider himself a great man or an expert in very much at all. The only thing he knows well are the bones of the dead. And though he saw it for only a fraction of a second, he knows what he saw.

That bone was fresh. Less than a year old. Flesh still hung to the joint, like gristle to a turkey carcass. It was not long enough to have come from a man and it had been found in the dark by a dog that pined to follow the scent of blood.

Matheson knows he needs to find Stone – and to quit this place. He cannot shake the vision that keeps flashing in his mind as he walks past the patricians and the angels in their big gold frames.

He cannot shake the memory of Wynn staring at the bone, something like fire in his eyes.

16

When sleep came, it closed over Stone like water. He spent the night five fathoms deep, in the blackest depths of unconsciousness. Here, now, he wakes as if breaking through ice. He pushes upwards, teeth bared and shoulders shaking, as he smashes into wakefulness and drags himself into the grey light of the day.

He sits up, chest heaving. Tries to get his breath. Blinks, hard, to clear the last remnants of the dream. He reaches over for his waistcoat to check the time then remembers he no longer has a watch. He fancies it to be about mid-morning, though there is so little light in Laura's room that he would not be surprised to find the moon still in ascendancy.

He lies down again, draws his coat over himself and presses his face back into the pillow he has made from his shirt and breeches. He shivers a little, and as he takes a breath, he catches the whiff of blood that was his companion as sleep engulfed him. He wonders if he is peculiar for finding comfort in the smell of Laura's blood, and what it says about him. But it offers a connection of sorts. He feels a closeness to her as he reaches up from his resting place upon the floor and tenderly strokes the mattress upon which they made love and on which she died, and fills himself with the scent of her life and death. He cannot make sense of his feelings but does not reproach himself for them. It is one of the few things about which he does not feel guilty.

A memory comes. A wisp of dream. The first man he killed. The simpleton on the road to Herat. He sees himself, skin darkened with oakum and dressed as an Afghan camel-trader. He sees the man's big, silly smile, as he saw through the disguise and began to say the word 'Feringhee' to himself, over and over. Stone sees what he did to him, remembers the sensation of blood gushing out from the hole in the man's side, the look of confusion and sadness in the poor fool's eyes as he emptied on to the rocky ground and fell forward to smash his face open on a jagged stone. Stone watches himself dragging the man's body behind a mound of boulders, then heaving rocks on to the still-warm corpse. He remembers that feeling of nothingness. That sensation of having changed. Of becoming somehow less, and more.

A cold breeze blows through the hole in the broken window and Stone begins to dress. He struggles into shirt and waistcoat while still lying beneath his greatcoat. He reaches out for his breeches and stretches to retrieve his weapons from within the depths of his tall hat.

The wooden door splinters as something smashes through the pane nearest the handle. Stone looks up to see a large leather boot sticking comically through the wood. He lunges for his hat, grabs the pistol and cocks it as the boot withdraws amid the mixed sounds of grunts and curses.

He swings the pistol at the door. Pauses, finger on the trigger. Then he makes a decision. He knows what is coming, and what he must do.

He drops the gun back into the hat, falls back to the mattress and is in the act of waking up, muzzy and afraid, as the door flies open and a large man in a spotless blue uniform bursts into the dingy gloom.

'Take him,' growls Sergeant Cooke, and steps aside as four police constables blunder into the room. Behind them, panting from the exertion and grinning like a gargoyle, Barrelman leans in the broken doorframe, froglike and vile in his stained green suit and top hat.

Stone makes a show of protestation as the constables rush him. He gauges their strength as they pull him, roughly, from the bed, and tries to cover his naked lower half with his hands, taking a blow to the kidneys for his pains. He aims a weak kick at a tall, gangly constable and sees the man jump backwards, awkwardly. Notes his poor defences and lack of balance. He forces fear on to his face as he is dragged before the big, bearded sergeant who stands, halberd-straight, by the damp wall.

Sergeant Cooke is not the biggest man Stone has seen but he is certainly an imposing physical specimen. He is several inches taller than Stone, broad across the chest and shoulders. The buttons of his blue coat strain to contain him. His dark hair is close-cropped and his beard is wiry and coarse. It has been shaved only at the chin, where a small, dimpled patch of pink skin pokes out like buttocks from the seat of a pair of furry breeches. He has deep-set eyes and a peculiarly simian appearance. Stone cannot help but wonder if he is in the presence of a gorilla that has been put into a suit and inexpertly shaved.

Cooke seems to consider the man before him. He turns slowly and raises an eyebrow at Barrelman, who grins and nods, causing sweat to fly off him in a fine rain. Cooke sucks at his cheeks and stares deep into Stone's eyes, as if reading what might be printed on the back of his skull.

Then he hits him.

Stone has taken better punches, but not many. The fist slams into his guts like a cannonball and he folds up around it. The strength leaves his legs and he sags in the arms of the two constables who hold him. The pain is a hot, sickening thing. He wants to fold himself into a ball and rock around the central spear of agony. He wants to curl up, like a baby. Like Laura . . .

Cooke hits him again. This time Stone's world goes black. For a second he is asleep again. Back on that Afghan road: warm blood on his hands and tears on his dusty cheeks as he heaves boulders on to the poor dumb bastard's body.

He wakes only a moment later. He has been allowed to fall to the floor. His face is pressed into the rotten timber. He is making a noise like a frightened cat.

'I'm Sergeant Cooke,' says the bearded man. 'These here are my lads. Tam Cooper you already know. And I presume that you're Meshach Stone. If not, you'll have to forgive me. You've just taken a punch that were meant elsewhere.'

Through gritted teeth, Stone hisses a curse. One of the constables kicks him in the small of the back.

'Aye, you'll be Stone. Barrelman tells me you've got a temper. Tells me a lot of things. I didn't give a shite about any of it, but when you start upsetting decent people, you become a problem I have to deal with. So I'm dealing. Pick him up, lads.'

Stone resists the urge to cry out as he is picked up once more. He sags against one of the constables who hold his arms, but whips his head up as the scarf that covers his scalp is torn away.

'By Christ, that looks sore,' says Cooke, appreciatively. 'And that'll be a musket ball, will it?' He looks down at Stone's bare legs. Nods at the ugly puncture wound in his thigh. 'You've been through the wars, eh? I've done my reading. Heard a lot about you these past few hours. You upset the good Dr Easter. Sent a runner to the chief constable himself, he did. Said you'd caused quite the rumpus, though that weren't what upset him. Said he needed to speak to you soon as we could find you. The chief constable likes to oblige the nobs so he sent a couple of my lads to look for you. Thankfully, they came to me first. And I decided that an important man like you needed to be shown some respect. Needed more than a constable wet behind the ears. So here I am, giving you a proper Hull greeting. You'll forgive me not delivering it earlier but I were busy running my city.'

Stone gasps as Cooke rakes his yellow fingernails across the wounds on his skull. He feels the skin tearing open and blood bubbling up between the cracks, like lava from broken rocks.

'Bet that stung,' says Cooke, wiping his hands on the nearest constable's sleeve. 'You'll have had worse, I'm sure. Great swashbuckling hero like you. Probably buggered day and night in Kabul, eh? They love all that, don't they, the darkies? I'm not a well-travelled man. Always felt comfortable within a day's ride of the Humber. But I do like reading about the places Her Majesty sends our brave boys. I'd love to see India some day but I have a delicate belly and I don't want to go all that way just to shite myself to nothing – can get that at home if you knows where to look. I read a bit on Afghanistan a few years back. I were just a constable then and not so wise, but it sounded an almighty mess. I don't envy you that trip back. You did well to survive it, though it don't look like you made it in one piece. So as a courtesy I won't break any bones. But you're not leaving this room without a lesson in manners. And if you go back to Dr Easter I'll make what they did to you in Kabul feel like a church picnic.'

Stone grits his teeth. He focuses on the throbbing pain in his head, then looks at Barrelman, who is enjoying every minute.

'Why?' gasps Stone, as pathetic and tame as he can muster. 'Why do I matter? Why won't you investigate?'

Cooke licks his teeth and glances at Barrelman, then snorts in incredulity. 'You're asking me questions? You don't ask me questions, Stone. The only man in this city who asks me questions is the chief constable and he only gets the answers he needs. You think we need more eyes on this city? It works, my lad. The cholera's come and that's a shame for all but it's doing no more than killing those who don't have much to live for. I'll be sorry to see many of them go cos they pay well and they know how things are, but don't expect me to be shedding a tear for them. I came from nothing and I fought to be somebody. Now I'm Cookie. I'm the one who says how things are. And I'm the one don't give a shite about some dead whores. Your whore died of cholera, my lad. That's what you need to tell yourself. She might have ended her misery by sticking a knife in her guts but that don't mean we all have to get in a fever and start looking for a madman. You understand, my pretty diplomat? You've seen the hell-holes of the world, have you? Well, you ain't seen nothing like Hull before. This little patch of Hell is mine. And I'm not ready for anybody to start causing trouble that don't suit my purposes. I'm sorry that you're going to leave this city with a limp and your pride hurt but, believe me, if I snapped my fingers you wouldn't be leaving at all. You'd be begging to be back on that road from Kabul, watching your friends freeze to death and cry for their mothers . . .'

Stone's captors have not noticed him shift his weight. They have relaxed their grip a little and are listening to their boss, enjoying the performance. They believe the man in their grasp is beaten.

They're looking forward to kneeling on his chest and hitting him until they're tired.

Stone's bare foot catches Cooke just above his knee. It is a powerful, expert delivery and the crack sounds like somebody breaking a tree branch. Cooke howls and falls like a toppled oak. Before his captors can check their grip on his arms, Stone has dragged the two constables close. He slams his forehead into the bridge of the nearest man's nose, then kicks the other in the crook of his leg. He falls backwards, and as he does so, Stone jumps on his chest.

'Stop him!' squeals Barrelman. 'Cooke, stop him!'

Still naked, except for shirt and waistcoat, Stone should not be an intimidating sight to the two remaining constables. But blood is running in trickles down his face and there is something cold and certain about the way he holds himself. Were they nearer the door, they would consider fleeing. But Stone bars their way.

The tall, gangly constable draws his club and swings it in a wide, clumsy arc. Stone blocks the blow at his wrist and the club tumbles on to the floor. He hits the man beneath the jaw and takes grim satisfaction in seeing him bite through his tongue. Behind him, he hears Barrelman squawk and turn. Stone grabs the remaining officer by the hair and smashes his fist into the man's forehead, with short, rapid blows. He spins the unconscious figure before he can fall and releases him with force, straight into Barrelman's path. The pimp falls heavily over the figure in blue and his tall hat rolls away, spilling coins and promissory notes among the tangled, blue-clad limbs.

Stone sniffs and rubs the blood from his face. He glances about him at the groaning, writhing men and decides he has time to get dressed.

Moments later, he has one booted foot on Cooke's ruined knee-cap. The big man is shrieking in pain. Barrelman has propped himself against the wall and is cowering under Stone's pistol. The four constables are either unconscious or wise enough to keep their mouths shut.

'That must sting,' says Stone, conversationally, nodding at the rapidly swelling mess of Cooke's knee. 'Going to be a while before that can even be set. You might walk with a limp for the rest of your days. But that won't be very long if you're not more helpful, so why don't you tell me again? Who killed Laura and why won't you do anything about it?'

Cooke makes fists. He has gone very pale and perspiration is standing out on his forehead. He seems to Stone like a man who has never been beaten. He wonders whether there is anything more pathetic than a beaten bully.

'It was cholera,' he hisses. 'She stabbed herself . . .'

Tutting, Stone puts the slightest pressure on Cooke's knee. The big man screams. Barrelman buries his face in his hands.

'Do you want to know why I saw Dr Easter?' asks Stone. 'Or do you already know? You do, don't you? You know somebody is killing women . . .'

'They're not women!' screams Cooke, furious. 'They're whores! They're just fucking whores! The city's dying, you fool! What does it fucking matter?'

Stone looks down upon the sergeant with contempt. Then he drops his knee directly on to the centre of the man's shattered kneecap. Cooke has only a moment in which to scream before Stone shoves his pistol into his mouth, breaking a tooth and causing him to gag. His cry is rattly and muffled: blood and wood and a dislodged incisor all block his throat.

'Don't!' yells Barrelman. 'For God's sake, he's a policeman!'

Stone scoffs. He wonders if Barrelman will make a break for it now he is no longer covered with the pistol, then realises it would take the fat man several seconds even to get up off the floor.

'They were your girls,' says Stone, to the pimp. 'Alice. Laura. You should give a damn. A thing like you understands the value of property. How much have you lost? Why are you afraid to admit what's happening?'

Barrelman holds himself like a frightened child. He rocks forward and back against the wall. 'I'm ruined,' he whispers feebly. 'Ruined!'

'I'm sure you have more girls,' says Stone.

'The cholera,' snivels Barrelman. 'Plague and pox have cost me dear. I can barely put food on the table. I needed money . . .'

Stone's face turns cold. 'You sold them? Sold their lives?'

'No!' wails Barrelman. 'Sold their names. I was afraid. And he had so much . . .'

Stone looks down at Cooke, wide-eyed and gagging around the pistol. He pulls the gun from his mouth and cuffs him across the head, then crosses to Barrelman, who squirms as Stone takes a handful of his lank, greasy hair. 'Who?' he demands. 'Who did you sell them to?'

'He was a big man,' stutters Barrelman. 'Came looking for me. I knew him, though not by name. Still don't, but there can't be many of his size. I did no wrong. I did no wrong!'

Stone tires of the man's whining. He presses the gun into his eye, then slides his dagger from his coat and presses it to Barrelman's other eyelid. 'Not looking good, is it? I can shoot you or stab you, Barrelman. There's another option, in which nothing bad happens at all, but I don't think you want that, do you?'

'Please!' begs the monstrosity at Stone's feet. 'I try! I pay what I owe. I look after my girls. I don't hurt them no more than they ask for and I helps them when they need it. They weren't earning. And he'd not done nothing to make me fear for them. They were just names. And I weren't to know.'

Stone applies pressure with the blade. A drop of blood wells up and dribbles on to Barrelman's cheek. 'You're a fat bastard, Barrelman. You know that feeling when you really need a piss and you think you'll burst if you don't get to drop your breeches? That's how I feel about killing you. I want to do it so much that I can't imagine not doing it. So make me grateful to you, and tell me what I need to know.'

A large stain spreads out across Barrelman's groin. The green suit darkens and the pimp begins to cry. 'Specialists,' he says, between bubbles of snot. 'When we met I told you about specialists. I knows what people like. They pay extra for it. The girls know it might upset them or hurt a little more but they're rewarded handsome, sir, I promise you.'

Stone flicks his wrist. He slices the faintest of nicks into the greasy tallow of the fat man's cheek. 'There's a girl at Dr Easter's,' he says. 'Irish. Not much more than a child. Somebody sliced her tongue so she couldn't tell what she saw. But when I mentioned your name she screamed and cried and broke my heart. I'm losing patience.'

'It weren't neither of us,' says Cooke, as he regains a little composure and shuffles so his back is to the wall. His face has gone a sickly green and there is sweat and drool in his beard. 'Just because we take our share from the unnatural goings-on doesn't mean we're bad men.'

Stone crosses to the sergeant. He stands over him and allows his face to betray the truth: he will kill everybody in the room if he has to.

'Barrelman's been running girls down here for years,' says Cooke, wincing. 'He pays his way, like they all do. I make no apologies for keeping the peace the way I choose to. You think the pay they give me is enough to compensate me for being a sergeant in bloody Hell? Don't judge me for guaranteeing my own pension.'

Stone says nothing. Just waits, unsure if he wants answers or a reason to put a pistol ball up the bastard's nose.

'Past couple of years, Barrelman's seen off the competition. He's the big man down here and I let him be. I keep the peace. Sometimes a customer gets a bit carried away with one of his girls. I make sure that customer knows not to do it again. Word gets around and soon everybody knows to respect the rules. It's not pretty, but everybody knows where they stand.'

'The Irish girl,' says Stone. 'Stop justifying yourself and tell me who cut her.'

'Weren't us,' says Cooke, petulantly. 'Ain't cut nobody. Not my way of doing business. I'll punch your guts till they're jelly and I'll crack your skull like an egg but I ain't got the patience for that kind of carry-on. And Barrelman wouldn't have the stomach. He's not a cruel man, despite what you may think. Not cruel like that, anyhow.'

Stone turns back to the pimp. Wonders if it would help the sergeant speak if he went over and cut the man's ear off. Cooke seems to read his thoughts. He gulps, painfully, and gets to the point. 'Past few months he's been moving up in the world. Helping the gentry, you might say. They have their needs too. And there are things that high-born ladies won't do. Specialists, like I said. That's what he made his name catering for.'

'He were a big man,' whines Barrelman, from the floor. 'Sought me out, beginning of winter. Said he had a fortune to spend and showed me enough of it to whet my appetite. Said he needed girls. Said they might come back a little sore but he was willing to pay for discretion.'

A trickle of dirty water falls from the roof beams as Stone looks up. The room seems to be getting colder. Unhealthier. He fancies he can see his breath form into tiny clouds, each one the ghost of a hope long since dead.

'Laura?' he asks quietly.

'She were a good earner,' says Barrelman, looking down at himself and moving his legs to hide the stain at his groin. 'Known her since she were a girl. She knew how to comfort a man. I told you that, did I not? Knew how to make a person feel all warm inside.'

'You sent her to the wolves,' says Stone, his teeth locked.

'Not at first, not at first,' says Barrelman, hurriedly. 'I had a new girl needed breaking in. Weren't so valuable. I tested the water with her. She weren't no looker but I wanted to see what I could get away with. Warts on her face like mould on cheese. He didn't mind. Came for her in a carriage black as your hat, he did. Picked her up without so much as a word and paid enough to put a man in a stupor. Brought her back as promised.'

'And?'

'She were fine, sir. Giddy, she were. Been living a fairytale. Good wine, nice food, soft sheets. Were even wearing silks under her rags. The big man weren't the customer, that were clear. But whoever entertained her did so proper.'

Stone turns to Cooke and receives the tiniest of nods.

'Who?' asks Stone, again.

'She don't know one nob from another, if you'll pardon the expression. Din't know where he took her neither. Shutters and curtains in the back of the carriage and there were a bottle to drink from that she weren't shy with. Half asleep by the time he opened the door. I tried to get some answers from her, cos you never know when such things will be useful, but she were still high as a buzzard. Said they'd blindfolded her with a rag of silk. Led her through open air then into a room bare except for bed, candle and the little treats they'd laid on for her. Smelt of paint and fresh straw, that's all she could recall. Told her to dress but not to wash, if you get me, sir. Must have been a bit like Napoleon in that regard, eh? Liked them dirty. So she did as she were bid. Fell asleep in soft sheets. Woke up in the half-dark with one of the nobs watching her. She couldn't tell me his face. Just a shadow. And he watched her for a while. Talked to her. Spoke gentle and polite as you like. She thinks he saw to himself in the end cos he didn't touch her. Then the big man came back and the silk went back on and she were brought back safe and sound.'

Stone licks his lips. He realises how dry his mouth is. Tastes the blood from his scalp.

'They were testing the water too,' says Barrelman, sniffing. 'I sent a more expensive girl next time. Didn't treat her quite so nice. Still got the flowers and the wine but he said some unkind things to her. Heard him giving himself what for, she did. Tugging on himself so hard it nearly came off. Made her keep the blindfold on the whole time. Pressed her face into the pillow and sorted himself out. Not to my taste but he'd paid for it . . .'

'You're a demon, Barrelman,' says Stone, trying to keep his temper.

'People wants their pleasures,' says Barrelman, snivelling. 'She'd took worse. They all had. She'd rather have that than some dirty sailor in an alley. You're one to judge. How did we meet, eh? You wanted to brush a whore's hair, did you?'

Stone feels an overwhelming urge to pummel the fat man's face until there is nothing left. He has to fight to control his breathing. Has to fight not to do bloody murder.

'Laura were one of 'em,' says Barrelman, and tears well up in his piggy eyes. 'His favourite, if you ask me, though he didn't show affection the way you or I would. Strung her up. No silk this time. Rough hemp, like you'd get on a sailing ship. Kept his voice soft as you like. Made her undress. Made her slip her hands through the rope and pull it closed with her teeth. Made her toss the far end into the shadows. He picked it up. Tied it off and pulled her hands over her head. Then he hurt her.'

Stone looks at the floor. He hates himself, the world and everything in it. 'How?' he asks.

'Put a brand on her, he did. Proper bloody scourging. A dozen lashes, regular as clockwork. Made a mess of her, though he cleaned her up nice as pie when she passed out. She'd screamed her head off but that didn't seem to stop him. Must have nice neighbours, eh? She made a noise to wake the dead.'

Stone cannot swallow. Cannot bring himself to speak.

'Gave her a pretty silk chemise for her trouble. She were sore for days but the big man was happy to compensate. Couldn't lift her hands for a week.'

Stone cannot help himself. He steps forward and stamps on Barrelman's huge, bloated stomach, feeling grim satisfaction as a rib snaps and the fat pimp emits a feeble squeal.

'What happened?' he hisses, pressing the dagger back to Barrelman's throat. 'He was getting more worked up, wasn't he? Working up to something . . .'

'He wanted more girls!' wails Barrelman. 'The next time the big man came he wanted three. Paid handsome . . .'

'He hurt them?'

'He just watched them – watched them hurt each other . . .'

'Whip?'

'And more.'

Stone can feel his heart thudding. He cannot help but remember the scarring on Laura's back, how she snatched his hand away as his fingers touched the striations in her flesh.

'There were no compensation when he brought them back,' blubs Barrelman. 'I weren't happy. They were a sorry state. No presents for them neither. I said a few things I shouldn't have, and when the big man told me not to get above myself, I threatened him with Cooke here. I told him he knew all about it and wouldn't be impressed.'

'He hurt you?'

'Just laughed at me,' spits Barrelman. 'Me! So I did what I'd said. I told Cooke. And Cooke reckoned the big man had been damn rude to enter his territory without even bringing him a little gesture of thanks for the safe passage. Next time the big man came, some of Cookie's lads were with me.'

'He wasn't happy?'

'He weren't scared,' says Barrelman, almost wincing at the memory. 'Just looked at me and told me I'd made a mistake. Then he whipped his horses and took off. It were months before I saw him again.'

Stone turns to Cooke. He takes a moment's pleasure in watching the policeman drop his eyes to the floor. 'And when he came back?' asks Stone.

'No carriage. No horses. No presents or nothing. Came to my house. My house!'

'He wanted more girls?'

'No, no, he wanted the same girls. The ones his paymaster had enjoyed before. Put a beating to me in my own home! I told him they weren't all still ripe, nor easy to find. Most had packed it in, gone back to family, got real work. I don't keep girls long – not unless they're special. I offered him the freshest meat. He wouldn't have it.'

Stone wipes blood from his brow. 'You gave him what he wanted?'

'What I could,' splutters Barrelman. 'I didn't know much about Rose. Just that she'd gone to family out towards the coast. Alice was with that idiot brother. Sarah was nursing her dying ma and I knew the street but not the house . . .'

'Alice,' says Stone. 'Her brother's going to get the rope or die in the madhouse. You know he did nothing to her. Nothing!'

'How do I know?' asks Barrelman, suddenly angry and rat-like. Spittle lands on his chin as he gasps his pain. 'People will do whatever their blood tells them! Cut her tits off, so they say. And? They weren't making me no coin . . .'

'And Laura?' asks Stone, his eyes cold.

Barrelman's mouth closes like a trap. He shakes his head, like a baby refusing the spoon.

Stone's knife takes the lobe of one ear. Barrelman feels the blood before he feels the pain, but then it comes like a locomotive. 'She were leaving me!' he screams, clasping one fleshy paw to his ruined ear. 'Had her head turned by some scarred soldier-boy, hadn't she? Said she knew he were coming back for her. Said she'd seen something in him – something that meant she couldn't spread her legs no more. What was I to do? After all the things I'd done for her, she were gonna leave me!'

'Describe him,' says Stone. 'The big man.'

'Beard and dark eyes,' blubs Barrelman. 'From the Valleys, judging by the little he said.'

Stone's head reels. He feels the floor lurch and it takes all of his strength to stop himself falling to the ground among the figures in blue. He concentrates on the vision in his mind. Focuses on her eyes. Lets the sensation fill him. 'You gave her up? Told the big man where to find her?'

'I just told him the building,' gasps Barrelman. 'He'd have found her anyways, no matter what I said. And I told Cookie afterwards. He said nobody would dare rip a whore on his patch.'

Stone crosses back to the bed. He sits down heavily, pressing his sweaty skin to the cool of the blade. 'And when you found her?'

'It were cholera! That's what she died from, no matter what you bleeding say!' shouts Cooke, from the floor. 'Nobody would rip a whore in Cookie's district. Nobody!'

Stone turns cold eyes upon him. 'You let them bury her. You stopped your bosses investigating, just so you wouldn't lose face. You're damned, Cooke. You're going to Hell when you die. But I'm going to give you a taste of it before I go.'

Cooke lets a little sneer creep onto his face. 'Do what you want, soldier-boy. Somebody's ripping whores, are they? There are hundreds dying every day. Somebody sliced a bog-trotter's tongue? Poor bitch. But at least at Dr Easter's she might live. Her family? They'll be in the ground before the sun's up. The plague's doing murder, Stone. Laura were a good girl. We all liked her. Nobody wants to think of her ripped. So tell yourself it were cholera and fuck off out of Hull. There's nothing for you here but pain.'

Stone stands. He presses the heel of his hand to his head and tries to control his thoughts. He is struggling to tell what is memory and what is vision. He cannot differentiate between the blades on that Afghan road, and the one that sliced upwards and sideways across the belly of the girl who could have redeemed him. 'Pain?' he asks softly. 'Pain I understand. Pain I live with every day. You're a bully, Sergeant Cooke. You're going to be a bully for the rest of your life. But I promise you, and your fat friend here, you're going to take a while to get your confidence back. It's going to be months before anybody runs at the sight of you or quakes at your name. Because for a while you're going to be doing nothing but healing. Pain? Let me show you how it feels . . .'

Moments later, the gulls and crows that sit on the roof of the crumbling building take off in a grey-striped swarm: their scream an echo of the sounds that erupt from within.

17

Matheson sits on the hard chair and looks at his own reflection in the half-dark glass of the bedroom window. He checks his pocket-watch and marvels at the hour. Early evening! In summer! And yet the room looks to have been drawn in pencil strokes. Goose-pimples continue to rise upon the bare skin of his plump forearms and each breath gathers about his face, like morning mist. The darkness of the room seems to be swallowing the light from the oil lamp. He fancies he can hear the sound of a vast throat opening and closing, gulping down the illumination like a drunkard with a quart of ale.

He rubs at his forehead distractedly, removes his spectacles and polishes them once again, then hooks them back over his ears and peers at the book in his lap. The words still seems blurred and indistinct. He cannot concentrate. He feels strangely untethered. There is a tremulous quality to his thoughts and he has noticed that his movements seem jerky and uncoordinated. He feels more than uneasy. He feels genuinely afraid.

Pushing out a long, slow lungful of air, he sets the textbook aside and considers again the letter in the pocket of his trousers. He nods, as if confirming his earlier decision. He needs to find Stone. He has no shame at the admission. Stone is his protector and friend. He has survived where others have fallen and Matheson has come to value his counsel. He is a comforting presence. Matheson has never been a fearful man. His zeal for discovery and enthusiasm for life have ensured that he is not troubled by anxiety. When he stands at the cold and dusty entrance of some new tomb and hears the voices of the dead screech past upon the wind, he feels only glee at what the next moments will bring. Here, now, he feels something far more primal in origin. It is a cold hand upon the nape of his neck. It is a handprint on a window in a locked room. He is permanently startled. His nerves are on edge and he jumps at every squeak of floorboard or creak of stair in this old, secret-laden house.

'You should have listened to Father . . .'

Despite himself, Matheson grins a little at his spoken thought. He gives in to a rare moment of nostalgic memory. He pictures the old man, sees the disapproval and disappointment in his father's gaze, remembers their last furious words, screamed at one another across the dinner table. He sees himself, flushed and impertinent, insisting he would rather go to Hell than subject himself to a lifetime of obedience in order to enter the gates of Paradise, then his father slumping back in his chair, as if shot through the heart. He recalls shrugging off his sister's embrace, stamping from the house and making up his mind. He would go to Europe. He would stuff himself to the gills with new experiences and discoveries. And then he would become the man his father wanted him to be.

Matheson sighs. He wonders if his father had seen this moment, if his faith had lent him some eerie gift of precognition and he had seen his errant son in a vision: sitting in this too-cold room in this too-big house, shivering and alone, an unnamed fear licking his insides and the image of a human femur scored into his memory like a knife wound.

He almost wishes he hadn't seen it, that he had turned away from the little rat-catcher before he produced his find. He wishes, too, he had not glimpsed Wynn.

Another shiver ripples through him and Matheson loses patience with himself. He pushes himself back from the desk. He has skulked up here long enough, has spent enough time confined to his room to be considered rude. For eight hours he has sat, read, paced and scribbled. He has ignored the growling of his stomach. He has heard the comings and goings of the household and ignored every knock upon his door. A little while ago he saw the handle turn and feared that some all-powerful force would cause the key in the lock to melt like ice. He imagined seeing it run down the painted wood, puddling on the varnished floor, the door swinging open and Wynn standing there, clutching the remaining bones and holding them out, like sticks for a fire. It had taken all his restraint not to yelp. He had found himself offering up a prayer, vouchsafing to excavate each of the good Lord's apostles if only he be allowed to escape this place and find his friend.

Matheson does not truly understand how he has become so consumed by fear. It cannot be the bone alone. He saw it for only a moment. It is possible he was mistaken. Perhaps it is indeed the bone of some long-forgotten priest, walled up inside his sanctuary. Perhaps it was from the corpse of a servant, killed by accident and never missed, stuffed into one of the many passageways and tunnels that criss-cross this great mausoleum. But he cannot convince himself of that. He knows bones. He has held them in his very hands. And that was a recent specimen. It showed none of the discoloration he has come to associate with ancient corpses. No, that bone had recently seen life. And if that were so, how could it have no skin? That is what so troubles Matheson. Somebody had stripped the flesh from it. They had taken a blade and butchered it so deeply that it had left grooves. And upon looking at Wynn, Matheson had seen something that turned his own blood to melted snow.

What does he know about the giant Welshman? He thinks again upon his brief association with Ansell's bodyguard, the first meeting in that stinking tavern. The pleasure the big man had taken in beating the drunkard to mulch. The unsubtle challenges he had made to Stone. The constantly unfriendly eyes. The delight he would have taken in breaking the bones of the little rat-catcher and his dog. He has seen him exhibit tenderness only once and that was to the lady of the house. Matheson cannot label the man a murderer on his fancies alone but he knows he does not want to be here for a moment longer. He will be sad to leave without having seen the reliquary and he will be loath to lose his new friend Phillip Ansell with such an uncourteous act, but he cannot stay. He needs Stone, the warmth of his companionship and security of his protection.

Matheson makes up his mind. He pats his pocket and feels the presence of the letters he has written to his sister and his friend.

He looks about him at the comfortable room. The sumptuous bed with its golden linen. The pale blue walls. The tasteful landscapes and portraits that hang in their wooden frames from the picture rail. He lifts the oil lamp and inspects them for a final time. The images are pleasant enough, but lifeless. He cannot imagine that Phillip Ansell chose them. The young master's own work is vastly superior to anything on display in the house. Matheson again wonders why his son's gift should so distress Lord Ansell. The painting is sublime: it captures moments so perfectly as to be almost unsettling. It imprisons the human condition at its most raw and exposed. He has never seen its like. Yet Phillip Ansell's paintings adorn not a single wall. His gift is not spoken of. And Lord Ansell treats him with utter disdain.

Matheson realises he is purposely delaying his departure. He does not want to leave the room. He does not like the picture he sees of himself skulking down the corridors and scuttling down the stairs, escaping the place without a goodbye. But he knows his own nature: he will be cajoled into remaining should he try to make his goodbye to Phillip. And knows he will betray his suspicions should he stumble across Wynn.

Softly, cautiously, he picks up the leather case that contains his archaeological tools and notebooks. He leaves everything else behind. He will send for such trivialities as his clothes. He plans to make his way on foot as far as his legs will allow him, then use coin to purchase carriage into the centre of Hull. He will take lodgings at a fine hotel and send messenger boys into the network of streets where he fancies Stone will be drinking himself numb. Together they will return to Reverend Verinder's house. They will finish their search for Simon the Zealot. And he will put the thought of the fresh femur from his mind.

Matheson unlocks the door as quietly as he can and peers out into the long, silent corridor. A tray of food has been left on the landing for him. Despite himself, he crouches down and lifts the lid that sits on the fine crockery. The stew is still warm and smells delicious. He spoons down several large mouthfuls, then takes a bite of the summer fruit pudding and swigs from the crystal goblet of fine claret. He apologises to his stomach for depriving it of the kitchen's exquisite cooking. Then he closes the door behind him and treads as quietly as he can along the corridor.

There is a flight of stairs and the great hall between himself and the front door. He knows there must be servant stairs but in this labyrinth of passageways and secret chambers he would not trust himself to find freedom. He has tapped every wall in his own quarters in the hope of discovering a hidden chamber but without success. The only way out is through the main body of the house. He is unsure whether to use stealth or speed. Fancies a mixture of both will serve him best.

Breathing as calmly as he can, Matheson scuttles down the long corridor, pressed as close to the shadows by the wall as he can manage. He looks up at the colossal pictures in their great golden frames, seeing martyrs and golden-haired cherubs, the serene faces of dying men and the tranquillity of beautiful women who press Christ to their breast and turn their countenances Heavenwards, even as soldiers and spears threaten defilement of their mortal bodies.

A dozen fat yellow candles blaze in an alcove at the top of the stairs. Ribbons of red flame rise up as if from a grey sea and black figures dance upon the wall. To Matheson they form a sea of souls. For an instant they are creatures in Purgatory: an ocean of the dispossessed reaching up to grab at those fortunate enough to be sailing on to Paradise. It sends a shiver through him. He doubles his pace . . .

'Diligence! Are you quite well, my friend? Would you permit me entry? I have some artefacts that may lift your spirits, and I see you have managed a little food.'

Matheson turns. Phillip Ansell is standing by the bedroom door. He is dressed in a patterned robe and is holding a small wooden box in white-gloved hands. Matheson realises that, from his position at the top of the stairs, he is invisible to his friend's gaze. He could stay there, pressed to the wall, then continue on his way. But what if Ansell should pass him? What if he sees him, hiding like a child, bag in hand, fleeing his warm hospitality? Matheson's heart races as he pushes back deeper into the shadows, peers into the gloom and sees the young master try his door.

'Are you sleeping? Travel will exhaust a person, will it not? I have stories I could share about my own time in the saddle. We have not yet properly spoken of how our dear Major Stone saved my life. Perhaps such a yarn would prove restorative.'

Matheson feels consumed by guilt. Phillip Ansell has shown him nothing but kindness. He has been a good and dutiful friend. Yet Matheson suspects his manservant of murder. He feels uncertain of how to proceed. He needs counsel and protection. He needs to get out of this place more than he needs to be a gracious guest. He pushes against the wall and sucks in his ample belly.

There is a soft click, and then a moment's imbalance. Matheson has to stuff a hand into his mouth not to exclaim. A sudden breeze causes the candle flames to dance and the shadows to lengthen. Almost without conscious thought, he takes a step backwards into the sudden space that has opened behind him. His feet scrape on loose stone. In an instant he has made up his mind. He turns and steps inside the hidden passage, grabs the edge of the wooden door and softly slides it back into place. He leans against it, panting, and wonders if he has made his position better or worse.

Slowly, he turns to look at his new surroundings. The passageway is lit by a series of torches held in brackets on the high, rough walls. There is a smell of animal fat. Unbidden, Matheson thinks, *Peasants*. It is not his own word. At home, animal-fat candles are used by the poor to light their homes. They give off a stink like the very devil and it seeps into hair, skin and clothes. To his father, it marks out a peasant. It is a badge of dishonour. Matheson is surprised to find them in this great house, more so to find them lit. They illuminate a long, narrow corridor. The floor is made of crude flagstones on which a variety of footprints intermingle and cross. He can see for perhaps twenty paces, at which point the passageway curves to the right.

'Meshach, as bodyguards go you are proving unacceptably inattentive.'

In the darkness, Matheson's whisper is swallowed. He feels a chill upon his skin. He has no choice but to follow the light.

As quietly and cautiously as he can, Matheson presses forward. His pack bangs against the rough wall and in the silence the sound is like a gunshot. He quickens his pace, reaching out to the coarse brick. Ahead, he sees a patch of faint grey light and steps into it. He turns and searches for the origin of the glow, feels air on his cheek and fumbles at the brickwork. A stone comes away in his hand . . .

He is staring into his own bedroom through a lighting bracket on the wall, directly at his own bed. Phillip Ansell is inside. He is pulling back the bedcovers. Looking inside wardrobes. Turning, hands on hips, trying to find his errant friend.

Matheson bites back a gasp and steps away from the viewing hole. He feels a sickness in his belly. Anger, too. Has he been spied upon? What indiscretions has he committed while under observation? He feels himself colour, then a sudden desperation to quit this place. Quicker now, he pushes on, following the passageway as it curves right. He hopes that it will begin to angle downwards. Hopes it will lead to a rear door and open fields. Instead he finds stairs leading up to his left. Panic begins to rise in his chest. He takes the only direction open to him, the stairs, and turns left into another long passageway. Again it is lit by animal-fat candles. And again every few paces are punctured by a soft grey radiance. Every room is speared by a viewing hole.

Matheson is almost running. He drags his bag and bumbles onwards. Despite himself, he peers through some of the viewing holes into large, lavish bedrooms, luxurious furniture draped in ghostly white sheets. He starts when he sees one of the maids dusting a fireplace. He turns his head and sees another polishing silver candlesticks and picking a back tooth with her little finger. He begins to question his own existence, to feel ghostlike, omnipotent, as he stares at those who cannot see him. Races on. Races on . . .

He stops short as his feet crunch on something brittle. Looks down. He closes his eyes too late. The image is already burned for ever into his memory. He is standing on a carpet of bones. Fresh bones. Each scored and scraped and de-fleshed as perfectly as the one the rat-catcher found.

Matheson's heart feels as though it will burst from his chest. He tastes acid and has to bite down on his hand to stop himself crying out. He turns back. Panics, as he realises he has lost his bearings. He cannot seem to order his thoughts. He's sweating and shaking and lost in this ghastly place. He needs a guide. A landmark. He presses his eyes to the nearest viewing hole and lets out an exclamation that echoes off the walls as if he had struck a bell with a hammer.

Lady Ansell is perhaps three feet in front of him. Her wrists are bound with rope and she kneels upon the floor with her head angled towards the chimneybreast to her left. She is naked, her fleshy legs drawn up under the bulging puddle of loose gut around her waist. Her skin is almost unholy. Her breasts are crimson with welts and sores. As she presses her face to the floor, she shows similar ruin across her broad back. Scabs have formed across her shoulders. Her face, which Matheson had expected to be open in agony, is instead held in a grimace of rapture and wanton, greedy pleasure.

Behind her stands Wynn. He, too, is naked. His hair is a matted sweaty carpet across his body and face and masks a similar degree of ruination. His excitement juts out obscenely in front of him.

Wynn reaches down. At his feet is a hair shirt.

In one movement, he drapes the coarse material about his mistress's flesh and presses himself to her.

Lady Ansell chews her lip in ecstasy as she continues to stare up at the picture of her dead daughter above the fireplace.

Matheson cannot take his eyes off the scene. He is still entranced and aghast as the rat scuttles across his foot.

Wynn looks up as he hears Matheson give a high-pitched shriek, which echoes off the walls of the chamber. Cold fury settles upon the giant's face. He crosses the room in three strides and slams a hand against a wooden panel.

Matheson squeals as Wynn swings open the secret door. He turns on his heels and thunders down the passage, yelping as his spectacles fall off and clatter on to the floor. He runs as if pursued by demons, expecting a hand to close upon his collar at any moment.

He blunders into total darkness, his way barred by fallen bricks.

He spins around, desperate now. Lost. He squeezes past fallen rubble and clatters into a long, sloping corridor. H runs desperately, and hears a sound he knows to be the screech of rats as he careers down the steep passageway.

Ahead he sees an area of softer darkness. He fancies he can see the soft haze of a glowing lamp. He scrambles forward, then feels his heart almost fold itself in two as a figure emerges and a brick smashes against his skull with an impact that causes a lightning storm to erupt in an explosion of purples and silvers against the blackness that swallows him like water.

Matheson is not conscious of what happens next. He does not feel himself picked up and slung over a greasy, sweat-streaked shoulder. He does not see his attacker descend the tunnel into the bowels of the earth.

He comes to on a cold earth floor. Sees, through the cracks in his vision, white lines and black wood. Feels dust upon his cheek and sticky black blood in his hair.

Somewhere nearby, stone is scraping on stone. An old hinge, unoiled, is creaking open and something heavy is being moved across an unyielding surface.

Matheson tries to form words but something is broken in his brain. He cannot smell, cannot swallow. He wonders why his father is looking down upon him so dispassionately. Why Meshach Stone is toasting his good health and smoking his pipe instead of drawing his blade.

And then a naked foot is pushing him through cold, empty air. He is landing, hard, on a surface of sticks and boulders. Something breaks in his forearm. He feels long-dead teeth against the bloodied skin at his neck.

He looks up as the light goes out, both within him and without.

The reliquary. The true resting place of the family's curiosities and artefacts. The place he had sought . . .

He fights through the fog for a solitary moment, manages a single thought, then gives in to the darkness knowing that he dies among the martyred, buried for ever among apostles and saints.

18

The wind blows in from the west, bringing with it the scent of cut grass and sawn wood. The stench of Hull fades as the carriage rattles and clatters its way up the rutted track.

Stone breathes deep, filling himself with a cleansing lungful of turned earth. He enjoys the sensation of heading west, leaving the pestilence and plague behind, even as he knows that he will return. First he has questions to ask the big man who cared so little for Barrelman's threats. And when he has his answers, he will return to do right by Laura's memory. He will find the girls who knew her and help set them free of a city that is closing on itself, like a rotting hand.

Stone slides the threadbare curtain aside and pokes his head through the small window. The sun is still up but its last rays have lost their battle with the cloud that has lain above the landscape since he woke. The evening is suffused with the sickly yellow-grey of a dying man's skin, and though the trees that bend under the attentions of the wind are thick with leaves, they seem to Stone as though they yearn to cast off their plumage and stand as stark charcoal skeletons; bleak signposts on the road into a fading city.

He pulls himself back inside. His next breath is all old leather, horse-shit and sweat. The carriage is an ancient, poorly ventilated contraption that threatens to come apart with each bump in the road, but Stone could find no other driver willing to make the long journey to Randall Hall. The rest are holed up in taverns, drinking themselves insensible and refusing to offer passage to anybody who has been within coughing distance of Hull's slums. Stone had to give over almost all of the money he took from Barrelman's purse, and the jerking of the vehicle causes his bruised ribs to sing with pain.

They are nearing the rear of Lord Ansell's property. Half a mile of dense woodland lies between him and his friend-employer. Stone's heart lifts a little at the thought of Matheson's big, round face, which will split into the warmest of grins when its owner spots him. He has missed his companion. The younger man looks upon him with such awe and appreciation that occasionally Stone stops despising himself and feels like a man of worth. He hopes that Matheson has enjoyed the past days, that he has made the discoveries that so energise him and which have brought him so far from home.

There comes a sharp rap on the roof of the carriage.

'Here, sir. Can't go no further. His lordship don't like no coaches without his own livery.' The driver's voice suggests that he would quite like to take a knife and draw the family's heraldic crest on the earl's fat arse.

Stone pushes open the door and steps down on to the muddy track. The rain has made the surface slippery underfoot but he keeps his balance as he reaches up and presses a decent tip into the man's hand. 'I can't ask you to wait,' says Stone. 'I'm sure you have reason enough to get back to the city. But a friend and I may need transport in the morning. If you were here . . .'

The driver holds up a hand. He's an old man, with thick white hair and grooves in his face that look as though his countenance has been repeatedly folded and unfolded. He shakes his head. 'Lord Ansell's man won't have it. Big man. From the Valleys. Sees us off if we come within a hundred yards of his boundary line. It upsets his lordship, they say. He likes to look out his window and see only things he owns. Likes it all stamped with his crest. I'm not one to talk out of turn but him and his man are well suited. Unholy terrors, though in different ways. His brute likes to dish out the slaps and kicks, so he does. His master likes to hurt you on the inside – likes you to know you're nothing and he's everything. Begging your pardon, sir, I wouldn't normally be speaking so free, but given you're not going in the front door

I has my suspicions you're not one of his lordship's bosom chums.'

Stone gives a little smile, turns his back on the wind and lights his pipe. He draws in a breath of tobacco, laced with the tiniest taste of his fine Turkish resin. He has added no more to the bowl, but the pipe stem retains the flavour. He realises how little he has needed its comfort these past hours. He has not taken a drink since last night and his hands are perfectly still. 'The big man,' he says quietly. 'Have you seen him on the roads? Driving a black carriage?'

The driver sucks his cheek and spits. 'There's a black carriage used to come in from the west in the winter months. No livery but well maintained. Fresh paint and chains well greased. Horses were fine beasts too. Could have been one of his lordship's vehicles painted black as your hat, though I wouldn't swear to it.'

'But Wynn,' persists Stone. 'The big man. You would have recognised him were he driving, would you not?'

The driver shrugs. 'I looks at the horses, sir. I tip my hat but don't recall who were at the reins. And it were dark. Couldn't rightly say.'

Thin-lipped, Stone smiles his thanks. He turns away and approaches the fence that marks the boundary of Lord Ansell's land. Behind him, he hears the driver urge the horses to pull to the left and, in a gentle thunder of creaking wood and protesting metal, trundle back down the lane to the Hull road.

Stone wonders if the man will survive the plague. Whether he has family dying of the cholera even now. Whether he will even survive long enough to spend the blood money Stone pushed into his dirty hand.

He places one hand on the expensive timber of the fence and vaults it in one fluid motion. He grins to himself as he lands. Matheson would have been excited to see that. Had he been present, Stone would have finished with a tumble, or performed a handstand on top of the fence. He would have brushed off the applause with some gruff words of dismissal but he would have enjoyed Matheson's delight. Perhaps he would have shared with him one of his stories. Told him about Bombay, Herat or that damnable road from Kabul.

It was on that road where it had all begun. Even after Herat, Stone had been in control of his mind. Even after the blood and carnage of the terrible siege, he could make merry and sleep soundly. He had enjoyed the occasional drink, and parts of his soul had festered with resentment about the childhood that had been taken from him by circumstance, but it was not until that hellish journey that he had felt himself pulled into the misery and self-destruction that have consumed him since. He simply saw too many terrible things to carry on being the man he once was. He sees them coming again. Akhbar's men firing their stolen muskets and charging at the weakening, crumbling line. Stone had survived by good fortune alone. The wound he sustained had rendered him unconscious. He woke to a scene of nightmare, alone on a mountain path carpeted with British dead. He had wanted to let death take him. But something had compelled him to stand and begin walking, all the while expecting a sudden shout or a pistol ball or the thunder of enemy horsemen. None came. As he walked, he ruminated on betrayal and the folly of the commanders who had not listened. He ground his teeth as hate colonised every particle of his being. When he staggered into Jalalabad, he was no longer Major Meshach Stone. He was a ghastly, bloodied spectre, a demonic, half-dead thing. He swore revenge and, ever since, has sought out debasement and numbness, violence and hate. He has killed, and killed again.

The pipe goes out as he makes his way through the darkening woods. He removes it and places it in his coat pocket, where it clinks against the side of his brandy bottle. Stone marvels at himself. Why has he filled himself for so long with drink, tobacco and laudanum when it has brought him such little relief?

He ducks under the branches of a rowan tree and emerges at the rear of the house. His boots are soaked from the long grass but there are still spots of Sergeant Cooke's blood upon the toes. He wonders who is treating the policeman's wounds. Presumably one of his whores will be looking after Barrelman. The fat pimp is only

186

alive so he can warn the girls to be wary. Stone has no other way of contacting the women he fears have been marked by a killer with a taste for his work.

Instinctively, he reaches into his pocket and grips the copy of the *Hull Packet*. He does not need to reread the story that brought bile to his throat when he glimpsed it on the table of the hotel where he dined. A young woman's body has been found in Patrington, broken so badly that the farmhands who discovered her believed she must have dropped from beyond the clouds. The story almost rivalled the cholera for column inches, though the article had given away precious little. Her name was Rose Holden and she had only recently moved to the village where she worked as a laundress with her aunt. She was a hard-working and Christian girl. She was seventeen and pretty. While the area's magistrates have not allowed themselves to speculate on local suspicions that she had been brutalised by persons unknown, investigations are advancing along the theory that she was run over by a cart. A wheel, showing signs of having buckled under great force, had been found near the poor girl's shattered body . . .

Stone bites down as he recalls the words. He is beginning to understand. There are pieces missing and he curses his abuse of his brain these past years, but he has some comprehension of the circumstances of her death. Hers and Laura's. They have been playthings. They have serviced a man of perversion. And now that man has taken their lives. Stone has half an idea who that man may be, but knows his own darkness well enough that he does not trust his judgement. He has too many questions to be able to make an accusation. He needs the counsel of a man he trusts and the influence that comes with the man's money. He needs Matheson. Together they will approach Chief Constable McManus. They will tell him about Sergeant Cooke, that suspicious deaths have been treated as the product of disease. He will do his duty by the woman who touched his soul. But, first, he will take bloody revenge.

'Major Stone! Good Lord, Meshach, is that you?'

Stone turns at the sound of Phillip Ansell's voice. He curses. He has lost concentration and allowed himself to blunder up to the house in a daze. Ansell is leaning out of a first-floor window, his face pale and his normally immaculate clothing ruffled and unkempt.

'Stay where you are. I shall be down directly.'

Stone feels like telling the young fop to go to Hell, but there is an urgency in his tone that persuades him to do as instructed. He leans against the great square bricks of the rear wall, looks up at the vast property and is overcome with a memory so vivid it almost takes his breath away. He remembers playing with his father. He would not have been more than four years old. They were throwing a ball between them. It was a simple, honest pleasure. Both had been smiling. The sun was shining and the sky seemed impossibly blue. He had felt safe. Loved. Warm. It could always have been like that. Should have been. Christ, how he wants to see the old man. A feeling he has not experienced for years is welling up in him, emotion he had thought drowned in drink. He feels a sudden need to uncork the brandy bottle and drink deep. He wants to stop his heart before it dares to suggest that he misses and loves the house of his childhood or the man who brought him home and tried to call him 'son' . . .

'Major Stone, I'm so pleased to see you,' says Ansell, as he stumbles from the large wooden doors on to the smooth pebbles of the rear courtyard. 'Is Diligence quite well? I will have his things fetched at once but, please, do reassure me that his condition has not worsened. Is he suitably lodged somewhere? Have I upset him with my tardiness and inattentiveness? I had so wished to make good on my promise but Father has been so intractable . . .'

Stone clutches the bottle in his pocket, feeling the pipe brush his fingers. He looks into the other man's face and sees only wide-eyed concern. 'He's not here?'

'No, no, he took to his bed earlier today and refused visitors. I finally gained entry to his rooms and he had vanished. I have the servants searching for him in case he came out seeking fresh air, but as the evening grows darker I fear he has left us. When I saw you approach I presumed you had come to retrieve his belongings. Is that not so?' Ansell's face falls as he realises the good news he had sought will not be forthcoming. 'Oh, Major Stone, I feel beyond consolation at the thought of his displeasure with me. He must have tired of the delays and simply taken himself off to somewhere more accommodating. Has he written you? Did he tell you where to meet?'

Stone pulls his hat from his head and rubs at his forehead. Could Diligence truly have departed this place alone? Could he have tired of Stone's company as much as he had tired of Ansell's failure to make good on his promises? Stone tries to believe it but cannot. He knows Matheson like he has known few others. Guilt floods him. He abandoned him here, with his enquiring mind, thirst for knowledge . . . and Wynn.

'His room,' growls Stone. 'Take me there.'

Ansell's eyes are filling with tears. He seems truly heartbroken at the thought of having disappointed his new friend. Stone remembers that look from years ago. He remembers the frightened, unworldly boy who had sought adventure on the road to India and found only danger and shame. Ansell has few friends and his father is a brute. He lost his dear sister and is denied the chance to indulge the one gift he was born with. Stone wishes he had time to offer consolation or a comforting arm. But his thoughts are entirely of Matheson. He grabs the young man by his shirt and drags him into the house.

'Wynn,' says Stone, as Ansell leads him through a hexagonal room containing fishing rods, birdcages and butterfly nets. 'He's here?'

Ansell shakes his head, opening a door into a long corridor lined with framed maps and mirrors. 'I sought him out when I discovered Diligence was missing. I presume he has gone to fetch Father from the train. Oh, I do hope all is well. He did seem truly weakened by this morning's unfortunate incident. I have reprimanded Goodhand. Even for a student of archaeology, such as our friend, it must have been a fright to see the bone clutched in his hand.'

Stone tries to silence the din in his skull. He concentrates on Ansell's words, then grabs the young man, who gives a high-pitched squeal somewhere between a laugh and a cry.

'Explain yourself,' demands Stone.

Snivelling, damp-eyed, Ansell explains the morning's events. He tells Stone about the secret door in the wall, the rat-catcher's grisly find and Wynn's rough behaviour.

'His room!'

Ansell runs up the stairs and Stone stamps after him, leaving dirty bootprints on the perfect floor. He follows him into Matheson's bedroom and shivers as a cold breeze dries the sweat on his skin.

'His things are still here but I believe he may have taken a single satchel,' babbles Ansell. 'Does he have the means to return to Croxington? Or could he perhaps have gone looking for you?'

Stone cannot help himself. He pulls the bottle from his pocket and gulps down the burning liquid as if it were water. He cannot fight the images that bubble, like a cauldron, in his mind. He suddenly understands. With Lord Ansell away, it is clear who has brought this fresh pain to his life. He sees Wynn brutalising his friend. To his very bones he believes that Matheson made a discovery that mirrors his own. Wynn is a killer and his master a man who takes his pleasure in the pain of others. Wynn has been killing to silence the whores his master so brutalised. Matheson discovered him. And now he has been snatched away from Stone's protection.

'Major Stone, you have gone quite pale,' exclaims Ansell. 'Is there a sickness in this house that all who enter must be contaminated with? I apologise with all that I am for bringing either of you into this place.'

Stone ignores him. He looks around him at the palatial bedroom and spots a discarded textbook with a sheaf of papers fluttering on the writing desk. He crosses to it and picks up the top page, angling it towards what little light comes in from the window. Unbidden, Ansell produces a tinder-box and sparks it into life.

'Please,' says Stone, under his breath.

Under the flickering light, he makes out the indentation of Diligence Matheson's neat handwriting. He slams the paper back on the desk. Ansell understands, and pulls a length of charcoal from his waistcoat pocket. Stone grunts his thanks. In broad, deft strokes, he colours the page black and watches the words become clear. He reads his own name and the looping signature of his friend. Angles the light again and holds himself so rigid that his shoulders crack under the tension of his pose.

'Major Stone?'

He turns to Ansell, folds the paper and puts it into his pocket, then forces a smile. 'We've worried for naught,' he says quietly. 'He has gone to see a physician of his acquaintance for a remedy to the malady that befell him this morning. He makes his apologies. He will be back before the dawn.'

Ansell's sigh of relief seems for a moment like air escaping an inflated pig-bladder. He sinks on to the bed, colour filling his cheeks. 'My word,' he says, 'but he knows how to give a fellow a fright. Could he not have left a note for me?'

'That's Diligence,' says Stone, with a flicker of a smile. 'He probably wrote it, then put it into his pocket. He has his mind on better things, does he not? He will be planning our next adventure, no doubt, and looking forward to the discoveries that you have promised him.'

Ansell is adjusting his clothing. He pulls a lady's comb from a pocket and begins to slick back his hair. He stops, as if arrested by a thought. 'You sought Wynn? Father should be another hour and Wynn will be with him, I have no doubt. Perhaps Father's manner will have softened and you will be welcome to spend the night in the house. If not, there are rooms aplenty where you would not be discovered.'

Stone concentrates on his breathing. On keeping the smile fixed on his face. 'I will speak to your father when he returns,' he says. 'I have much to apologise for and will sleep where he bids me as we await our friend's return. And, yes, I believe Wynn and I would benefit from a similar discussion. I am at your disposal until then.'

Ansell seems gleeful at the thought of some time with the man who rescued him so long before. 'Would you care to see my own humble rooms, Major? We could talk over old times, could we not? And you could share with me some of your adventures. I love a story and have so few opportunities to talk with those who have seen the world as it truly is.'

Stone drops his empty bottle on Matheson's bed and follows the young master from the room.

The letter, folded in his pocket, seems to burn against his skin. It is all he can do not to begin tearing at the walls, searching for the body of his friend.

Stone knows what Wynn has done, and why.

He knows, too, that before the night is through he will seek redemption in blood.

PART THREE

My dear Meshach

*I write these lines swiftly, knowing that I will have to copy them out
again and again, despatching errand boys into the heart of the
cholera district in a bid to find you and bring you to my aid. I am
quitting Randall Hall. This morning I made a discovery which I
believe places me in great peril. I know bones, do I not? And that
which I saw today was not from some long-forgotten corpse but
from a female in her prime and recently departed of this world.
What is more, I believe cruel indignities were heaped upon her. She
was stripped of flesh. Stripped! I swear this to be true. And, though
I chastise myself for the suspicion, I believe that the guilt lies with
Lord Ansell's manservant Wynn. He saw the suspicion in my eyes
and I fear the consequences. I do hope all is well in your heart and
that you have managed to arrange a decent and fitting burial for
the woman who brought you the happiness you so richly deserve.*

Your friend,
Diligence

19

He had expected opulence, luxury, golden drapes and birds of paradise: an orchard of blooms. Instead Stone is led into a room as soulless and Spartan as a monk's cell. The bed is little more than a prison bunk, over which a drab grey blanket has been neatly folded. The only other furniture is a writing desk, a hard-backed chair and a solitary shelf upon which rests a battered, leather-bound Bible. Shutters bar the window and the walls have been painted a yellowish white that puts Stone in mind of the moon's appearance on clear winter nights. One colossal threadbare tapestry hangs from a bare pole on the wall to Stone's left, reaching to the floor and almost as far as the window. It is a Biblical scene on cloth: Christ stares out, face mouldy, the threads of his wounds mottled and unpicked.

Stone imagines trying to sleep beneath that gaze, the sensation of being watched, judged and labelled a sinner by those hand-stitched eyes. He opens his mouth to speak, and sees his breath escape into the ash-coloured air. He watches as it disappears into a nothingness so complete that it almost takes the strength from his legs.

'Please,' says Ansell, pointing at the chair. 'I don't expect us to share a bed.'

Stone waits for him to give his girlish laugh, but he remains silent. Stone stays where he is, leaning against the door, unsure if he should make some apology, then return to the colour and light of the corridor. Before he can move, Ansell crosses to the bed. From underneath he pulls out an oil lamp, which he lights with his tinder-box. He uses the flame to ignite his small cigar, then places the light in the centre of the room. It gives off a soft glow that casts peculiar shadows on the bare walls.

'Not what you'd imagined?' asks Ansell, sitting down on the thin mattress and puffing his cigar. 'You should feel honoured. You're the first friend I have allowed in here. Father would be furious.'

Stone softens his demeanour slightly at use of the word 'friend'. He nods stiffly and crosses to the chair, sits down and begins to play with his pipe. He can't think of a damn thing to say.

'Kerosene,' says Ansell, after a time. He is pointing at the lamp that burns between them. 'A miraculous invention. Discovered only a couple of years ago by a gentleman named Kesner. Canadian, I believe, though I never found opportunity to ask Diligence if the two were acquainted. I anticipate its use in the houses of both rich and poor within the decade. I urged Father to invest but, as with so many of my proposals, he met the idea with derision. Still, I have sufficient purse to import enough for my own needs. It creates day from night, does it not? And the light it emits lends a quality to painting that enchants and irritates in equal measure. Is it real? Is it an affectation? Should art be authentic? These are the questions that trouble me as I lie awake. Truly, we live in a remarkable age.'

Stone listens attentively. He feels dizzy and sick. The liquor is crying out for company and he feels his hands begin to shake. He turns the pipe between his fingers and concentrates on his breathing. He considers the young, flamboyant man on the hard mattress, staring at the light as if it were the soul of God. 'I'm not sure I would have recognised you,' says Stone, at length. 'You were a different man when we parted in Bombay. Younger, yes. But it's more than that. You weren't so . . .'

'I wasn't so much of a peacock, you mean?' asks Ansell, giving a little grin. 'No, I was still finding my way, Major Stone. Still trying to be what Father wanted me to be. I dressed as other men dressed. I spoke as other men spoke. And I lived a lie so the truth of my nature did not bring shame upon the family.'

'And what is the truth?' asks Stone, softly.

'I am not like other men,' he says flatly. 'I cannot dress and act and talk as they do. I was born with a blessing that my father views as a curse. I see beauty, my friend. I see it and I can recreate it. But Father does not want some limp-wristed popinjay as a son. He does not want my name in galleries and journals. Does not want me to strip men and women and make their bodies immortal on paper and canvas. He has tried to cure me of this accursed gift for nigh on thirty years. I fear he will soon stop trying. He is mellowing a little. He allows me to paint for Lady Ansell so that he does not have to think of any other means to comfort her. Allows me paper and pencil so that I may create sketches for my own enjoyment from time to time. Perhaps he is preparing to disinherit me and this is his gesture of compassion. But I fear not. He is not given to such feelings.'

Stone watches as the shadows from the oil lamp flicker in the hollows and lines of Ansell's face. There are no tears in the young man's eyes. Just a great sadness.

'I remember your gifts,' says Stone, lighting his pipe. 'I may not have said so at the time but your paintings were extraordinary. Luminous, you might say. I have been tempted to sketch from time to time. I have an etching in my wallet that once brought me comfort, though I have not been able to look upon it for a time. Your own works should not be hidden away.'

Ansell shrugs. 'I did sunsets and mountains the way others had done before. I mimicked the art I loved. I had not yet found that which truly inspired me.'

Stone considers the young man, then tries to give him some kindness. 'I'm no expert but I could tell you had a formidable talent. If you were my son I would have encouraged it. It's not your fault your father is a bully.'

'A bully?'

'I know his type,' says Stone. 'Old-school officers. Happy to face the musket balls and to lead a charge at the enemy. Fearless in battle and willing to die before dishonour. Good, solid British gentry. And utterly dead inside. They don't value their lives so they don't value the lives of others. Nor do they appreciate the things that make life tolerable. Were your father to give in to a love of beauty, of art, of poetry, he would not hold his own life so cheap.'

Stone looks up and sees Ansell staring at him intently. His mouth is hanging open, like a dog waiting for a bone.

'I have thought upon my father each night for years,' he says quietly, 'and never once considered him as you just spoke. I wonder, Major Stone, how you see so clearly.'

'I know pain,' says Stone, candidly. 'Inside and out. And I have lost friends, lost part of myself, through the folly of rich men who do not value life.'

'The march from Kabul?'

'That and more,' says Stone, filling his lungs with smoke. 'I was conceived on the battlefield. I'm the bastard son of a rapist, raised in a mansion and reared for war. There are parts of me missing. Perhaps those parts recognise something in you.'

Ansell pulls at the neat strip of beard around his jawline. 'You were only the second man to strike me,' he says, at length.

'Your father?'

'He never raised his hand. The whippings came from Humphreys, in my youth. Have I spoken to you of Humphreys? Perhaps not. He was a soldier from Father's regiment who joined the household while I was still a boy. Whipped me on Father's instructions. Do not ask the indiscretions for I remember them not. Humphreys whipped me until my thirteenth year, when he began to punish me as a man. A closed fist to my flanks. He could deliver the blows so perfectly it would cause me to lose consciousness. I pissed blood more days than I did not. I don't think he experienced pleasure in the act. He was serving his master.'

'And your father?' asks Stone, quietly. 'Pleasure, I mean. In the act.'

'I do not believe Father considers pleasure. He considers duty and responsibility, and he has procreated as one should. But he is not given to laughter or gluttony or expressions of contentment. We both struggle to believe we share blood.'

Stone says nothing. He keeps his expression neutral even as he pictures Lord Ansell, sitting in the darkness, touching himself as he watches prostitutes whip one another. He relights his pipe and looks again at the bare room, turns away from the face of Jesus on

199

the ancient tapestry and wonders how one who so loves colour and life could exist in a space so devoid of joy.

'Did I hit you?' he asks at last. 'I don't recall.'

Ansell grins. 'Straight to the jaw,' he says gleefully. 'You checked that my companions and I were well, of course, and settled things with the locals. You had a face like thunder and it cost you dear to buy our safety. My companions had the wit to say thank you and naught else. I asked if we could stay until dawn so I could finish the painting of the sunset I had begun. You hit me. Knocked me out cold. I woke over the back of your horse, bumping along with a headache straight from Hell. You didn't speak to me until we were nearly back at Bombay. Then you told me I was a damn fool and that I could have been killed. It was time I grew up. And when I responded sullenly, you told me that wherever I went, the thing I was fleeing would always be within me, and not without. It was the first advice I ever listened to. For that I thank you. For the punch, I thank you again. Our meeting changed my life. It persuaded me to return home. To try to be what Father wanted. I have failed, but the activity has been the making of me.'

Stone tries to remember the brief time he spent in Ansell's company a decade before. The man had been different then. He had been playing a part, trying to be his father. He had barked his orders and snarled his discontent, mocked those beneath him and sneered at things he did not understand. Stone had seen through him to the frightened little boy who had run away from home to paint pretty pictures in exotic lands. Somebody who was so terrified of life that he had run at it as if over the side of a cliff. He had been plummeting towards an impact that he seemed powerless to stop. He and his companions had strayed into the tribal lands of an angry and proud people, and had Stone not discovered them, they would each have been decapitated with a single swing of a blade. Stone had handed over all the gold in his purse and a pair of beautiful pistols before the tribesmen would allow Ansell and his friends to go free. He has no memory of hitting the young man, but certainly does not doubt his account.

'Can you still do your tricks?' asks Ansell, suddenly. 'The hand-stand? Jumping on to your horse?'

Stone looks at the sudden gleam in his eyes. It makes him think of Matheson, and as his friend's face fills his mind, he feels the familiar coldness in his gut. 'They aren't tricks,' he says, half to himself. 'It's a form of prayer. A way that better men than I praise their God. I was lucky enough to be taught. I tried to tell Diligence all this but he still liked to see.'

'But can you? The fire . . .'

'My body is coming apart,' says Stone, smiling. 'If I tried to jump over my horse I'd split in two.'

'You're being modest,' chides Ansell. 'How I would love to see such a feat again.'

Stone wonders when he witnessed any such demonstration. Then a memory bubbles up. He recalls his negotiations with the tribal chief, the dank, musty heat of the tent and the angry faces that snarled at him between beard and turban. Stone had stood there with his blackened skin and dirty clothes. He had apologised for the error of the Feringhees and promised that no such trespass would again be committed. He had told them he was a horse trader. One who had devoted himself to a good life and decent acts. He had shown them the skills he had learned from Dalip, performing for the elders like a damn clown. Belched fire. Leaped from a standing posi-tion over the back of the chief's horse. Had made them like him. Saved the intruders' lives, and his own. It was his first diplomatic success, and he had lied his way through the whole damn affair. He had trembled as he left, even as the womenfolk looked angrily after them and hissed furious curses from behind their men. Stone can still see the cold venom in their eyes. The way they gabbled at their men and demanded that the Feringhees be put to the sword.

'Father used you as a role model when I returned,' says Ansell. 'He held you up as an example of how a man should be. Capable. Strong. Adaptable. Useful.'

'He didn't seem very fond of me when we were introduced,' says Stone, absently picking at a missed spot of dried blood upon his wrist.

'He felt betrayed after your court-martial. Desertion: the worst crime a soldier can commit. He felt you had let yourself down, and him by extension.'

Stone shrugs. 'I didn't desert. I walked away. Everybody was dead. There was nobody to report to. I didn't even know who I was when I woke up in that pile of bodies. I slept inside the body of a dead horse. I had more blood on my skin than inside it. They only found out I was alive because I was recognised in Jalalabad, and the court-martial was held in my absence. Father spoke up for me. So did many of his influential friends. They sold my commission and word reached me that I was no longer a fugitive, merely a damned disgrace. People like your father were a long way from my thoughts. I didn't know him and he didn't know me. I let people down, Phillip, but in more ways than losing my commission. I've made a life out of it. I've failed so many people in so many ways.'

'You're a hero to Diligence,' says Ansell, gallantly.

Stone drops his head. He fears his friend will never again look at him with the forgiveness and affection that have made his life tolerable these past months. He fears Diligence is already beneath the ground. 'Wynn,' says Stone, suddenly, as bile rises in his gullet. 'He has been your father's man for a long time?'

'He took over from Humphreys. He's not as good with the kidney punches but he can wield a whip and stamp on a face better than any man I have seen.'

'He was a groom?'

'He was everything. Came from one of Father's estates and brought with him a cloud of menace I have so far failed to paint correctly. He's a brute. Always has been. Fiercely loyal, though. And we have had no problems with debtors since his arrival. People pay, or he hurts them. He's good at it. And he has kept me safe when my nature has brought me into danger.'

'You have an affection for him?'

'As one would have for a vicious dog that one has the power to command,' says Ansell, thoughtfully. 'He is a useful man. And there is a heart inside him, I know it. He dotes upon poor Lady

Ansell. He has been more of a comfort to her than any other since poor Grace's passing.'

'I find that hard to picture,' says Stone, and a flash of anger shows in his face. His mind is suddenly full of Wynn. He feels a rush of hatred for himself, despising himself for sitting here inert when he has so much to avenge. He shakes the picture away and focuses on Wynn, sees him sticking the knife into Laura's guts, taking Diligence by the ear and breaking the poor bastard's neck with one twist of those big, dirty hands.

'People will surprise you once in a while,' says Ansell, half to himself. He cocks his head, as though he has heard something. 'I believe Father is home. That suggests the next few minutes will be most unpleasant for both of us. Would you like to take your leave or simply endure the brow-beating?'

Stone's chest feels tight. His temper has ever been a curse and now it threatens to engulf him as violently as an August storm.

'I want to speak to Wynn,' he says, through locked teeth. 'We have much to discuss.'

'Something brews between you two,' says Ansell, quizzically. 'Is it a battle of warriors? The challenge of two fighters who wish to test their skills? Or is it more than that?'

Stone breathes out slowly. He decides to tell the truth. 'I've tested myself in many ways. I have more pressing concerns than proving myself the superior fighter. I wish to ask him about the dark cloud you have failed to paint. I wish to ask him why he took himself to Pig Alley and butchered a girl, and so many others, for his own damn enjoyment.'

Ansell seems to freeze where he sits. His face elongates in the light from the kerosene lamp. As he speaks, his voice gets louder and a sudden harshness clips his words. 'I do not understand, Meshach. Wynn is a brute and capable of much, but the crimes you accuse him of are an act of evil. He is my father's man and has served the family well. I must ask you for proof before I can allow you to confront him in such a temper.'

'I will speak to him as I please,' says Stone, surprised at the young man's change in tone, the anger within him taking hold.

'He was seen. He procured women for the enjoyment of a rich man. Do you need me to tell you whom I believe that man to be? And then he sought them out to silence them. He was seen by a pimp and a working girl. He butchered a young Irish girl's mouth so she would not tell what she saw. Even now a simpleton languishes at Dr Easter's rooms, facing the rope for Wynn's crimes. Do not test me, sir.'

Ansell stands. His whole demeanour has changed and when he opens his mouth next it is to shout: 'You offend me, Major Stone. You offend this house with your mad accusations. You will forgive me for my candour but you are a drunkard and an opium-eater and it angers me that you would weave my family into the nonsensical narrative you have constructed in your drugged stupor. I insist you leave this—'

He yelps as the door crashes open. Wynn stands in the doorway, like a fairy-tale monster. He brings with him the stink of horse-sweat, animal fat and blood. His black eyes lock upon Stone. 'You were told to stay outside,' says Wynn, and spittle froths from between his yellow teeth to dribble into his matted beard. 'That means you're a trespasser. And that means I can throw you out or kill you.'

Stone stands. He clamps his pipe between his teeth and stretches, like a cat. He feels himself grow calm and peaceful. He feels the gaze of the threadbare Christ and revels in the half-light and ragged serenity. 'Like you killed Diligence?' he asks, smiling. 'Like you killed them all?'

'Diligence?' asks Ansell, startled. 'But his letter—'

'Diligence is dead,' says Stone, flatly. 'So are the women your father likes to beat for his own pleasure. And Wynn has had his fun keeping them silent.'

A look of contempt flickers across Wynn's face, like sunlight on tar.

'Whores? You can't kill whores, Major. They're already dead. There's no life in them. That's why you can use them as you wish. They're for sale. Every part of them has a price. Even their heartbeat.'

Ansell turns upon the great bear of a man. His face twists in shock. 'Wynn, these are lies, are they not? Major Stone is in drink. Should we not talk of these things when everybody's temper has cooled?'

'Where did you bury him?' asks Stone, reaching into his belt for his pistol and pointing it at Wynn's vast chest. 'Diligence. He deserves to be buried at home.'

'Take these with you,' says Wynn, pulling a pair of spectacles from the folds of his coat and tossing them at Stone's feet. 'He won't be able to see the coffin lid without them.'

Both Ansell and Stone look at the spectacles as they clatter noisily on to the wood. The light of the lamp reflects on one cracked lens. Ansell looks back up at Wynn and moves towards him, blocking Stone's view of the giant who so richly deserves a pistol ball through the heart.

'Phillip, move.'

Wynn grabs the young man by his hair and picks him up, holding him in front of his chest like a shield. With a roar he charges across the bare room and throws Ansell straight at where Stone stands, arm outstretched, pistol held impotently in his hand.

Stone and Ansell crash heads with a sickening thump. Ansell falls to the ground and as Stone brings his hands to his face to try to mute the ringing in his ears, he feels a fist the size of a maul hammer thud into his guts. Bile shoots into his mouth and he begins to choke on it as another fist takes him in the ribs, pummelling the flesh and bones pounded by Cooke and his men just hours ago.

'Come on, soldier-boy,' growls Wynn, taking Stone by the rag around his head. 'Show me how a hero fights. Show me what the rich boys pay you for.'

Stone reels as a fist slams into the side of his head and his legs go out from under him. He spills to the floor, knocking the kerosene lamp with a flailing hand. By miracle alone it skitters across the floor but does not tip or smash.

'You like that?' asks Wynn, as he boots Stone in the ribs. 'Imagine I'm an Afghan, if it helps. Get up, man! Show me why they tremble at your name.'

Wynn picks Stone from the floor and shoves him, bodily, into the corridor. There are stars exploding in his vision and he barely registers the half-light of the long hall, with its solitary candle and its great frames containing so many disapproving faces. He turns, clutching his ribs, just in time to see the fist coming towards his jaw, like a cannonball. Instinctively, he snaps his head to the right, grabs Wynn's arm by the wrist and brings the elbow down, sharply, against his shoulder. There is a crack as the joint breaks like a branch.

Wynn's bellow is like the roar of an angry bull. He cradles his broken arm and lashes out with a kick but Stone has had a moment to gather his senses. He catches the leg, holding the muddy black boot, then drives his elbow into the gristle and cartilage above the big man's knee. Something pops and Wynn howls. He falls to the floor, trying to hold both arm and leg and finding himself lacking the necessary limbs.

'They would hang you, Wynn,' says Stone, shaking the fog from his mind. 'They'd hang you in a flash. But I don't want to give them the chance. I don't want his lordship to assert his influence or for you to slip away from your cell in the night. I'm going to open your throat. And I'm going to watch as you bleed to death.'

Wynn is wriggling backwards, his upper half disappearing into the gloom of Ansell's room. Stone shakes the last of the mist from his head and steps forward, drawing the blade from his coat.

'Hold, you blackguard!'

Stone turns to see Lord Ansell standing at the top of the stairs, a pistol cocked and pointed at his head. His face is a mask of fury. There is no doubting his resolve. He would pull the trigger as readily as crush a spider.

'He's a murderer!' yells Stone, angrily. He drops his head and lets the blade fall to the floor. 'He killed your whores,' he says, though there is a sudden weariness in his voice. 'Killed them all, for you . . .'

Lord Ansell snorts in derision. He gives his braying laugh and shakes his head, as though amazed at the other man's stupidity. For a moment it seems he is willing to shoot him just because he can. 'Mr Stone, you are a fool to credit such a blunt instrument with the wit to make his own choices.'

Stone stares down the barrel of the pistol. He raises his gaze and stares into eyes that must have witnessed, and enjoyed, the spilling of so much blood.

'Burn! Burn!'

Stone whips his head around at Wynn's shout but is too late to duck the kerosene lamp. It strikes him full in the face and smashes in a blizzard of glass, fuel and flame.

Stone's hands fly to his face, fuel upon his tongue, penetrating his bloodied flesh. He squints through eyes full of tears and oil. Sees, too late, Wynn's colossal figure, dragging itself upright and lunging at him with vast, powerful arms.

Stone and Wynn tumble backwards with their arms locked. They stagger and wheel, fumble and seek weakness in the other's grasp. Neither man sees the flames take hold upon the hallway rug. Neither sees the ruffled reds and oranges and golds as they creep through the twilight and lap at their ankles.

Stone feels wood at his back. Feels arms, stronger than his own despite the big man's injury, squeeze at ribs that could splinter like chicken bones beneath the Welshman's weight. He wriggles and squirms, seeking leverage, a place to punch. Wynn senses the movement and pushes forward.

There is a moment of imbalance, a fraction of a second in which Stone is sure he will regain his footing.

And then both men are falling over the banister towards the hard tiled floor two storeys below.

Instinct makes Stone throw out his hands. It could be called miraculous that his grip holds.

Half blind and in agony, Stone swings over the void. Through the haze, he realises he has not heard the crash of impact. He looks round . . .

Wynn is hanging by his fingertips, only feet away. His broken left arm is useless at his side but the strong right looks capable of clinging to the edge for far longer than Stone's weakening grip.

'Let go!' hisses Wynn. 'His lordship will pull me up. Nobody will help you.'

'You let go, damn you!' growls Stone, through the fiery throb in his forearms. 'You're a murderer. You'll fall straight to Hell.'

Despite it all, Wynn's face splits into a grin. 'I've done terrible things, soldier-boy. I'll do plenty more. I'm loyal, see. Never served Her Majesty but I'm a soldier and this family's crest is my flag. You're a dead man. Dead as your prying, spying little friend. Dead as the whores that bastard is butchering . . .'

'It was you, Wynn,' splutters Stone. 'I know it was you.'

Wynn grimaces. 'It doesn't matter what you believe. You'll be dead in a heartbeat.'

He turns his broad, bearded face upwards, up at the chandeliers and the high ceilings. At the concerned face of Lord Ansell, reaching slowly down, proffering a hand to his great brute of a hireling.

'My lord! Please,' bellows Wynn, panic creeping into his voice. 'A rope, or an arm!'

Stone feels the heat above him. Sees the flame in the corner of his vision. Smells the kerosene upon his clothes and skin.

Slowly, painfully, he lets one arm go and drops it to his chest. Takes a fistful of his lapels in his hand. Wrings the fuel from the garment on to the palm of his hand. Laps it into his mouth. Reaches up and ignites his sleeve.

Wynn sees him move. Aims a kick that does nothing but weaken his grip.

Stone feels the flame kiss his skin. He looks through the fire into the widening eyes of the evil man who denied him redemption.

And spits a plume of flame straight into his face.

Stone's eyes refuse to close. He watches it all: sees the fire engulf his enemy as he hangs above the darkness. Sees him let go.

Sees, and hears, as Wynn falls, feet first, into the great empty space below.

Stone has no strength to pull himself up, no strength to picture the people he has avenged. He feels his fingers slip, then a blessed moment of absolute weightlessness; the peace of hanging, unsuspended, over nothing.

A gloved hand grabs his still-flaming wrist.

He opens his eyes as Phillip Ansell hauls him back from the brink. A rug is bundled about him and well-meaning hands beat out the flames.

Stone hears his name repeated over and over – angry voices and promises to have him whipped bloody and hanged until dead.

Stone gives in to the darkness, hoping to wake into light.

20

The pain has been awake for several minutes by the time Stone returns to consciousness. It has had time to take hold, to reach a crescendo, so that his first breath comes out as a gasp, a riposte to the concerto of agony playing within him.

'Christ!' he manages, and folds himself into a tight ball. His hand feels as though it is still on fire. His left shoulder is throbbing and he feels barely able to lift it, while his face is puffy and swollen, aching from his scalp to his back teeth. It takes him several minutes to gather himself, during which he wishes that he was dead.

Slowly, he takes hold of his senses. He is lying not on a hard wooden floor but upon a soft mattress. There is a blanket covering him and a pillow beneath his cheek. He raises his head and feels pain explode, like distant cannon fire. He opens his eyes in increments, his pupils shrinking then dilating, and uses his good hand to rub at his temples.

Through the haze, he realises where he has been deposited. This is Diligence's room. He has been placed in the bed of his dead friend.

Stone raises his hand to his face. A bandage has been wrapped around his palm. His swatch of silk is still bound about his skull. His boots, greatcoat and hat are missing but his dignity is preserved by his breeches. The tails of his long, white shirt hang loose.

In stockinged feet, Stone pads painfully to the door. He tries the handle and finds it locked. With each step sending waves of pain through him, he crosses to the window and pulls back the thick curtains. It is not yet dawn. Only the softest of light permeates the canopy of grey cloud and fine rain that suffuses the grounds and turns the forest into a sea of spilled ink. Stone looks down at the courtyard below. He is on the second floor, and though he fancies he would be able to climb down unseen, he doubts his pulled shoulder or burned hand would allow him to do so without suffering lethal injury.

Stone shivers. He holds himself tight, as if expecting to come apart. He tries to put together the last thing he can remember. He has a half-memory of Wynn falling into blackness, then Phillip Ansell hauling him to safety. Had Lord Ansell spoken? Were there threats and promises? He seems to recall screams and the sound of tears. He returns to the bed and sits down painfully. He waits, hoping he will begin to feel something. What would be the right sensation? Should he feel glad at having killed Laura's murderer? Fear, at what Lord Ansell intends for him? Gratitude at his life having been spared? He considers his lordship and finds that the poison within him has not dissipated. He will find no measure of peace until he has despatched him into the same fire and darkness as the man who killed to protect him.

Stone feels wetness in his eyes. He hears his breathing stutter. He fears he is about to weep and knows that, if he does, he may never stop. He feels as if he is fading. That his spark is flickering out. He searches inside himself and encounters only a hollowness: an impression of having been cut off from pleasure and pain, certainty and doubt. He feels like a half-thing, a soul untethered and directionless.

He lies back, stares up at the ceiling and waits for sleep, or death, to claim him. Neither does. After only a few moments his thoughts become clearer. He screws up his eyes and opens his mouth wide, cracking his jaw and feeling new waves of pain run from his ears to his toes. He feels as though he has been run down by a horse. And yet it is becoming bearable. He can stand, should he choose. He can search the room for a weapon. Perhaps Matheson left something useful. He knows that whoever locked the door has done so to keep him prisoner. And prisoners have gaolers. Gaolers can be hurt . . .

He drags himself upright and staggers to the wardrobe. Inside, Matheson's clothes remain where they were left, neatly folded. He takes his friend's work coat, a soft brown leather garment that still smells of the eye-watering fluids used to cure it. He slips it on and finds comfort in wearing it. He can see no boots, but pulls on a second pair of stockings to protect his feet should he make it outside. He searches through Matheson's remaining possessions, hoping to find his tools, then curses in disappointment when his hands touch only papers and cloth.

Stone pushes out a breath and steadies himself. He thrusts his hands into the coat's pockets in the hope of useful discovery. His fingers close on a stub of pencil and a sheaf of papers. He cannot help but smile. His mind fills with images of Matheson and their long journey through Spain. He curses himself for every time he shot down the younger man's ebullience, and shakes his head in regret at the harsh words he threw at his employer when he woke him from a drunken slumber to admire a sunset. He wishes he could share just one more of those accursed conversations. Wishes he could listen to him prattling on about saints and sinners, bones and tombs. He crouches once more and roots around under the bed. Had he the energy he would consider snapping one of the planks from the bed's frame to be armed with something harder than his own brittle bones, but the effort seems beyond him. Half-heartedly, he searches in the dark, empty space beneath the bed. His fingertips touch paper. He retrieves it and holds it to the little light that dribbles in through the curtains.

Like so many of the images in this great house, it is a biblical scene. It shows an elderly man crucified above a writhing mass of anguished mourners. It is a powerful image. Stone has never seen agony so perfectly captured. He is used to serenity and peace in the faces of saints. In this martyr's eyes there is fear of what lies beyond and a look of utter torment at the wounds inflicted upon him. In the faces of the mourners he sees at once grief and glee. Their countenances are locked in rictus screams and their eyes gleam with horror and excitement at the torture they witness. A Roman officer stands off to one side, face impassive, all-knowing, one hand concealed by the jut of his sword. Stone peers closer. Angles the image. Snorts. The centurion is familiar. More than that. He is Lord Ansell.

Stone does not need to look at the signature. He knows this is Phillip Ansell's work. Knows, too, the location of the Roman officer's hand. This image, this depiction of true martyrdom, is also a work of vicious satire. Ansell has transformed his father into a Roman general, righteous in his demeanour, who pleasures himself at the murder of a weak, innocent man. Stone almost gives in to laughter. He wonders if Matheson recognised the likeness. Whether any of the faces in the crowd are similarly recognisable. Whether Lord Ansell fought to bury his son's artistic ambitions because he knew the boy would not resist mocking him for the joy of all who cared to look.

Stone scans the faces, the tear-streaked cheeks, ripped dresses and dirty feet. Sees sweat-smeared cleavages and matted body hair . . .

His hand turns to a fist. He creases the paper as he looks into the eyes of a young, dark-haired girl, hands held up in prayer as if bound at the wrist, a look of defiled innocence in her horrified eyes.

Laura.

His legs weaken. He reaches for the bedpost and grips it with his burned hand. Phillip Ansell knew her. Knew her well enough to draw from memory.

He examines the image again. Could it be a falsehood? Could he be seeing her face now as he has seen it in the faces of so many strangers since she took him into her embrace? He focuses on every pencil stroke, the fine detail of the lace at the edge of the dirty smock. She is wearing the gown she wore when he lay with her; the gown she would not let him remove for shame of the wounds on her back.

Stone's world begins to spin. Suddenly he feels trapped. Trapped in a way that matters. He scans the vast canvases on the lavishly decorated walls and half expects to see his own father staring at him – fears that he will see his dead wife in the eyes of the child suckling serenely at Mary's breast.

'Will you be wanting a way out, Mr Stone? I have space for company, see.'

Stone's head jerks up at the sudden rush of whispered words in the empty room. He fears his own madness. He has known soldiers who hear voices and mumble replies, who become pitiable simpletons holding conversations with long-dead comrades and invisible persecutors. He drags himself upright, holding up his hands as if warding off blows.

'Follow my voice, Mr Stone. By Christ, but you look like you've been thrown from a building!'

Suddenly Stone recognises the voice and follows it to a large canvas hanging in an alcove beyond the unlit fireplace. The frame hangs askew and a small face protrudes from a triangle of perfect blackness exposed by its movement.

'Mr Goodhand!' He feels like kissing the bumpy, nightmarish face. Relief and gladness flood him.

'Bloody labyrinth this place,' mutters Goodhand, pushing the picture further out of Stone's way and reaching out a hand to help him into the concealed passageway. 'Felt like a mouse in a maze, I have. It does me good to see a friendly face, even if it's been beaten. Are you quite well?'

Stone half stumbles into the cold, damp passageway. It is gloomier in here than it was in the bedroom but he can see a candle flickering some way in the distance. He can smell the same animal fat he had noticed on Wynn's clothes.

'You did for that big bastard, then?' asks Goodhand, brushing Stone down and apologising as his hands slap at bruised flesh. 'My God, you messed him up.'

'You've seen him?' asks Stone, stuffing Ansell's drawing into his coat and wincing as his stockinged feet land heavily on a sharp stone. 'He's dead?'

'Dead and being mourned like a Viking chief,' says Goodhand, quietly. He reaches into the depths of a satchel at his waist and pulls out the body of a terrier. 'Broke his back, he did. Would have broke mine had it not been for the dog, see. Wynn had me by the hair. Dog went for him and I got away. I've been slinking about this bloody place for hours!'

Stone tries to control his thoughts. He wonders whether Goodhand had done Wynn a specific ill or was just another gentle thing he wanted to break. 'Why did he wish you harm?'

'Saw him, didn't I? I'm a small man but my mouth runs away with me. The dog here found a bone, see. I showed the young master and your friend, the round-bellied chap from over the water. Found it in one of these passages. Wynn heard me say it. Knew what else I must have seen.'

Stone puts his face close to Goodhand's. 'What did you see, sir?'

'Him and her ladyship playing their games. Saw him beating her like she were an animal and her loving every damn second. Does terrible things, grief. She's serving her penance and turning it into a pleasure, sir. I didn't want to see. Just happened across the spyhole. And she wriggling while he whipped her bloody as a lame mule. Not to my taste, see. But it's a secret he wouldn't want finding out. Not if he cared for her, and it looked like he did, in his way. Held her, when he were done. Dressed her wounds and stroked her hair and put the picture of her dead daughter close enough to bring her comfort. She's wailing now. Wailing for her dead lover the way she wailed for the girl. You're welcome to come and listen. I knows the way. But his lordship will be back with the magistrate soon enough and I'm thinking that escape would be a better future for you than what that bastard has in store.'

Stone is trying to make sense of what he has learned. He leans back against the rough stone of the passageway and feels his heart race. 'My friend,' he says suddenly, 'you say Diligence was there. And there was a bone . . .'

'Scared him, see. Looked like he'd seen a ghost. Took to his rooms the second I went back into the tunnels looking for the nest.'

'The nest?' asks Stone, trying to keep up.

'Rat's nest. Believe me, there's a beauty to be found. I've seen rats here big as a dog, Mr Stone. They know the tunnels better than anybody. Secret chambers and priest-holes, safe-rooms and bloody false doors. It's a wonder anybody has any secrets in this house and yet it's full of them. Now, can I urge us away?'

Goodhand has already begun to make his way down the passage. Breathing hard, Stone follows him. He watches the light grow stronger and breathes shallowly as the stench of animal fat grows thick and cloying in his nostrils.

'Mr Wynn knew the hidey-holes like a king rat,' says Goodhand, over his shoulder. 'These candles are his work. Kept it nice for himself. Knew the way to her ladyship's rooms and no doubt enjoyed taking a few peeps at the young serving girls along the way.'

Inside Stone, hope is rising. Could Diligence have found a way out? Could he have discovered a hiding place to conceal himself until Stone's return? He remembers the broken spectacles. Could he have dropped them? Perhaps Wynn simply picked them up in one of these secret chambers. Stone hardly dares to imagine that his employer is alive. And yet the thought revives him.

'Downwards to the servants' stairs,' says Goodhand, over his shoulder. 'Best way from here.'

'What's that way?' asks Stone, nodding in the direction of the narrow staircase that curves away into the darkness to his left.

'Her ladyship. Weeping and wailing, no doubt. Clutching the young master's drawings as if they were skin and bones.'

'Drawings?'

'He does sketches of the poor dead girl,' says Goodhand, dismissively. 'Sketches her for her ladyship's comfort. Not to my taste, but they seem to bring her as much relief as the whip. Now, can I urge haste?'

Stone shakes his head. The light of the passageway glimmers feebly and the only noise he can hear over the rushing of his blood is the spit and sizzle of the flame eating into the candles. 'I need answers,' he says. 'Please, Mr Goodhand, take yourself from this place. You owe me no more good turns, but I urge you to seek out Chief Constable McManus. Do whatever you must to make him listen. Tell him that a murderer lives within these walls. Tell him fresh murder will be done before the day is out.'

Goodhand stands immobile, torn between the desire to flee and a sense of duty to Stone, with whom he shared a fireside and who treated him like a man twice his size. 'His lordship will ensure you swing,' says Goodhand. 'The young master has spoken in your favour. He has accompanied his father to fetch the magistrate and ensure that the hearing is fair. But do not expect his lordship to be moved in his resolve. He believes you have murdered one of his household and perhaps even killed your friend. Whatever answers you seek, are they worth your life?'

Stone does not even have to think about his response. He gives a nod and squeezes Goodhand's shoulder, then turns to face the stairs.

Moments later, he hears the little man's footsteps receding into nothing while he hauls himself into the absolute blackness of the upper corridor. He wishes he had asked Goodhand for a tinder-box and gives a little grunt of exasperation as he shuffles forward down the uneven passageway. He feels a breeze upon his cheek and reaches out for the wall. Touches ancient, rotten wood. These must be the spy-holes that provided Wynn with such enjoyment. He wishes he were passing through in daylight so he could see even the slightest silhouette.

He shuffles on, dry earth and tiny pebbles beneath his feet, stifling a curse as he stubs his toe on loose brickwork. Finally he sees the light.

Stone feels like exclaiming with joy at the shaft of radiance emanating from the wall. He hurries forward, steps into the rectangle of illumination and angles himself to face it.

Lady Ansell stands within. She is wraith-like in her mourning clothes, clad and veiled entirely in black. She is on her knees as if scrubbing the floor. The carpet is covered with squares of cream-coloured paper, all decorated in the same expert hand. Her dead daughter smiles up at her from a hundred different angles. Lady Ansell sobs and gulps. For a moment she seems to Stone like a pig gobbling filth. Then he chides himself for the unkind thought about a woman whose grief has made her mad.

Stone knows he should not trouble her. He should turn and follow Goodhand to safety.

He knows that her mutterings will be the testimony of a madwoman and will bring him only grief.

He braces himself against the wall, puts his boot to the panel through which he peers and steps into her ladyship's bedroom. He finds himself utterly untroubled by her scream.

21

Lady Ansell pushes herself backwards as if the devil himself has materialised through the wall. Beneath the veil her face splits in an expression of untamed terror.

'Lady Ansell, my name is—'

Stone does not get the chance to finish. She springs to her feet with an unexpected agility and lunges at him with her arms outstretched. Stone raises his hands as if to defend himself from claws but the attack he expects does not come. Instead she flings herself at him as though she is embracing a returning child. 'You came,' she splutters, pushing against him and squeezing him with fleshy hands that cause his wounds to sing with pain. 'They told me you were dead. Taken like she was. Who would have taught me had you gone? Who? Who?'

Stone tries to slip from her grasp but she holds him as if he is a barrel and she is tossing in a raging sea. 'Lady Ansell, please, you are mistaken . . .'

'To think you would go and not say goodbye. To leave me without comfort. Without redemption.'

Her hands press hard into his bruised ribs and Stone cannot stop himself reacting with aggression. He shoves her away, and she tumbles backwards, her feet tearing the drawings of her daughter before she lands heavily on the floor. 'I am not your lover, Lady Ansell,' says Stone, his face hard as he looks down upon her. 'I am not the man who beats you for your pleasure. Wynn is dead, Lady Ansell. I am Meshach Stone and I will be heard and answered.'

Lady Ansell is sprawled upon the floor. Her black dress has ridden up to reveal bare feet and hairy, flea-bitten legs. She pushes back her veil, as if it were a lock of hair, and looks upon him with unfocused eyes. 'Wynn takes care of me,' she says, her lip trembling. 'You are not Wynn.'

Stone shakes his head.

'You came through the wall. I feared you were his soul, come to haunt me. Then I prayed that it were so. I would rather be haunted than alone. Were you a ghost you could seek out Grace. You could bring her to me. You could bring us both peace.'

Stone feels a sudden burst of pity for the pathetic creature at his feet. He reaches down and offers a hand but she looks at it as if doubting its very existence.

'They said he fell,' says Lady Ansell, to herself, 'fell, fighting with a bad man. Are you the bad man?'

'Lord Ansell would say so,' confesses Stone. 'Many others would too. But Wynn was not a good man, my lady. You must know that.'

'Good and bad, good and bad,' she mutters, looking down at herself as if trying to understand why she is on the floor. 'I was good, and bad things happened. Now I try to make it right.'

Stone glances around the room. The bed looks as though it has not been slept in. A picture of the dead girl gazes out from the mantelpiece on to a room painted in pinks and crimsons. Two oil lamps burn upon a table, throwing a harsh glow on to the varnished wood of the dressing-table and wardrobes. There is no art on the walls, though there are patches of discoloration that suggest large frames hung there once. Leather straps flop limp from the foot and head of the bed.

'Wynn was your lover,' says Stone, softly. 'I understand so little, my lady. Please.'

Lady Ansell picks at the hem of her skirt, like a little girl. 'He brought me comfort. So few do. So few do.'

'Since your daughter died?' asks Stone.

She lunges for one of the drawings and presses it to her breast. 'Found me. Found this.' She pulls up her sleeve to show ugly white lines scored into her wrists. 'Bound me. Nursed me.'

'You wanted to die?'

'I wanted to be with Grace.'

Stone squats down and looks at the nearest picture. 'May I?' he asks gently.

Lady Ansell gives a tiny nod and he examines the image. The girl was a beauty. Her eyes sparkle and the soft lines of her jaw suggest a face given to laughter. 'This is Grace?' he asks. 'Phillip drew this for you?'

'He and Wynn have sustained me. His drawings. Wynn's rope.'

Stone shakes his head, placing the drawing by his feet. 'Why does he beat you, Lady Ansell?'

'I have sinned,' she says matter-of-factly. 'I offer my skin in exchange for Grace's torments.'

Stone winces as he stands. He closes the door to the passage-way behind him, then turns back to Lady Ansell. He looks at the pitiful specimen and sees too much that he recognises in her expression. He knows that agony can feel like a healing, cleansing thing. He has fought and whored and done terrible things to himself and others in some desperate attempt to find something that feels like atonement. He has never found it. Has simply pushed himself deeper into the darkness with each new act of penitence.

'An exchange?'

'She is in Hell,' says Lady Ansell. 'I saw it. I allow myself to be debased and defiled so that her soul will not suffer. I bleed for her.'

Stone tries not to lose patience. 'In Hell, Lady Ansell? Please, I need to understand why you would allow that hellish man to hurt you.'

'He hurts me as I command,' snaps Lady Ansell. 'He beats me because he loves me. He will not let me die. He knows that if he denies me the lash I will finish what I began. I will watch my blood flow and go to Grace in Paradise. Wynn will not permit that. He needs me. So he hurts me as I instruct him and I promise not to die.'

Stone feels weak. He needs food, a drink. He staggers to the dressing-table and finds water and brandy. He takes a sip of water and a swig of liquor, and feels the liquids act as a balm upon his fraying temper. 'Why do you hurt yourself?' he asks, as gently as he can. 'Why do you believe your daughter to be damned?'

Lady Ansell buries into herself, pushing her fat cheeks into her shoulder like an infant. 'I saw,' she says, with an impish, unexpected grin. 'The lady found her soul. But she burned. Burned while lost between worlds.'

Stone wants to grab the woman by her mourning clothes and shake answers from her. Instead he forces himself to be calm. He squats so he can lock eyes with her. 'Which lady? Which lady found Grace?'

'Lily,' says Lady Ansell, eager now and full of smiles. 'Do you know of such blessed people? Those who can contact departed souls? My grief for Grace threatened his lordship's sanity. He gave in to my pleading and found a spiritualist. I wanted it to be a private affair but he insisted it be done in the glare of society. I invited the ladies of note from the great houses. We gathered to see Lily bring Grace back to me. I needed only a few words from her. I sought only a crumb of comfort, the knowledge that we would meet again and that she loved me still. Lily found her. I saw her bring forth Grace's soul. She became my daughter before my very eyes. Grace spoke to me. She told me she was content. Happy . . .'

Lady Ansell screws up her face as her world fills with memories.

'What happened, my lady?'

'Lily burned. The fires of Hell caught her dress. Wynn says it was the candle but I know what I saw. I had a vision, sir. I saw her soul. Saw him!' Lady Ansell spits this last. 'Saw my husband. Her father. Saw him cavorting with his whores. And I saw Grace disappear as the fire ate Lily's skin before my eyes.'

Stone feels a chill upon his own skin. The light of the oil lamp seems to flicker as a breeze plays with the images upon the floor. 'You had a vision?' he asks, desperation creeping into his voice. 'A vision of what?'

'His whores!' says Lady Ansell, turning angry eyes upon him. 'I have never denied my husband the pleasures of their company. There are things he wishes from a woman that he would not ask of a wife. I saw him writhing with the whores of Babylon. I saw Grace leave Lily's burning body and her soul enter theirs. I saw her vanish in flame and darkness, even as her father rutted and writhed in the smoke . . .'

Stone pushes himself up and crosses back to the dressing-table. He swigs the brandy straight from the bottle and hands it to Lady Ansell. She takes it wordlessly and sips without wiping the rim.

'You saw your husband fucking whores,' he says, almost whispering. 'And you believed your daughter's soul had entered one of them.'

'Ripped from Paradise,' snivels Lady Ansell. 'Torn from Heaven because I could not let her sleep. Wynn was my only comfort. He helped me make sense of it. Helped me see. He told me he would find the whores. I dared to hope that one of them was carrying a child. And that child could have contained Grace's soul, could it not?' She looks at Stone, eyes filled with zealous hope. 'I could have found her again. She could have been restored . . .'

Stone refuses to give her the nod she craves. He bites his lip and tries to keep the snarl from his face. 'He kept his word to you,' he growls. 'He found the whores he thought your husband had used. He sought their names from a pimp called Barrelman. And then he killed them for your pleasure . . .'

Lady Ansell shakes her head, angry and uncomprehending. 'Killed?' she asks. 'Wynn would not kill. Wynn wept every time he struck me. Wynn sought them out to bring me comfort. He sought names so that if they were with child we could bring Grace home. He saw all the girls from my vision. None was carrying. Somehow Grace has escaped me. Her soul is lost. And so I punish myself in her name.' She turns beseeching eyes upon him. 'Would you hurt me, sir? There is a whip beneath the bed. You may abuse me as you wish. I sense Satan about me at all times. He has turned my debasement into a pleasure, which I do not understand. But I yearn for the lash now. I yearn for the bite and sting of the hair shirt. Please. Phillip will bring me an etching this evening. I can look upon my daughter's smile. But I need to feel the sting to know she is not being tortured in Hell . . .'

Stone sinks to the floor and leans back against the bedroom wall. He looks at the bandage upon his hand and notes that already it is turning yellow from the wound that seeps beneath it. He feels broken, somehow vile and contaminated. He has a moment's desire to cut Lady Ansell's throat. She is beyond comfort. Past redemption. She sent a monster to seek out women based on a vision she conjured through flame and madness.

'The girl,' says Stone, softly. 'The séance. Lily. She burned?'

'Burned half to death. The ladies left us and fled home through the snow. They left Wynn, Phillip and me with a half-burned girl and a fading vision of Hell. Phillip gave me to Wynn's care. That was the night I begged him for the whip for the first time. The night we reached our understanding . . .'

'And Phillip?' asks Stone.

'He saw to Lily.'

'Saw to her how?'

Lady Ansell gives him a childlike, innocent smile. 'Flip the mattress,' she says guilelessly. 'You will like it.'

Stone drags himself up. He refuses to let go of the bottle, even as Lady Ansell reaches out to take it. He crosses to the bed and takes hold of the edge of the mattress in his good hand. He lifts it and sees the splashes of colour beneath. The crimsons, reds and greys daubed in Phillip Ansell's hand.

'Christ,' says Stone, resting the mattress on his shoulder so he can take the jumble of images in his fist.

'Good, aren't they? Real,' says Lady Ansell, her manner entirely friendly and proud. 'He saw Hell too. We thought he was ill and sought help for him. But he was not sick. He was blessed. I have seen Hell and it is as Phillip painted. He sees things as they truly are.'

Stone grips the painting. He looks into the terrified eyes of a half-burned woman as pottery shards tear into her skin and flesh is peeled away from her body, like meat from a carcass.

'He made her look like the others. Like the priests in the wall. The bones, you see? He put her with the rest. This is a house full of bones. It was not murder – she would not have healed. She was a half-dead thing. And he had waited so long to be allowed to make his art the way he wanted to . . .'

Stone drops the top image to the floor. In the picture beneath he sees a blond-haired saint, roaring in pain as her breasts are sliced clean through with a priest's jagged blade. In the next, a skinny, red-headed, dirty woman is being roasted upon hot stones. He sees Laura – her insides are being pulled from the crimson cross carved into her gut. And he sees a young girl screaming as her limbs are smashed upon a great wheel by a shapeless form wielding a hammer.

'Why?' asks Stone, and his voice catches in this throat. 'Why . . .'

He turns at the movement behind him. Phillip Ansell steps into the room from the passageway and shoots Lady Ansell through the eye with Stone's pistol. He stands, emotionless, in the opening, blood and smoke settling upon him like rain. He turns to Stone, not even looking as Lady Ansell slumps to the floor and the blood from her wound spills across the endless images of her dead child.

He pulls a second pistol from his waist and levels it at Stone. 'I made them pretty,' he says.

22

Stone tries to speak but his tongue feels like a boulder in his throat. He looks down at the ugly wound in the back of Lady Ansell's head, turning her greying hair to a sticky mess of burned jam. He looks back up at Phillip Ansell and wonders, for a moment, whether he could make it across the room and get his hands around his neck before his finger tightens on the trigger.

'Don't,' says Ansell, shaking his head. 'You wouldn't get more than a step, Meshach. And I don't have to kill you. A bullet in the belly and you're mine to play with until I decide you've had enough. I don't want to do that. It has to be right, you see? The face has to look right!'

Stone tries to work some spit into his mouth. He tries not to betray the tightness in his chest or the stuttering of his breath. 'You might miss,' he says, trying to sound confident. 'One pistol ball, one chance. I've faced a lot of pistols . . .'

'I won't miss,' says Ansell, flatly. 'I never miss. I've been firing pistols since I was a boy. Do not test me.'

Stone looks about him desperately. His gaze stops on the sketches of the murdered girls. He turns cold eyes on the man who stands, motionless, in the shadow of the secret panel, half in darkness and half in light. 'They weren't art,' he says, teeth locked. 'They were people.'

Ansell grins excitedly. 'You understand!' he exclaims. 'You are so very right, Meshach. They were just people. And I made them into something significant. Something powerful and beautiful and raw and real. Do they not speak to your very soul? Have you ever seen their like before?'

Stone cannot help himself. He curls his lip and takes a step towards the doorway. Ansell's finger immediately tightens on the trigger and Stone is forced to arrest his movement. He feels so helpless. He has no fear of the pistol ball ending his own life but he wants to stay alive long enough to tear Phillip Ansell's heart from his chest and make him see how fucking pretty it looks. 'You killed them!' he shouts, his chest heaving and the pain in his ribs dissipating under the flood of his fury. 'You ended their lives just so you could paint how they looked when they died!'

He grabs at the nearest canvas, staring into the agony of the girl who had healed some of the fissures in his soul. The woman with whom he could have made himself whole again. Laura. The gentle spirit who had made the mistake of telling Barrelman she wanted to live a new life. 'You did this for your own pleasure. Don't pretend it is anything sublime. It was murder. It was evil.'

Ansell gives his girlish laugh, then grins as if he has been caught eating a cake in the pantry. 'Meshach,' he says soothingly, 'there's a plague out there. People are dying in agony in their own shit and puke. Nobody's dying fat and happy in their beds in beautiful white sheets and the last rays of summer sun. Now is the time! Now is the time that death doesn't matter. But I can at least make its victims into something exceptional.'

Stone feels sweat run down his neck, tracing a cold path to his navel. He tries to concentrate. To order his thoughts. He cannot bring himself to beg this evil man for answers.

'The saints,' he says quietly, looking down at the canvases. 'The martyrs. You've been creating them.'

'Bravo, my friend. I grew tired of serenity. Does it not sicken you? I live in this great palace of art and not one painter has captured the moment of martyrdom as it truly was. These men and women did not go to their graves with their faces masks of perfect peace. They were not fair-skinned and golden-haired and cleaner than a virgin princess. They died in agony. They met their God screaming and roaring and yearning for the pain to cease. I have captured that. Look. Look at her!' He gestures at the image of a blond-haired, plain-faced woman, locking her teeth around a scream, her hands bound to a stake, as a curved blade cuts into her exposed breasts. 'St Agatha of Sicily. High born but steadfast in her faith. She rejected the advances of the Roman prefect Quintianus, and in his temper, he had her taken to a brothel. There she refused to yield her virginity, so Quintianus had her tortured. She was beaten. Stripped. Humiliated. Her skin was pierced with needles and her breasts cut from her body. When she came to be executed, a great earthquake shook the island and saved her from burning at the stake. She died in prison. Have you seen her image in the great galleries? There is a painting by Piero della Francesca, venerated as a masterpiece, in which she proffers her breasts on a silver platter. She might be asking if one would care for a scone! Where is the blood? The frenzy? The agony and rage? Only in my work can it be captured. I draw from life and from death.'

'For whom?' asks Stone, swallowing bile. 'You aren't a religious man. This is no act of worship or prayer.'

'Don't be deceived,' chides Ansell. 'I venerate my Lord in a way you cannot comprehend. I pray even as we speak. I am ever involved in a conversation nobody else can hear. I was blessed, do you not see? I was born into privilege and wealth but with a character my father despised. He shut me away. He tried to beat the beauty out of me. He kept me from prying eyes and punished any word or gesture he thought unfitting in a gentleman. Mother allowed it. My true mother. She was too afraid of him for anything else. They kept me in a bare room with only a Bible and a Foxe for instruction and diversion.'

Stone bites his cheek. He remembers the discovery of the incongruous letter 'x' beneath Alice's nails. He remembers a book one of his sergeants had on the Kabul road. John Foxe's *Acts and Monuments*. A record of Protestant martyrs, written centuries before and filled with woodcuts of the blessed dead in their final moments.

'John Foxe,' he says quietly. 'Your father thought that suitable for a child?'

'He positively insisted upon my devouring it. And devour it I did. Every word. Every story. Every woodcut. They were my nursery rhymes and bedside tales. Beheadings. Burnings. Disembowelment. I had never seen beauty, Meshach, but in that book I glimpsed my calling. I would draw what I saw. I would steal charcoal. Pencil stubs. None of the beatings would stop me. It was only that poor creature who gave me some respite,' he says sadly, pointing at the corpse of Lady Ansell. 'When Father remarried she took pity upon me and allowed me freedoms I had not before enjoyed. We visited the great galleries to see the art of the masters. I admired them, but felt no affinity with their blobs of paint upon canvas. They did not match the pictures in my head. The people were too clean, the teeth too white. It was all so angelic! I wanted to show the pain of sacrifice. The truth of it. I imagined seeing a painting of my own upon those great walls, imprisoning a perfect moment. Immortalising it. Father would not permit it, of course. Even with my new freedoms he saw my work as blasphemous. And this in a house filled with the bones of saints! He saw no sacrilege in collecting skulls, teeth and the rags that mopped up the blood of martyrs. And yet my daubings were an act of evil! We fought, Meshach. Fought endlessly. And yet I knew I could help him see – that if I showed him the potential of my gift he would embrace it as a blessing. I knew I had to capture something on canvas that had the power to astound. I took one of the maids and whipped her bloody, then chained her in the grotto where you spent such an uncomfortable night. I was disturbed in my work by one of the household – stopped before I could put more than a handful of lines upon the canvas. Father had me beaten so badly I could barely walk or see. And yet I managed to escape . . . I had made contact with a group of like-minded fellows planning a great adventure overseas. We took ship to India. They wanted to paint sunsets. I wanted to hurt somebody beyond endurance, then paint what I saw. I found a native girl on an empty mountain pass, took her by force and began to bind her. She was too slippery. She escaped my grasp and alerted the savages. I believe they would have killed us all, had you not interceded on Father's behalf. I could have died there and then, without ever beginning my great work.'

Stone wants to reach out to support himself. He wants to slither to the floor and puddle into nothing.

'When I was sent home it was to a different kind of father,' says Ansell, whose arm has not wavered despite the weight of the weapon in his hand. 'He no longer sought to beat my gifts out of me. No longer believed himself capable. My sister had blossomed into a fine young girl. Elegant. Pretty. Presentable. I do believe he may have been happy. I had never felt as trapped or alone. I found friendship with one of the servants. Truly, companionship was all I sought. Father believed me a sodomite. He had my friend whipped from the house and swore he would see me cured of such ills or see me dead. He took me to the man who created that damnable asylum and demanded I be turned into somebody new.'

Stone feels a window open in his mind. 'Dr Easter,' he says, as he tries to keep himself from falling into the blackness that is closing in on all sides.

'A well-intentioned fellow,' says Ansell, warmly. 'He has done much to care for the mentally infirm. Father paid him handsomely to talk to me about how I saw the world. I must confess I was rude to him. I did not see myself as in need of a physician. I continued to draw. My images became more powerful and yet still they seemed false. They were works of imagination. I had not truly seen suffering. I began to hurt my sister. I did not do it for pleasure, you understand, I needed to see tears and pain and the flicker of terror that comes when you fear for your life. Father near lost his mind. He had me sent away to Dr Easter's care.'

'You were a patient at the new asylum?' asks Stone, incredulous.

'That had not yet opened. No, I was a patient in a place since condemned as unfit for a human. I would declare it unfit for swine. I was kept in a cell to wallow in my own filth, fed on slop and forced to listen to the shrieks of a hundred lunatics. I refused to eat. Grew thin to the point of delirium. I saw my Lord, Meshach. I believe that the visions I experienced told me to live. They told me that I was blessed and insisted I live on to complete my great works. So I ate. I spoke to Dr Easter, obeyed the warders and used the paints and paper they gave me to draw sunsets and landscapes and the asinine serenity they all wanted to see me achieve. I made progress. They spoke of my being returned to my family. By then

Dr Easter had opened the new asylum. The rooms were hospitable and the comforts plentiful. I was transferred there and allowed more freedom. I began to dress and act in the way I felt comfortable. I became what you see.'

'The daguerreotype machine,' says Stone, understanding. 'It was you who destroyed it . . .'

A ripple of madness crosses Phillip Ansell's face, like the wake from a ship. 'A machine that can capture perfect moments? He showed it to me as if it was a miracle. Bade me sit still as he focused it upon my face. He showed me how I appear to others. It was blurred. Indistinct. I was a half-thing, and an ugly, misshapen one at that. I felt anger like never before. I smashed the damned thing. To capture a person as they truly are is the blessing of an artist, a servant chosen by a higher power. That is I, Meshach. I!'

Stone keeps his eyes on the pistol. It has still not wavered. He realises that the man must possess a strength and stillness to match his own. He is not the foppish dandy he appears. He must have spent countless hours in his various cells, building his strength, using his body as clay and sculpting it into a thing capable of making art from human suffering.

'I returned home to a house of misery and darkness,' says Ansell. 'My sister had died. An influenza, we believe. She was never a strong child. Her passing had turned Father to stone and driven Lady Ansell mad. I had no gaolers. I was free to drink and gamble and act every inch the scandalous fop. I was given Wynn as my protector and permitted to act as I saw fit. I ventured into low places and breathed in the fetid air of the slums. I felt a stirring in my blood I had not known before. This was true humanity. This was a place of medieval squalor. I yearned to immortalise such scenes but not even Wynn could permit me to set up an easel in the shit and mud of the street.'

'So you brought them home,' says Stone, feeling in his breeches with his bandaged hand and wishing that somehow he could conjure a blade.

'Father had begun to insist I enjoy a woman,' Ansell says scornfully. 'He had Wynn bring me a whore. He sought her out from a fat pimp in the worst slums of Hull. I will confess I was terrified. I had no desire to touch a woman, or any other creature for that matter. She turned up drunk and stinking of the gutter. I hid in the shadows of a bedroom in the guest wing, like a frightened child. A dress had been laid out for her, and treats to make her feel like a lady. Eventually she ate and drank and tried to coax me forward. She lifted her skirts and touched herself. I felt nothing but revulsion. I banged upon the floor until Wynn came and took her away. I told Father I had lain with her. He doubted my word until I asked him for another. That seemed to please him. That was the pattern in the months that followed. Wynn would bring me a whore. I would watch them marvel at the fine silks, the food and the wine, and I would sit in the darkness. I began to appreciate the performances. Sometimes I would instruct them to hurt one another. I liked to see their faces as the slaps and kicks landed. Once my mind went black. I came to with blood upon my face, a whip in my hand and the whore gone. I came to enjoy those women. I was content to do so for as long as I could sustain the lie. Then he brought me her.'

Ansell nods at the half-covered canvas showing Laura and the jagged X in her midriff. 'She had something I wanted to draw,' he says reverentially. 'Some light. Some beauty. I took my belt and bade her hold her hands aloft. I whipped her sore, Meshach. I must confess to a hardening I had not felt in any other act before. I emptied myself in my breeches and sketched her as she bled. My mind turned again to the stories of my youth. I entertained hopes of turning those vile creatures into the images of the martyrs who were my companions then.'

'The spiritualist,' says Stone. 'Lily.'

'A true blessing,' says Ansell, and seems about to clap his hands at the memory. 'Lady Ansell yearned for her daughter. I had come to know a gentleman in one of the better taverns who had in his employ a failed actress. She made a living fooling the rich and famous into believing she could communicate with the dead. Father was away in London and Wynn would have agreed to anything that might bring Lady Ansell comfort. We hired her and she was as good as her word. She was in communication with my dead sister when she caught fire. Whether candle or gin or the presence of the devil himself, she was clothed in flame. Lady Ansell's madness turned those flames into a vision. I did not see Father with whores the way she did. I was too busy looking at opportunity. At the ugly, livid wounds upon the body.'

Stone opens his mouth but finds he has no words. His mind is too full of sickening images to speak.

'I acted as the man of the house should,' says Ansell, proudly. 'I took over. Bade Wynn take my stepmother to her room, saw the guests to their carriages, and then came to take care of Lily.'

'You skinned her,' says Stone, recoiling. 'You cut the flesh from her skeleton . . .'

'I heard a proverb in one of the taverns I frequent. Something about the skill of killing two birds with one stone. I did just that. I rid the house of a troublesome body and made something beautiful in so doing. You know of Hypatia, do you not? My childhood tutor was a great lover of her story . . . the pottery shards biting into her skin as the crowd dragged her from the temple and destroyed her physical form. I did the same. I carried Lily to my private place in this house of secret chambers. I treated a failed actress with the reverence of a saint, as one whose name still echoes through the ages. I painted her agony. Then I put her bones in the upstairs temple. I do confess to smiling at the thought of Father praying there, venerating an actress from the gutter. He would have continued to do so, had Wynn not seen the skeleton. He was not fooled. He has seen much death, has Wynn. He told me he knew what I had done and took the bones away. He knew the secrets of this house almost as well as I. He found a place for her. I do believe he would have told Father about it, had Lady Ansell not tried to end her own life. Then he was given his task of finding the whores she'd seen in her vision and buying their child. Neither of them saw or heard me as I listened. It was not difficult to follow him as he terrorised Barrelman. I do not understand how his mind worked but I believe he had become convinced by Lady Ansell's ramblings. In his simple mind, the prostitutes he brought home for me and the ones his lover saw in the flames were the same. He wanted to serve his mistress and could not lie or deceive her. For you or me, he would have brought home any old strumpet with a baby in her belly. Wynn could not do that. What he felt for his mistress was genuine. He carried out her wishes. He was brusque in his dealings with those pitiful women – gave them coin and blustered away, shamefaced. Lady Ansell did not find her reborn child. But I found opportunity.'

Stone forces himself to be still. With a bullet in his belly he will not be able to avenge the women this ghoulish thing had killed. 'Laura,' he says pleadingly. 'The dark-haired girl . . .'

'A masterpiece.' Ansell pauses and smiles. 'Diligence spoke of a girl who warmed your heart. Was it she? Good Lord, you should thank me for making her immortal as I did. But I see nothing in your eyes other than a desire to hurt me. You may try, Meshach, but you could never hurt me as I did her. I wonder, did she think of you as the blade went in?'

Stone swallows. His throat is too dry and his eyes too unfocused to give in to tears so he just looks at the other man with utter hatred.

'She died hard, Stone. Fought like a tiger, too. She was my favourite, truth be told. I planned to paint her as St Symphorosa, whose seven children were martyred alongside her for refusing to worship pagan gods. But I saw no practical way to tie an anchor to her neck and throw her into the river. She would have sunk before I could paint her. And, besides, she was too beautiful to pass for a woman of middle-years in those dark times. I cheated a little. Foxe spoke only briefly of a young nun disembowelled by an amorous landowner. I brought a little imagination to the scene. I was with her a long time. I watched the light go out in her eyes. Truly it was a moment of beauty. Look at the canvas. Does she not seem timeless? Immortal? Like the other whores of her company. I turned a washer-woman into St Catherine of Alexandria! Broke her upon the wheel and sketched as she begged and pleaded and moved towards God. I created St Agnes from a gin-soaked whore. She was roasted alive, though the fire would not kill that most sacred of women. She, like my St Agatha, was decapitated by the very Romans who failed to make her give up her virginity. I did not feel it necessary to do such a thing to my model. It was the agony of the fire I needed to see. The rest I found able to create myself.'

Shadows flicker in the room and a sudden gust of wind causes the ends of the climbing ivy to scratch at the panes of glass. Stone feels himself shiver as he reaches for the canvas and crumples into all-consuming grief as he looks upon Laura's face: hands above her head, tied at the wrist, and the sadness, the despair, that fills her even as her blood leaks out. Worst, most powerful of all, is the tiny spark of hope. The merest ripple of belief that she will be rescued; that this will be stopped.

'I went back a few days ago,' says Ansell, chattily. 'She was still there. Rotten. Green. Legs drawn up like she had stomach ache. That's how they found her, I believe. Cholera, was it not? I had been reading the periodicals and journals for mention of her death but none came. There has been so little interest I feel almost cheated. But what is my work when weighed against the mass murder of God, eh?'

Stone cannot speak, just stares, so full of hate and remorse that he fears he may burst open.

'I did not know my work to be truly blessed until I learned that your path was to cross mine again,' says Ansell, grinning madly in the yellow light. 'Imagine my delight when we received correspondence from your Mr Matheson, asking for access to the reliquary. He spoke of his companion and friend, the mighty Meshach Stone. Father declared the request damnably insolent but I saw opportunity. I have only practised my art upon women. What joy to witness first the utter destruction of your heart, then to immortalise you. To paint your suffering and hang your likeness on the wall. There is something artistic about the very notion. Poetic, even.'

His mention of Diligence Matheson causes a fresh wave of anger. 'What harm could you wish Matheson? Why would you allow Wynn to kill him? You justify your crimes as art. What art could there be in his death?'

'What death?' asks Ansell, smiling. 'Diligence's heart still beats, even if his skull requires a fresh bandage. He will be a part of my next creation. I wish to turn you into St Sebastian. Do you know the story? He was a soldier who turned to Christianity. His emperor ordered him shot to death with arrows. Miraculously, he survived that, and being thrown into the river. He resumed his post and gave his emperor a nasty shock when he removed his helmet and remonstrated with him for his treatment of Christians. The emperor recovered, of course, and had the poor man beheaded. But I do believe that the image of his arrow-littered body would make for an exquisite work. Diligence will be the soldier who refuses to shoot. He will lie upon the floor, bleeding and insensible, having been beaten by his fellows for refusing to add his arrow to the dozen that pierce your body. Can you see it, Meshach? Can you comprehend?'

Stone smells something rich and energising in his nostrils. He hears a sound in his head like the approach of a train. Diligence lives! If he himself can stay alive, keep this deranged man talking, he could yet find a way . . .

'Would you be so good as to bring my canvases?' asks Ansell, politely. 'We are going back down to the chamber, and now that you have murdered Lady Ansell, I cannot trust her to keep them safe. I enjoyed her madness and she learned to appreciate my art in her last weeks, but I could not spare her. You saved me from the difficult task of disposing of Wynn. Loyal though he may have been, I know he had begun to suspect me. When he saw Lily's bones he knew what I was capable of. And who knows if he turned his lover's mattress and saw my sketches? I do not believe he would have gone to the constables but he could have told Father, and Father would have had me locked up once more with no access to the women I need for my creations. No, I mourn him, but it is better he is dead. There is just one extra little thing to arrange so I can continue my work. When Father returns he must find his wife dead and you missing. I will be injured, of course. They will look for you for a long time. Your name will be damned. But they will never find you. I found the priest-hole only through luck. I was a mere child, fleeing a beating. A trapdoor within a trapdoor, a chamber within a chamber! The design was fiendish. Father believes the room at the top of the east tower to be a sacred place, built to harbour priests during the purges. He has not studied the art as I have. Sometimes a hiding place was built to be found. It was a double-bluff. The true chamber where the priests secreted themselves had not been entered for two centuries before I stumbled in. It had worked a little too well. Their bodies were still inside. Over the years I have taken their bones and exchanged them for those Father reveres. I enjoy such naughtiness. I create my art surrounded by saints and their artefacts. Does that not seem somehow fitting? Now, if you would be so good . . .'

Stone gathers up the canvases, rolls them carefully and places them inside his coat. Ansell moves in a slow arc away from the opening in the wall. He gestures for Stone to enter the chamber, then follows him four or five paces behind. The sweat on Stone's body seems to freeze as he enters the darkness once more. He has to clamp his teeth together to stop his jaw trembling. He glances over his shoulder to gauge the distance between himself and his captor and is rewarded with a tut.

'Past the stairs,' says Ansell. 'Squeeze past the pile of bricks. Wynn was too big to go further but you and I will manage. Keep going. It begins to slope down sharply so watch your footing.'

Stone hears true madness in Ansell's words. He cannot tell whether he is considered the man's mortal enemy or a best friend with whom he has had sharp words. He finds his feet skidding and agonising pressure on his aching ribs as he manoeuvres himself through the opening, and then he is tumbling down a slope. He manages to grab the wall and realises he can hear the angry screech of nearby rats.

'They live behind the walls,' says Ansell softly as he makes his way down the slope with practised steps. 'Goodhand would be in his element. It was a pity he found Lily's remains. Wynn must have left them somewhere indiscreet. The man was never a thinker. That said, I shall miss his useful company. And I am not sure he deserved to die so brutal a death. Truly, Meshach, you are a monster.'

Stone stumbles on, his legs shaking. He longs to spin and knock the pistol aside. Longs to stick his thumb deep into the young man's eye and not stop pushing until he feels brains. His hands are pressed into fists that shake and his fingernails dig into his palms. He wishes he knew where to find some soothing thought within himself. He wishes he could picture placing his head on Claudia's belly and feeling her stroke his hair, or conjure the taste of Laura's mouth and the hungry, tender kisses she stole from him in the darkness. But all he can think of is his inadequacy. He cannot push away the lone, malicious thought as it grinds into the very front of his brain: he's just like you. That is what threatens to overwhelm him as he staggers over the stones and bones towards the blackness ahead. He is a man of violence, a man who has chosen blood as his area of proficiency. He has hurt people for reasons less elevated than Ansell's, has killed people to silence them, or because his employers told him to. Yet he sees no repentance in Ansell, only pride in the man's eyes when he talks of his crimes. Where Ansell has been devoured by darkness, there remains in Stone at least the possibility of light. His humanity has not died. It was resurrected in the arms of a woman who looked into his soul and breathed new life into his heart.

'Do you feel the breeze?' asks Ansell. 'To your left. Push aside the rag by the fallen stones then climb down the ladder. The wood has crumbled but it should support your weight at the edges.'

Stone does as he is bidden. In darkness as black as a jackdaw's feathers, he climbs over rubble in his stockinged feet. He stumbles and grazes his knees on the fallen brick. And then he is lowering himself into the dark, feeling splinters of ancient wood skewer his soles as he descends into the cold, draughty chamber below.

His bleeding toes touch dry earth. He collapses and lands upon something brittle and hard. He grabs for the object, swinging it in the direction of the opening.

'Not even close,' says Ansell, from some distance away. 'I spend a lot of time in the dark, Meshach. But, out of respect for you, I will again demonstrate the wonders of kerosene.'

Stone pushes backwards, reaching out to feel the coarse texture of brick and wood. A match strikes and slowly the room fills with soft light.

They are standing in an underground chamber eight feet tall, four feet wide and twelve feet long. The sagging ceiling is held up with struts of blackened timber and the earthen floor is littered with bones and swatches of cloth. At the far end of the room, almost eclipsed by shadow, there is a fleshy bundle. Ansell makes no move to stop him as Stone runs towards it, crushing bones beneath his feet. He bends down and rolls his friend over. 'Diligence! It's Stone. I am so sorry. Can you hear me? Can you see?'

'Touching,' says Ansell, levelling the pistol at where Stone crouches. 'Still breathing, is he? I do hope so.'

Matheson's eyes flicker and he emits a low hiss. Stone searches him for wounds, and flinches when he touches the mess at the back of his skull. 'Diligence, wake up . . .' Stone beseeches his friend, then wonders at the wisdom of it. He looks up at the sagging roof and the beams that hold it aloft. They are far below ground. God alone knows how many tons of earth would descend should the struts give way. Stone was trained as an artilleryman. He understands pressure points and weakness, knows where to push and just how much pressure it takes to create a breach.

'Sleep, my friend,' he whispers. 'You don't want to be awake for what's going to happen next.'

23

'I must ask you to disrobe,' says Ansell, apologetically. 'Do you see the column to your left? Old wood, is it not? One wonders at the brawny hands that felled it and brought it here to this most sacred and secret of places. Remove your shirt and stand against it. Diligence looks rather perfect where he is, though I would ask you to angle his face so I can see the bewilderment and pain upon it. That's better. Yes, thank you.'

Stone watches as Ansell moves, swift and light, between the bones. Still keeping the pistol aimed at him, he reaches down and retrieves a bow and quiver. He is unarmed for only a fraction of a moment, and then he pulls back the string, an arrow notched in the groove, and trains the weapon on Stone. 'A primitive weapon, yet devastatingly lethal. I am not as skilled with it as I am with a pistol but at this range that hardly matters.'

Stone looks at the point of the arrow. His guts feel full of eels and ice. 'You think one arrow will stop me getting to you before you notch another?' he asks, slipping out of his coat and glancing down at the bones upon the dirty floor.

'Depends where I place it,' says Ansell, smiling. 'And, besides, you won't have your hands free. Move to the post and feel around.'

Stone spits as his hands close upon the manacles. 'You expect me to tie myself up? Why would I do that? To stop you shooting me? You're going to do that anyway.'

'You'll do it because if you don't the first shot I fire is going right through Diligence's head. The painting doesn't need him. It will work just as well if he's a corpse.'

Stone sets his jaw, locks eyes with Ansell and dares him to try. 'The second you loose that arrow I'm coming for you,' he says.

'Yes,' says Ansell, smiling. 'But Diligence will be dead.'

'I thought he *was* dead until moments ago.'

'And I have resurrected him for you. Here among the bones of saints. Do you wish his death to be re-enacted? Do you seek that pain again?'

Stone knows what an officer would do. He knows he should let Diligence die, then use the opportunity to kill Ansell and avenge those he has murdered. But he cannot. He finds himself unable to sacrifice him. The thought of his death is impossible to bear.

He shuffles over to the creaking wooden strut, kicks his jacket away from his feet and slides out of his shirt to reveal a torso striped with more scars than a body should be able to endure. He looks down and sees that Ansell's paintings have slid from the discarded coat and are lying in the dirt at his feet.

'Lock the chains,' instructs Ansell. 'I will put the first arrow in your thigh. I don't want you to die before I've picked up my pencil, do I?' His girlish laugh sets off the squeaking of the rats, which echoes against the low ceiling.

Stone puts his back to the column and closes the metallic chains with a snick. He is immobile, his bare skin pressed against soggy, brittle wood.

'You grew up down here, did you?' he asks, looking around contemptuously. 'This is your secret, special place? You and the rats, doing your little drawings and moaning about Papa thinking you were a waste of seed? It's sad, really. It pains me to think of that little boy.'

Ansell stares at him down the length of the arrow. '*You* feel sorry for *me*? Look at where we stand. Look who holds the bow.'

Stone manages a smile. 'But I'll be dead soon, Phillip. You'll have to go on living. Just think, you'll have your paintings and your bones and it will be you and Papa in this big house. You with your bare bedroom and your book of martyrs. Did you know you left an *x* under one the girls' fingernails? Scratched the cover, did she? Were you reading to her as she bled to death? I bet it upset you, her scratching that book. I bet you don't like it when your precious things are roughed up.'

240

Slowly, deliberately, he brings his bare foot down on the edge of the nearest canvas. In the flickering lights of the kerosene lamp, he places a blob of blood on the intricate shading in the bottom corner.

'Damn,' says Stone, fixing his gaze on Ansell. 'I've spoiled it. I'm so sorry. I hope it doesn't rip when I move . . .'

He draws his foot back, like a bull pawing the ground. There is the satisfying sound of paper tearing. The rats squeal in response to Ansell's shout of anguish.

'Don't, Meshach,' he says, starting forward then stopping, suddenly, as he struggles with the voices inside him. He wants his drawings. But he doesn't want to get so near Stone as to leave himself exposed. 'They're blessings. Immortal! To do them again would be to have made the first ones for nothing . . .'

Stone watches the tip of the arrow waver. He looks up to where the timber joist meets the fragile roof of compacted earth and old stone. He braces himself against the wood and tries not to let his intention show. 'Fire your damned arrows,' he says, staring deep into the recesses of Ansell's skull. 'Make your little drawings. But don't go thinking you're an artist. I've seen true art. You've got a talent for sunsets. But all this? This suffering and pain and anguish? Seen it all before, son. Big market for it in Spain. There's one man who keeps his most sinister stuff to himself so the public think he's another of those serene portrait artists you seem to hate so much. But get him drunk enough and speak loud enough and he'll show you how he sees the world. You're an amateur. You're the pitiable son of a bully, and you can't even do the one thing you were born to do. Blessed? You're not even worth a curse.'

Ansell looses the arrow with shaking hands, just as Stone pushes back against the timber with all the strength that remains in his body. The arrowhead spears into his left biceps with a wet thud that sends hot pain shooting to his wrist and fingers. He does not stop. He plants his feet, grits his teeth and pushes again, feeling dirt patter on to his upturned face even as blood pools in his palm.

'What are you doing?' shouts Ansell, as the rats begin to scream. 'The roof! The bones. My work . . .'

He tries to fasten another arrow to the string but drops it as his hands start to shake. Earth begins to tumble through the gap in the chamber's roof as Stone gives a final almighty heave and the strut gives way, sending him toppling to the side to land heavily on the dirt and shattered bones in a cascade of soil and rock. He slithers along the length of broken wood and cries out in triumph as he slips the manacles from the splintered top. In one movement he brings up both knees and slides himself through the loop made by his tethered hands, leaving himself cuffed at the front and not behind.

Ansell is staring, immobile, the bow hanging uselessly by his side. A large hole has opened in the roof. Like the beginnings of an avalanche, dirt and dust and small boulders are beginning to tumble through. He can see his drawings on the floor. Can see them being buried for ever, here, in this sacred place.

Stone's hand touches something solid. Something reassuringly brutal and hard. He picks up a bone. Three old dagger-length nails have been driven into it just above where the bone meets the ankle joint. Something flashes in his memory, then disappears as he looks over at where Diligence is beginning to stir, the earth raining down upon his semi-conscious form.

Ansell is shoving the dirt aside, raking through the growing mountain of fallen earth as he grabs for his paintings and howls.

Stone knows this will be murder. He doesn't give a damn.

Ansell yelps with elation as he pulls a canvas from the mound and clutches it to his breast, as if he has saved a baby. He stuffs it and the others into his shirt and turns, furious, to go and stamp on Stone's guts . . .

The nail goes into his neck, just beneath the jaw. Its blunt, rusted head goes through the soft flesh and up into his mouth, skewering his tongue. It pushes through his top lip and enters his nostril, closing his entire face around the scream.

He looks into Stone's eyes, inches from his own. Sees his own madness reflected back at him. Sees something else too. Sees a demon in Stone's eyes. Sees a capacity for blood and violence that could eclipse his own.

Stone says nothing. Just grimaces, then pushes him back into the pile of dirt.

Ansell's face is nailed shut. Blood is dribbling down his shirt and on to the tattered canvases. One of the nails hit bone and has clattered to the floor.

Stone picks up the pictures and tucks them into his breeches. He darts forward as he spots a crevice widening in the roof. He grabs Matheson's hand and hauls him up. 'Move, Diligence! Please, just give me a few moments of wakefulness. Then I'll let you sleep as long as you want.'

Matheson squints at him, uncomprehending and dizzy. There is mud and blood on his face and drying in his ear. 'Meshach!' he exclaims. 'Meshach, Lady Ansell and Wynn are having liaisons . . .'

Stone rolls his eyes but feels like laughing as he hauls the Canadian to his feet. He feels a sudden pain in his arm and changes sides so as not to force the arrow any further into his flesh. Together they scurry down the chamber, dodging falling masonry and collapsing roof beams.

Suddenly Matheson stops. Amid the carpet of bones he has glimpsed something. Something that causes his eyes to gleam.

'Those nails are from the time of our Lord!' he cries. 'Crucifixion nails. We must rescue them, Meshach! This is what I came to find!'

Stone pushes Matheson in the small of the back. 'Go, Diligence. We've got moments. Just moments!'

Matheson looks fit to erupt in tears of frustration but gives in to Stone's urgings and stumbles on.

'There!' shouts Stone, over the sound of falling rubble. He bends and grabs at the earth. 'Climb! Climb!'

Matheson begins to haul his ungainly frame up the cracked and broken ladder. A boulder falls from the ceiling and crushes the oil lamp, plunging the chamber into darkness. He screams as something furry and sleek brushes his hands, followed by what seems like a million more.

Stone leaps to the side as the rats pour into the tunnel. He watches them fill the chamber, like sewage, then pushes Matheson by the rump, bleeding and shouting and climbing in the face of a torrent of vermin.

He isn't sure, but above the sound of the screaming rats, he fancies he hears a muffled cry for help. Fancies that Phillip Ansell, half buried by fallen rocks, has torn the nails from his mouth and screamed.

And then a plump hand is grabbing his wrist and hauling him into the cool, dark safety of the sloping passageway. He is lying on his back, and the wide, anxious face of Diligence Matheson looms over him like a full moon.

Below, the screeching of the rats increases in volume, then is lost amid the sound of the collapse.

They are spared the sound of teeth closing upon human flesh.

The saints rest beneath the earth, untouched. The fresh corpse is not similarly sacred. Before the last of the earth has fallen, it has been reduced to little more than bone, nicked with the indentations of a thousand biting mouths.

Above, Stone allows himself to be embraced by his friend as he lies shirtless and bleeding, scarred and near numb with pain, upon the cool rocks of the passage that leads up to the house. Lord Ansell may be back. The magistrates will have arrived. The hangman's rope already feels tight around Stone's neck. Suddenly he feels a reverence for life, a desperation to live. He has so much to redeem, so many wrongs to set right before he can allow himself peace.

Painfully, he sits up.

'That was Phillip,' stammers Matheson. 'I thought I was in a dream. But what a dream! He spoke of shooting you full of arrows! That I would be a corpse! And those bones, Meshach. You understand what they signify? My God, to think they could be buried there for ever . . .'

Stone feels a breeze upon his face. Feels the blood and sweat and dirt on his body and reaches into his breeches. He pulls out a stack of muddy, creased paintings and hands them to Matheson, who peers at them through the gloom and grimaces at their content.

'He signed them,' says Stone, tiredly. 'Signed them all.'

'Will that be enough for Lord Ansell?' asks Matheson. 'He could say they were forgeries! And what of Wynn? You're in no state to fight him.'

Stone pulls himself upright and begins to shuffle up the slope, nodding to Matheson, who follows him like an obedient dog.

'He knows,' says Stone, as they climb. 'Always has. He'll be happy to believe that his son has fled. He's just killed his step-mother. Run away to paint that which inspires him. Ansell won't want scandal. He'll bluster, but he's just a bully, and bullies are easy to frighten. Besides, he has fresh grief to bear. Just do as I do, Matheson. Just lie.'

In the darkness, Stone hears Matheson gasp. 'I am not given to lying,' he says haughtily.

Stone reaches back and presses something into his hand. He says nothing, just squeezes Matheson's pudgy fingers and pushes on towards the light.

The gloom recedes under their tired, painful steps. Both men use their hands as shovels when they reach the fallen rock. They pull back boulders and dirt, and grin as the first spears of light bathe their faces.

Matheson has the presence of mind not to speak.

Just holds the crucifixion nail in his palm and feels the dried blood of Lazarus warm his skin.

Author's Note

Well hello, dear reader. Glad you survived. Don't scrape the blood and muck from your boots just yet. You can hang on a moment before hitting the shower. Thanks for making it to the end. I very nearly didn't, but that's another story . . .

I normally write books set in the present. They feature a giant Scotsman called Aector. If you like the McAvoy series, you'll have no doubt thought the same thing that I always do when I discover that an author I enjoy is busy luxuriating in a self-indulgent project, such as writing a book that doesn't involve their usual protagonist, instead of doing their duty and serving up the next instalment. I can only apologise. I hope you think it was worth me getting distracted by.

I read a lot of books, pamphlets and old manuscripts during the research process. Some were interesting and others astonishingly dull. If you have an interest in the world through which Meshach walked, I'd urge you to read the terrific memoir written by Rev James Sibree. It is thanks to his ministry that Hull survived the catastrophe with its soul intact. If you want to look into the heart and mind of a genuine good man, read his *Fifty Years' Recollections of Hull; or Half-a-Century of Public Life and Ministry*. Or try the DS McAvoy series . . .

The Zealot's Bones came to me in its entirety while I was lying on a trampoline in the back garden of the house where Meshach and Diligence were staying during their sojourn in Croxton. I point this out as proof that when it looks like we are lying down and staring at the sky, creative people are often very hard at work. So, y'know, leave off.

I'd like to say thank you to everybody at Hodder for taking a chance on a work of historical fiction by somebody who had never written any before. Ruth, you are a lesson in patience, good-humour and vision, and I can only apologise for continually dragging a good soul like yourself into the muck and blood of my twisted imagination. Kerry, you're a trouper and you've got me through some difficult times. Cicely, you have far too splendid a name for a girl from Yorkshire. Naomi, you're a star. Rosie, thanks for looking after me. And Nick – how do you put up with it all?

Thanks, as ever, to my agent Oli Munson. I have no doubt that there are times when seeing my name in your inbox causes a desperate desire to switch your phone off, but you deal with your most demanding and pitiful client with avuncular forbearance. Thank you for putting up with me.

A tsunami of gratitude must go the way of my fellow writers. It's been a difficult couple of years and without the friendship and understanding of a certain fine body of chaps and chapesses, I may well have buckled. Thanks to all of you.

On the personal front, I have a habit of thanking people for being in my life and then driving them away before publication, so I'll try and break that particular curse this time around. Of those duty bound to stay with me henceforth, I'd like to say a quick thanks to my dad. Thanks to you I'm short, round, bald, beset with gastro-intestinal problems and mental illness. But I'm moderately clever and occasionally funny, and that's probably down to you. Mam, I reckon I get most of my weirdness from you. Cheers! Bernard, I've come to the conclusion that you're one of the good guys and I really appreciate all your kind words and support over the years.

Elora. Never forget that weirdness is merely a side-effect of awesome and that love expands to fill the space required. Whatever comes at us, we will always walk through it together.

Finally, here's to you, my love. You're my enchantress; an immaculate sky above my desolate earth. I will always endeavour to be remarkable. I will always fight to be yours.

I don't know if Meshach will be back. That's really rather up to you.

D.M. Mark, 2017